TITANIC 2020

COLIN
Bateman

A division of Hachette Children's Books

First published in Great Britain in 2007
by Hodder Children's Books

5

A catalogue record for this book is available
from the British Library

ISBN-13: 978 0 340 94445 5

Typeset in Bembo by Avon DataSet Ltd,
Bidford on Avon, Warwickshire

Printed and bound by CPI Bookmarque, Croydon, CR0 4TD

The paper and board used in this paperback by Hodder Children's
Books are natural recyclable products made from wood grown in
sustainable forests. The manufacturing processes conform to the
environmental regulations of the country of origin.

Hodder Children's Books
a division of Hachette Children's Books
338 Euston Road, London NW1 3BH
An Hachette Livre UK Company

For Matthew

To save a lot of time, right here at the start, let's be sure of our facts:

1. In this year, 2020, as the new *Titanic* prepares to set sail on its maiden voyage, nobody can doubt it is the finest, most luxurious cruise ship in all the world. It's unsinkable.

2. The original *Titanic* was built in Jimmy's home town of Belfast. It sank in the early hours of April 15, 1912.

3. Jimmy's great-grandfather helped build the first *Titanic*. Jimmy's great-grandfather was *useless* at building things – no wonder it sank.

4. Everyone said that *Titanic* was 'unsinkable' as well. 1,500 passengers and crew died when the *Titanic* went down. Moral of the story – don't listen to what people say. And learn to swim.

5. History is dead boring. If you really want to learn about the old *Titanic*, go rent the movie.

6. Can't think of a 6, but I'm sure something will come to me.

7. Nope, still nothing.

Prologue

This is the bit before the story really gets going – i.e. before **The End of Civilization As We Know It** – which kind of goes some way towards explaining what Lucky Jimmy Armstrong was doing stowing away on the new *Titanic* in the first place. It's sort of exciting, although not as exciting as the rest of it – what with **the plague** and **the mutiny** and **the flesh eating dogs** – but it's worth bearing with it so that you understand that he wasn't really there out of choice, that he was just trying to do something right for a change.

The year was 2020, and not much different. Sometimes Lucky Jimmy Armstrong was sick to death of hearing about the *Titanic*. You would think *he* had actually sailed on it or something, instead of some mouldy old ancestor who'd gone down with the flimsy pile of junk. But, like it or not, Lucky Jimmy Armstrong was doomed to have the *Titanic* figure largely in his life. His granddad was always talking about it, his parents were always talking about it, and since they'd started building a *new Titanic* just down the road from his school – and you could see it taking shape, day in, day out, because it was the size of a city – all of his teachers and most of his fellow pupils were always talking about it as well.

Now, as an extra-special treat, they were about to get a tour of this new *Titanic.**

There were thirty-eight boys and girls from East Belfast High on board a bus designed for half that number. They were crammed into seats and standing in the aisle, pushing, shoving, yelling, pinching, punching and swearing as they baked in the heat of a sweltering June morning. They wanted off, but the driver, the rotund Mr Carmichael, wouldn't let them until the teacher in charge, Mr McDowell, gave the all-clear, and he didn't seem to be in the slightest hurry – possibly because he was already standing on the dock, enjoying the cool sea breeze as he discussed the tour with the guide provided by White Star International, the owners of the *Titanic*.

Eventually the doors slid open and Mr McDowell's appearance was greeted with a sarcastic round of

* Actually, I've just remembered 6, which is why Lucky Jimmy Armstrong is called 'Lucky' Jimmy Armstrong. It's a sarcastic joke. Ever since Jimmy's great-grandfather went down on the *Titanic* the family had been plagued with ill luck. The Armstrongs attract accidents and controversy the way summer flowers attract bees. *This* 'Lucky' Jimmy Armstrong, thirteen years old, was simply following in the family tradition.

applause. 'All right, all right,' he said. 'Keep it down. If you'll all just get off in an orderly fashion and form yourselves into two neat lines . . .'

In the stampede that followed Mr McDowell was almost crushed. He yelled for order, but was completely ignored. The White Star guide looked at them apprehensively – it had been his idea to invite pupils from the local school. He had thought it would be good publicity, but now he wasn't so sure.

Mr McDowell waved his hands in the air. 'All right . . . settle down now . . .'

Jimmy was slapped from behind. 'Aaoow!'

'Armstrong!' Mr McDowell snapped. 'Stop that right now!'

'It wasn't me, sir!'

'Just be quiet!'

Jimmy glared back at his mate Gary, who sniggered.

'OK, now. Mr Webster here has very kindly agreed to act as our guide—'

'Aaoow!' Jimmy spun. 'You quit it now or I swear to God I'll—'

'Armstrong! I won't speak to you again!'

'Sir, he—'

'Armstrong, I'm warning you. Another word and you'll go right back on that bus.'

Out of the corner of his mouth, Jimmy hissed, 'I'll get you for this . . .'

Mr Webster, a red-faced man with thinning hair, held up a hand as the pupils began to edge towards the gangplank. 'Now, while it is our great pleasure to have you on board, I have to warn you that we are just adding the finishing touches, so the ship is still classified as a building site. I can't emphasis enough the importance of staying with the group, not wandering off, not—'

'Aaoow!'

This time Jimmy couldn't help himself. He twisted round and thumped Gary hard. Gary yelled in pain. His hand shot to his nose in a vain attempt to stop the blood that was already flowing.

'I warned you!' Jimmy spat. 'Don't say I didn't . . .' But before he could finish his blazer was grabbed from behind and he was yanked out in front of his classmates.

Mr McDowell towered over him, his face flushed. 'Armstrong – I've had it up to here with you!'

'It wasn't me, sir!'

'You didn't punch Higgins?'

'Yes sir, but he was hitting me!'

'It's always someone else with you, isn't it, Armstrong?'

'No, sir . . . yes, sir, but he was . . .'

'You're a troublemaker, Armstrong. You always have been and you always will be . . . Now get back on the bus.'

'Sir?'

'Get back on the bus! I'm not having you spoiling today for everyone! You've already let your classmates *and* the school down. If I let you on here you'll probably sink the boat on us! Now get on the bus!'

Jimmy seethed. He hated Gary Higgins, he hated Mr McDowell, he hated Mr Webster and now that he thought about it, he hated the *Titanic* as well.

There was still no sign of his classmates an hour later. The bus driver, Mr Carmichael, took pity on him, climbed out from behind the wheel and eased his considerable bulk down the aisle.

'Thought you might want some company,' he said, squeezing into the seat opposite.

Jimmy looked him up and down. 'No thanks.'

Carmichael ignored him. 'Did you see this?' He had a colour brochure in his hand, with a picture of the new *Titanic* on the front. 'They left this for me to read. It has all the facts and figures. I get to go to a hundred different places with schools like yours every year, but all I ever get is the brochure. Got to stay on the bus.' He began to flick through the pages. 'Still, thought you might be interested.'

'Nope.'

'Like how much that big bucket cost – says here, six hundred million dollars.'

'Not interested.'

'It weighs one hundred and forty-two thousand tonnes.'

'Don't care.'

'It has a helicopter pad and an ice rink and a cinema.'

'Boring.'

'It has fifteen decks.'

'Yawn . . .'

'Thirteen hundred crew . . .'

'Nearly asleep now.'

'. . . and they come from sixty-five different countries. Two thousand passengers will join the ship when it arrives in Miami—'

'Could you just be quiet?' Jimmy snapped suddenly. '*Please*.'

'Then there's all the food. The passengers will get through twenty-eight thousand eggs a week. Imagine that.'

'I don't care! Please, just shut your big, fat cake hole.'

Carmichael blinked at him for several moments. Then he said, 'And they'll eat eighteen thousand slices of pizza. Plus twelve thousand pounds of chicken . . .'

'God almighty!'

Jimmy jumped out of his seat and charged down the aisle. Carmichael, taken by surprise, took several moments to lever himself up out of his own seat and follow him.

Jimmy stared down at the bus's instrument panel, trying to decide which button controlled the doors. He just wanted to sit on the edge of the dock and breathe in some nice, cool sea air. But the bus was old and decrepit, and whatever symbols the buttons and levers and switches had once possessed had long since been worn away.

'Step away from the controls!' Carmichael shouted as he trundled down the aisle. 'Don't touch that . . .!'

But he was too late. Instead of gambling on one button, Jimmy pressed them all. He spun around, confident that the doors would open, freeing him to jump from the bus.

Jimmy Armstrong was not known as 'Lucky' Jimmy Armstrong by the teaching staff of East Belfast High. He was more commonly referred to as 'that damn boy', 'that idiot boy Armstrong', or simply as 'Trouble'. As in, 'Here comes Trouble.'

But sometimes it was a two-way thing. For instance, this time, as Jimmy saw the swing doors at the far end of the corridor open, the headmaster come through, flanked by two police officers and followed by Carmichael the bus driver and his teacher, McDowell, he was able to think to himself, *Here comes trouble.* The driver was soaked to the skin. McDowell's face was so pale he looked like he'd been raised from the dead. There was smoke coming out of the headmaster's ears. The omens were not good.

The headmaster, Mr McCartney, rapped on the smoked-glass panel in the wall above Jimmy's head. It slid open immediately and Mrs James, his chubby-cheeked secretary, peered out.

'Were his parents called?' the headmaster asked.

'Yes, Mr McCartney, but they're refusing to come. They've had enough.'

The headmaster looked down at Jimmy. 'Right – inside with you!'

Mr McCartney grabbed his arm and led him into his office. He pushed Jimmy towards a chair then turned to his companions and said, 'Five minutes, gentlemen, please.' He rolled his eyes, then closed the door on them and crossed to his desk. He sat glaring at Jimmy for nearly a minute, drumming his fingers on the desk the whole time. Finally he said, 'What are we going to do with you?'

Jimmy shrugged.

'Shrugging isn't good enough any more, Jimmy.'

Jimmy shrugged again.

The headmaster sighed. 'Just to be absolutely clear, Jimmy, as to the sequence of events – and please, correct me if there are any inaccuracies. First of all, on arrival at the dock, you were warned to keep quiet several times by Mr McDowell. Then you gave young Higgins a bloody nose. As a result of this you were sent back to the bus. When Mr Carmichael tried to engage you in conversation you told him to "shut his big fat cake hole". After this you ran up the bus and pushed a button which released the handbrake, causing the bus to roll backwards and almost fall into the water. Mr Carmichael managed to stop it just in time. Shaken and upset, he pursued you outside. You deliberately stepped out of his way, causing Mr Carmichael to stumble over a mooring rope, as a result of which he fell over the edge of the dock some ten metres into the water below. Luckily for you, he was immediately spotted by Harbour Police and rescued.' The headmaster cleared his throat. 'Now, Jimmy, would you say that that was a fair and accurate summary of what you achieved today?'

'I was just trying to get the doors open.'

'Did anyone give you permission to do that?'

'No, but what was I—'

'ENOUGH!' Mr McCartney banged his fist down hard on the desk. 'In all my years of teaching I have never, *ever* come across such blatant indiscipline, such disrespect, such . . .'

Mr McCartney stood abruptly and crossed to a window. He studied the flowers and bushes in the school garden. His left leg seemed to be vibrating uncontrollably. His lips moved silently, as if he was counting. He turned to face Jimmy again, but remained by the window. 'Tell me, Jimmy, what would you do in my situation? Faced with this kind of behaviour.' Jimmy stared at the ground. 'Come on, Jimmy, I'd really like to know.'

'Well, I'm sure you could get another job.'

Mr McCartney shook his head sadly. 'Always something funny to say, isn't there? As long as there's a laugh you don't care whether someone has a broken nose or is nearly drowned or whether you almost lost us a school bus worth tens of thousands of pounds! As long as you can come out with some smart-aleck comment! Well how about this for a great laugh,

Jimmy – you're expelled! Get out of my office! I never want to see your face again!'

Jimmy wandered around the city centre, browsing in the shops, but as the day wore on he was gradually drawn closer and closer to home, until, at just after seven that evening, he found himself perched on a small hill in an overgrown stretch of wasteland just behind his house, trying to work himself up to facing his family's fury. He had hoped that his parents would go out to the pub, as usual, but by nine o'clock it was clear they weren't going anywhere. They were waiting for him. It was dark now and he was starving. He was beginning to contemplate eating flowers and weeds or licking a rusty Coke can when a voice suddenly came out of the darkness.

'Hey – Jimmy . . .' Jimmy shot to his feet and was already halfway down the other side of the hill when it sounded again. 'Jimmy . . . Jimmy – it's only me.'

Jimmy peered back up the hill. He could just make out the outline of a slightly stooped figure standing where he had been just moments before. 'Granda?'

'Who else? Jimmy lad, you've been sitting up here for hours.'

'What? You've seen me?'

'Jimmy, we've *all* seen you. When are you coming down?'

Jimmy shook his head, but now felt confident enough to join his grandfather on the brow of the hill.

'You're just like your dad,' Granda said. 'Stubborn.'

Jimmy shrugged.

'Well, if you're going to stay out here, maybe you could make yourself useful.'

Granda removed a small brown envelope from his back pocket. 'The other day I was up rooting around in our roof space amongst all the old stuff my dad left behind when he died. And guess what I found.'

'A lot of unpaid bills, with our luck.'

'No, Jimmy. Look.' He upended the envelope and a single copper coin fell into his palm. 'I think this is Lucky Jimmy's lucky penny.'

'His *what*?'

Jimmy squinted at it. It was about five times bigger than a normal penny, and though it may well have been made of copper, it had long since lost its shine.

'I thought it went down with him on the *Titanic*,' Granda said. 'Believe it or not, lad, there was a time when everything went right for the Armstrongs. The first Lucky Jimmy was given this as a child, and he grew up to get a job on the *Titanic*, and free passage to America. In those days it was like winning the Lottery. Anyway, I'm thinking maybe that the first Lucky Jimmy decided he'd had all the good luck a man needs, so before he left he passed it on to his little brother, so that he could have good luck as well.'

'And then he went out and drowned.'

'Perhaps he thought he was doing the right thing.'

Jimmy, who was barely acquainted with the concept of doing the right thing, shook his head. 'He shouldn't have bothered. I mean, look at our family. If they made a documentary about us it would be called *The Armstrongs: One Hundred Years of Disaster and Catastrophe*.'

Granda flipped the coin up into the air and caught it. 'What if the coin *was* good luck, but somehow by giving it away too soon, the first Lucky Jimmy turned it to bad luck? If the coin's been in our roof space ever since, maybe that's what's been keeping us back. Maybe it's been responsible for everything that's gone wrong.'

Jimmy shrugged.

'Well, lad, if you're not coming home yet anyway, how about doing an old man a favour?' He flicked the coin towards his grandson and Jimmy's hand instinctively snapped out and caught it. 'If it *has* brought us all this bad luck over the years, then why don't you take it down to the water and chuck it in? Maybe it'll make its own way back to where it belongs, in old Jimmy's pocket, and maybe that'll turn our fortunes around. What do you think?'

'I think you're barking mad,' said Jimmy.

'I'll give you money for chips.'

'Deal,' said Jimmy.

And *that* was how it really started, doing something stupid for his old granddad, just to put off getting yelled at by his parents. Little did Jimmy know, there and then, trudging through the darkened streets towards the seafront, that he would never see any of them again.

The New Titanic

Ten minutes after leaving his granda, Jimmy was standing on the shore, coin in hand, preparing to skim it out over the calm water. As he pulled his arm back to throw it the moon made one of its occasional appearances from behind a cloud, throwing its pale light over the shore and illuminating, less than a mile away along the coast, the massive outline of the *Titanic*. Jimmy stopped. That *bloody* ship. It represented everything that had gone wrong for him that day. The punch, the bus, the near-drowning, the expulsion – he could trace them all back to the *Titanic*.

Anger gripped him again. The red mist descended.

He was Jimmy Armstrong, they couldn't treat him like this. Every single one of them owed him an apology. And they also owed him a tour of the ship. As he stood staring at it, it came to him that the only way he was going to get to do that now was if he organized it himself. Sure, wasn't it sitting there empty, doing nothing? And wasn't he doing nothing but waiting to get yelled at? Well stuff them all! He was going to have his tour, *right now*.

Jimmy looked at the lucky penny. He still intended to throw it into the sea, just like Granda wanted, but there was something he was going to do first. He was going to find the most public part of that ship, somewhere they couldn't fail to notice, and he was going to use the coin to carve *Jimmy Armstrong Was Here* right into it, so deep that they'd never get it out. That would definitely show them he wasn't to be messed with. It wasn't the brightest idea, but it was perfectly in keeping with many of his previous ones.

There wasn't any problem getting access to the dock itself; it was just a case of climbing over a couple of fences. There was a security hut at the end of the pier, but by coming at the dock from the rear he was already behind it. There was a barrier across the road, but it was raised to allow the trucks carrying supplies access to the half-dozen gangplanks that had been lowered on to the dock. Two of them were wider than dual carriageways. Vehicles rumbled across to deposit their goods directly into the bowels of the ship. The others were narrower, with teams of workers carrying boxes scurrying back and forth along them. It was undoubtedly busy, but it wasn't constant. Jimmy, standing hidden behind a pile of discarded wooden crates, observed that there was a one- or two-minute period between the end of one delivery and the beginning of the next that might allow him to zip up a gangplank undetected, even if those on either side were still busy.

There was a moment – a very brief moment, admittedly – just before he made his charge for the *Titanic* when Jimmy paused to consider if he was doing the right thing, if he was about to turn a bad situation into a terrible one. But then, as criminals and politicians often do, he was able to justify his actions by reminding himself that *he* was the one being victimized and persecuted and he was just standing up for himself, and more, striking back! It was his *right*. And if he did happen to get discovered, he could just act stupid. He was still in his school uniform. He could say he had been on a tour of the ship earlier in the day and got locked in one of the cabins by accident. Or that he'd slipped and fell and knocked himself out. There were a million stupid things he could say. He was an expert on stupid.

So, having convinced himself, Jimmy thundered out of the shadows and up the gangplank, his heart hammering. He was going so fast, and the gangway finished so abruptly, that he almost took off as he reached the end. He skidded to a halt against a tower of cardboard boxes before ducking down and around them until he was out of sight. He took a moment to catch his breath before cautiously peering out. There were a dozen similar towers around him, all awaiting redistribution around the ship. Dozens of men in different-coloured overalls were hard at work driving, carrying and shifting – but for the moment he was safe. However, with the ship being stocked up, all of the lower decks were going to be just like this, brightly lit and buzzing with activity. He had to get to a safer location. Already workers were back on the gangplank he had used. He had to get moving, and *now*.

Jimmy took hold of the closest box, quickly tested it for weight, then heaved it up on to his shoulder and began walking. In a few moments he found himself clear of the immediate distribution area. He turned into a long, straight corridor. There were two men coming towards him, chatting in a language he didn't recognize. Jimmy moved the box slightly forwards and at an angle so that even as they squeezed past they couldn't see his face. Words were spoken, but he couldn't tell if they were directed at him; he just grunted and kept walking. He came to a set of stairs, looked both ways, then set down the box and darted up them. At the top there was an elevator which opened as soon as he pressed the button. He selected the ninth floor at random. The doors eased shut and Jimmy breathed a sigh of relief.

But it was short-lived.

As the elevator rose out of its resting place he suddenly realized that its walls were made of glass, and now he could be seen from virtually every point of the hollowed out central section of the ship. He was passing up through a vast shopping mall four decks high and running virtually the entire length of the vessel. It glistened with chandeliers and was lined with exclusive designer shops and soda fountains and wine bars. He would *definitely* have been seen – if there'd been anyone there. But the mall was completely empty. Not a soul. Like a very well-kept ghost town. After what seemed like an eternity he was finally hidden again in the darkness of the lift shaft.

The elevator pinged. Jimmy tensed as the doors slid open – but there was no one there. He stepped out. He listened. No voices. No footsteps. He ventured forward and peered down long, straight, half-lit corridors, then moved cautiously along them. He hesitantly opened doors to cabins, looked inside, then hurried on. Gradually he began to relax. There really wasn't *anyone* this high up. He ran down the corridors, not out of fear, but with an exhilarated lope, like a zoo animal released into the wild. And not just on the ninth. He worked his way up to the highest level, the fifteenth, taking time on each floor to study the framed floor plans which decorated the walls at regular intervals, familiarizing himself with the layouts and noting the areas to avoid.

Below him there were ten decks devoted to the guest cabins – although each deck also had some other kind of attraction, like a library or a cinema or restaurant. Beneath the guest cabins was the shopping mall and a formal dining area which itself had three levels. Lower down there was the crew quarters, the kitchens, storage areas and medical facilities. Beneath that the huge turbine engines which powered the ship. His teacher had been right, it was like a floating city. And just like that fat bus driver had said, there was even a helicopter pad – and an ice rink. He had never ice-skated in his life, but when he found boxes of brand new skates he thought *why not?* and glided out on to the pristine ice. He fell over. He fell and fell and fell and laughed and laughed and laughed. He was there for half an hour and never managed to stand unsupported for more than a few seconds. But he loved it. His legs were sore, his knees raw, but he was having a ball. When he had finished he returned to the fifteenth deck and sauntered out into the cool night air. Up here, so high, all by himself, the disasters of earlier in the day felt like they had happened to someone else. He imagined that the *Titanic* was his to command. He would sail it across the great oceans of the world, he would have fantastic adventures!

It was now almost four o'clock in the morning. He was thirsty and hungry. There were restaurants aplenty on board, but they wouldn't open until the passengers arrived. If he wanted food he would have to venture into the kitchens far below – and he could see over the side of the ship that supplies were still being loaded from the dock. It was just too dangerous. He was having the time of his life, no point in risking it all for the sake of a rumbling tum.

Then he had a brainwave – the mini bars in the

cabins. Jimmy chose the biggest and best of the Presidential suites and helped himself to Diet Coke and Toblerone. He lay back on a huge bed and stuffed his face.

This was the life!

He was no longer just the Captain – he was the owner. All of this belonged to him. He was the Jimmy Armstrong who went to America on the *Titanic* – but this time he survived. He became wealthy and famous and now here he was, not leaving but returning home to the city of his birth. He should celebrate! A toast to his success! Jimmy opened the mini bar again. Champagne!

Why not?

Jimmy opened a bottle. The golden liquid foamed out over the plush carpet. He didn't even consider cleaning it up. One of his servants could do it in the morning. The champagne was slightly bitter, but he found that the more he drank the nicer it tasted and the happier he felt. He hated Gary Higgins with a passion, but part of him wished he was here now, to enjoy this with him. Or his mum and dad. Or Granda.

Granda, it's all mine! The Titanic*!*

Except he wouldn't call it that.

Jimmy raised the bottle.

'I name this ship – the *Jimmy*! May God bless all who sail in her!'

He giggled, then collapsed back down on to the bed. He took another swig. He was so relaxed. Jimmy's eyes flickered. It had been a long day, and his adventures on the *Titanic* had been as exhausting as they had been exciting. But he knew it had to end. He had to go home. Face the music. First, though, if he just closed his eyes for five minutes he could recharge his batteries. Then he could sneak off before first light.

Jimmy closed his eyes.

Five minutes.

Maybe ten.

Surprise

He was dreaming.

Or, no, he wasn't.

The voices had started out in a bizarre adventure featuring talking hamsters, but they no longer seemed to exist inside his head, but outside it. They had been squeezed out and replaced by an unbearable pain sweeping through his entire body. For the first time in his life Jimmy realized why his dad was so miserable in the mornings, and, quite often, in the afternoons. *Too much alcohol.* Now Jimmy was suffering from his first hangover. To make matters worse, there was a blinding light coming from the balcony window. And those annoying hamster voices were getting louder, and louder and . . .

Jimmy bolted upright.

Daylight!

I've slept straight through!

Voices, outside in the corridor.

Oh no, oh no, oh no, oh no . . .

My head!

I'm going to throw up!

I'm going to vomit on the bed – and get caught doing it! Get up!

Jimmy rolled off the bed and staggered to his feet. The cabin seemed to be revolving around him. The voices were so close. He looked about him in panic. It was too late to escape from the room itself. *Hide! Somewhere! Anywhere!* He stumbled towards the cupboards, then the balcony and the bathroom, but finally threw himself under the bed. He curled himself in a ball and sucked in his breath to try and stop himself from heaving up.

Pass by! Pass by!

But of course they didn't. If they had to choose one cabin on the entire ship to stop at, it just had to be his.

Because he was, of course, Lucky Jimmy Armstrong. So although the ship was supposed to be empty of passengers until she reached Miami, *of course* the only non-crewmembers on this trip wanted *his* cabin.

'This is us,' said a man.

'Oh darling, it's wonderful,' said a woman. There was the sound of a kiss, and then the woman's voice grew more serious. She called out to someone else: 'Darling, will you hurry up please?'

'What's the rush?' It was a girl, further away, sounding annoyed.

Jimmy saw two pairs of shoes enter the cabin. One pair sturdy and black, the other slim, red and high-heeled. A few moments later a third pair joined them: trainers, with pink laces.

'Isn't it beautiful, darling?' the woman asked.

'S'all right,' said the girl.

'Your room's just through there,' said the man.

The trainers moved to the right. There was a slight pause, then the girl said: 'Is that it? It's tiny.'

'It's not tiny, darling,' said the mother.

'It's actually extremely large for a cruise ship,' said the father.

'Still small,' said the daughter.

Jimmy squirmed. He just wanted *out* of there.

'Oh for goodness' sake,' said the father. Jimmy saw the man's shoes move rapidly across and stop at the foot of the bed. 'Look at this.'

'Champagne?' said the mother. Then Jimmy saw her knees as she bent down along the side of the bed. He sucked his breath in. 'Chocolate wrappers. George? And look – someone's been sleeping in my bed!'

The girl laughed.

The mother snapped, 'It isn't funny, Claire.'

But Claire evidently thought it was. '*Someone's been sleeping in my bed!*' she mimicked. 'Do you think it was Goldilocks?'

The father tutted. 'Your mother's right, Claire – this just isn't good enough. Someone's head will roll for this. We're moving to a different suite.'

Claire snorted. 'Just straighten the bed and put the wrappers in the bin, Dad.'

'That's not the point,' said the mother. 'This is your daddy's ship, Claire, it has the best of everything. What kind of message does it send when the chief designer and owner comes on board and he's presented with a room full of rubbish?'

'Exactly,' said the father. He marched out of the cabin.

The mother said, 'Claire, you could show a little more interest. This is a big moment for your father.' There was no response. Jimmy suspected there was a shrug. She sounded like a spoiled brat. Jimmy's own shrugs were entirely different, of course. Claire's mother tried again. 'Darling – when you're older you'll look back on this and really appreciate the fact that you were one of the first passengers on the new *Titanic*. It's an historic moment.'

There was another pause, then Claire said: 'We could have flown.'

'Claire!' The mother stomped out of the room.

Claire let out a long, sad sigh before reluctantly following her parents. Jimmy waited until their renewed bickering had faded, then crawled out. He rose gingerly to his feet, feeling dizzy and sick. If this was what alcohol did to you, he was never going near it again. He checked his watch. *God almighty!* It was after eleven in the morning! The ship and the dock would be a hive of activity! How was he going to get off undetected?

Don't think about it . . . head too sore . . . just do it.

He moved to the door and peered out. The family was just disappearing along the corridor to the right.

Jimmy turned left, and, moving as quickly as his frail condition would allow, came almost immediately to a set of elevators. He pushed the call button.

What was I thinking of? I came on board to scratch my name and teach them a lesson! And I haven't even done that! He felt in his shirt pocket. The lucky penny was still there. *I should have thrown it in the sea when I had the chance!*

He glanced at the lights above the doors, which showed the elevator moving steadily upwards.

Relax. What have you done that's so wrong? Snuck on to a boat and eaten some chocolate. Drunk some champagne. Ruffled a bed. Hardly the crime of the century. You've nothing to be ashamed of. Hold your head up.

And he would have held it up if he could have. He just felt so ill. The whole ship seemed to vibrate around him.

Ping.

The elevator was empty. Jimmy stepped in, pushed the button for Deck Three, then pushed himself against the back wall as it descended past the shopping mall. For extra protection he shut his eyes, as if somehow his not being able to see anything meant that no one else could see him. He was still half drunk.

Ping.

The doors slid open.

Two men stood opposite him. They wore crisp white short-sleeved shirts with fancy designs on their arms, and black baseball caps.

One was saying, 'But Captain, this is our best opportunity to . . .' but stopped as he saw Jimmy. They both stared at him in confusion.

'Who the hell are you?' the Captain demanded. He was a stout man with a a neat grey beard.

Jimmy did his best. He stepped out of the lift and said, 'It's all right, I'm with the school tour.'

It was a gamble. The ship was bound to be having lots of other school tours.

'*What* school tour?' demanded the other one – a taller, thinner man.

'That one,' said Jimmy and pointed to his left. As the two men turned to look, Jimmy charged off to his right. A moment later they came charging after him, the Captain shouting and his companion yelling into his radio. Jimmy skidded around a corner and ran at full pelt down the corridor. It was busy with crewmen, moving back and forth, in and out of doors, carrying boxes and sacks and wheeling equipment, chatting and singing in half a dozen different languages – and luckily, none of them English. Even as his pursuers shouted after him, Jimmy dodged in and out, in and out, barely changing his pace at all.

I can do this!

I can do it!

The adrenaline was pumping through his body, banishing the headache, quelling the sickness.

Freedom!

Escape!

Jimmy crashed through the doors at the end of the corridor and out on to the deck, then turned frantically, searching for the nearest gangway on to the dock.

But there wasn't one.

For the simple reason that there was no dock.

In fact, there was no land.

The *Titanic* was at sea, steaming fast for America.

3

The Anxious Stowaway

Announcements were made by the Captain over the public address system, appealing for Jimmy to give himself up, telling him that he wouldn't get into trouble.

Yeah, right.

He had *stowed away*. There was no land in sight *anywhere*, in *any* direction. He was in BIG TROUBLE.

They followed up their appeal with a deck by deck, cabin by cabin search. But the ship was too big, and the crew was too small. Even though he only had a few hours' experience of the layout of the *Titanic*, he had thirteen years' experience of being chased, and he put it to good use. He was constantly one step ahead of his pursuers. And sometimes two.

Jimmy was torn between being frightened by what he'd done and hugely exhilarated by it. There was a slightly sour feeling in his stomach, and it wasn't just the after-effects of the champagne. His parents, once they got over the urgent desire to slap him around the head, would be going frantic. His granda, who had sent him on a mission to throw away the lucky penny, was probably blaming himself, convinced that Jimmy had somehow slipped and fallen into the water and drowned.

On the other hand – what a story he would have to tell when he got home! Some boys skipped off school for an afternoon and thought they were pretty cool. Even getting expelled was relatively commonplace. But running away to sea on the *Titanic* – now there was a tale worth telling!

The easiest thing would be just to give himself up. What was the worst they could do? Shout at him? It was the early afternoon of the first day at sea – if he surrendered now, they would almost certainly be compelled to return to Belfast to hand him over.

But what if he . . . stayed hidden?

Wouldn't they get to a point of no return – where it made more sense to continue on to America and send him home from there?

Absolutely!

The more he thought about it, the more sense it made. Avoid them for a few days – then give himself up and enjoy the rest of the cruise in style! Maybe they'd fly him home first class as well!

No problem!

Jimmy enjoyed a snooze in a cabin on Level Ten, then sat on the balcony enjoying a Toblerone. As the sun fell the temperature went with it and a cool wind blew up, so he retreated back inside. It was time to move – he had already decided it wasn't safe to spend too long in any one place. Besides, there was a lot more of the ship still to explore. But as he peeked out to make sure the corridor was clear, he was horrified to see two officers hurrying straight towards him. Jimmy let out a surprised yelp, then hurtled out of the room and ran as hard as he could in the opposite direction. They raced after him, shouting at him to stop, but he was too young and too fit, and even though they had radios to call in help, he was soon able to lose them.

A little later, Jimmy took the stairs down to Level Six, selected several books from the large public library there, then wandered along the corridor until he found a cabin he liked. He was completely relaxed again. They had stumbled on him by chance, and that was something you couldn't plan for. But they'd wasted their opportunity and he remained confident in his abilities to avoid them. Jimmy closed the door, switched on a bedside light, liberated another Toblerone from the mini bar, then lay back on the bed and leafed through a book about Florida. He wondered if there was any possibility of jumping ship once he arrived in Miami. He could hitchhike up to Orlando, and go to Disney, or any of the other huge parks up there. Maybe this would be his life from now on. Living wild, on his wits, on the road, a tramp, a *super*tramp. He could be a modern-day Robin Hood, stealing from the rich and . . . keeping it. Jimmy laughed and closed the book. It was easy to dream on this ship. The ship itself was a dream. He returned to the mini bar.

Peanuts this time, I think.

He sat quietly munching on the edge of the bed, trying to imagine what the *Titanic* would be like with its thousands of passengers on board – if he was still a stowaway then, it would surely be even easier to avoid detection. He could just lose himself in the crowds and cruise the world for ever.

Still hungry, Jimmy opened the mini-bar door again and selected a small glass jar containing jellybeans. As he looked for something to drink – definitely *not* champagne – his eyes fell on a price list stuck to the inside of the door. Toblerones were $6. He guessed that was about four pounds! Diet Cokes – which were only half-sized cans anyway – cost *five times* as much as at home! If the passengers were prepared to pay that much, they were crazy. At the bottom of the price list there were payment instructions:

There is no need to keep check of your purchases from the mini bar. Each time you remove an item it is automatically registered to your account, which you may settle at the end of the voyage.

Jimmy smiled. He was stuffing his face at someone else's expense. Well, they could afford it. They probably wouldn't even notice.

He was just opening the jellybeans when the thought struck him.

He studied the payment instructions again.

Each time you remove an item it is automatically registered to your account.

Every time I remove something it'll show up on the computer! They'll know there's nobody supposed to be in this cabin. That's how they found me earlier! And I took another Toblerone fifteen minutes ago!

Jimmy dropped the jellybeans and dashed out into the corridor, fearing the worst.

But it was empty.

Maybe he was crediting his pursuers with too much intelligence. Or perhaps capturing him wasn't all that important when there was a ship the size of the *Titanic* to navigate across the Atlantic. He was just turning back into the room when he heard the *ping* of an arriving elevator, followed by hurried footsteps.

They were coming for him!

Naked Bum Man

It was a close call, but he still escaped. When he'd put enough distance between himself and his pursuers he even had the confidence to stop at the end of the corridor and perform a little victory dance. Then he'd nearly had a heart attack at the sound of footsteps coming towards him from the stairs – but it was a cleaner, and she was as surprised to see Jimmy as Jimmy was to see her. She even made room for him to pass as he charged towards her.

Thinking about it later Jimmy was surprised that they hadn't learned their lesson after their first attempt. Once again they had tracked him down, only to leave him with a means of escape. If they'd come at him from both ends of the corridor he would have been theirs. Not that he was complaining. He had worked out their mini-bar master plan. Now if he was hungry he simply took what he wanted and moved quickly to a different floor before they had a chance to trap him.

But it was hunger that was the real problem.

Toblerones, nuts and jellybeans were rapidly losing their attraction, and after spending a second night on the ship in a small cabin on the eighth level, he woke with an overwhelming desire for a proper breakfast. He wanted cereal. And bacon. And sausages. And eggs. Fried. Scrambled. Boiled, in a cup. With toast soldiers. The fact that he usually made do with a Diet Coke at home was neither here nor there. He was famished and nothing else would do but that he had to throw himself back into danger by staging a raid on the crew kitchen and restaurant far below. With the passengers still to board, he figured, none of the many restaurants were yet functioning, so it was the only place hot food was going to be available.

What he needed, he decided, was a disguise.

The school uniform was a dead giveaway. He needed to blend in. There was at least a hundred crew on board – ten times that number would join in Miami – but they were surely all still getting to know each other. Another strange face wouldn't be so remarkable – even if it did look very young – especially if he was wearing the right clothes. Jimmy had already observed that the sailors wore white uniforms, while the engineers wore blue overalls and baseball caps, the catering staff green and the cleaners red. He didn't think he would ever pass for a sailor, but if he could get hold of a set of overalls and matching baseball cap, then he would surely be able to pass unchallenged. It was just a case of having the nerve to go for it.

Nerve was never a problem for Jimmy Armstrong.

After studying the relevant floor plan Jimmy

pinpointed a store room on the second level which looked a likely place for the crew uniforms to be kept. When he got there he discovered that it was situated at a busy crossroads of corridors. It took nearly an hour of patiently watching in a dark stairwell before he had an opportunity to dash across and try the door – but it was locked. Before he could try and force it footsteps sounded on the stairs behind him and he had to bound across the corridor and seek refuge behind the first door that would open.

As he slipped in he found himself confronted by a man's bum.

It was white and flabby and spotty. Like a full moon beaten with a stick.

He was in the men's locker room. Luckily, the sound of his panicked entrance was covered by the water pounding against the tiled floor of the shower cubicles. Jimmy darted behind a row of lockers just as the bum, along with the man attached to it, moved into the shower. Thankfully, Naked Spotty Flabby Bum Man was the only other occupant of the room. As NSFB man began to sing something vaguely Japanese he became enveloped in steam, which allowed Jimmy to venture out and remove his red overalls. He held them against himself. They were slightly too long in the arms and legs, but with a bit of turning up, they would do rightly. He changed quickly, lifted the man's baseball cap off a second hook, and discarded his by now rather stinky school uniform in a bin. Jimmy made sure his cap was pulled down hard over his face, then stepped out of the locker room into the busy corridor. At first he moved hesitantly, sure he was about to be rumbled, but very soon he realized that nobody was paying him any attention. He was one of them!

And now for food!

The canteen doors were open, and with the breakfast rush apparently over there were only a few crewmen still eating or choosing their food from a long buffet table. Jimmy walked purposefully up to the hot food selection, lifted a plate and began to load up. He was so hungry he could have just buried his face in the scrambled eggs and sucked it up. But he had to stick to the plan: stock up then get back up to the guest cabins to enjoy his feast in comparative safety.

When he couldn't pile anything else on to his plate, Jimmy turned for the door, only to find an angry-looking chef blocking his way. Veins bulged at the side of his head as he barked something incomprehensible. Jimmy shrugged and tried to move past, but the chef remained exactly where he was.

A voice from behind Jimmy said, 'If you want me to translate, he's saying you can't take food out of the restaurant.' Jimmy glanced around. There was an old man – at least as old as his granda, sixty maybe – sitting at one of the long bench tables. 'If I were you, I'd shift your butt, because Pedroza there is as mad as a bag of spiders. Only this morning he took a knife to some guy for tramping egg into the carpet.'

Pedroza's eyes blazed down. Jimmy backed away.

'Jimmy, why don't you join me?'

Jimmy froze.

'C'mon Jimmy. I just want to talk.'

Jimmy turned slowly. The old man nodded at the seat opposite. Jimmy looked around the restaurant: there were four other crewmen still eating, but apparently paying no attention. Pedroza remained in the doorway. Jimmy cursed himself for getting caught so easily.

'How . . . how did you know?' he asked as he lowered himself warily on to the bench seat.

'Well there's this . . .' The old man unfolded a sheet of paper showing a photo of Jimmy, one he recognized from school. 'They sent this out to us when we reported a stowaway. I thought if I sat here long enough you might turn up. Hunger does that. Nice try with the overalls, but you do look about twelve.'

'I'm thirteen!'

The old man put his hand out. 'They call me Scoop.' Jimmy just looked at it. 'It's not my real name, obviously. My nickname. You know where it comes from?'

'Do you sell ice cream?'

Scoop laughed. 'Nice one. It's a name they gave reporters in the old days. When they got exclusive stories, they'd call it a scoop. And I was one of the best. Scoop Morrison.' Jimmy shrugged. Scoop withdrew his neglected hand. 'Well, lad, you've certainly been giving us the runaround, haven't you? Pity it all has to end, eh?' Jimmy shrugged again. Scoop leaned forward and lowered his voice. 'Or does it?'

Jimmy just looked at him.

'See, kid, they're really mad with you upstairs, the havoc you've caused.'

'Havoc? I stole a couple of Toblerones!'

'Jimmy, lad, you think Mr Stanford's tearing his hair out because of a few bars of chocolate? He's tearing his hair out because he'll have to turn this ship around and take you back to Belfast. If he has to do that there'll be a delay in getting to Miami, which means the passengers will sue him for millions of dollars for ruining their cruise. Do you see? And I tell you, kid, if Mr Stanford *is* sued for millions of dollars you can be damn sure he's going to sue *you* for exactly the same amount.'

'He can sue me for whatever he wants. Haven't got it, and my family haven't got it either.'

Scoop blew air out of his cheeks. 'All right, Jimmy, we're getting ahead of ourselves here. Let me just say, if you're found, the Captain will have no alternative but to turn the ship around. We're only two days out.'

'What do you mean, *if* I'm found?'

Scoop smiled. His teeth were as white as snow, but appeared to be slightly loose in his mouth. 'Well, I was just thinking, *I* don't want to go back to Belfast; the Captain certainly doesn't; Mr Stanford – the owner – well it's the last thing on earth he wants to do. But the problem is that the others're so good and honest they would feel duty bound to turn the ship around if you were captured. I, on the other hand, am not particularly good *or* honest. So if I was to give you the chance to stay lost, and thus ensure our continued journey to America, what would you say?'

'What do you mean, *stay lost*?'

'At least until we dock in Miami. I'll organize food for you. Somewhere to sleep. I can be pretty certain you won't get caught.'

'Why would you do that? What's in it for you?'

'In exchange for helping you out, I would like you to help me.'

Jimmy's eyes narrowed. 'How?'

'Well, walk this way and I'll show you.'

It was only when the old man *rolled* backwards that Jimmy realized he was in a wheelchair. He had no legs beneath his knees. Scoop, seeing Jimmy's look of surprise, patted the space where they'd once been. 'Let this be a warning to you – I dropped a slice of pizza last night and *that* crazy fella . . .' he nodded at Pedroza, who was now back behind the buffet table, then made a chopping motion with his hand, 'sliced them off in anger – *whack! whack!* He's keeping them on ice until my table manners improve.' Scoop nodded gravely, then turned his wheelchair and began to roll towards the door.

'What a lot of crap,' said Jimmy.

But he followed, nevertheless.

Scoop

The long straight corridors were perfectly suited to a speeding wheelchair. Jimmy had to run at full pelt just to keep up. Scoop finally ushered him into a suite on the eighth floor. There was no bed or cupboards or mini bar, instead almost the entire floor space was covered by large cardboard boxes.

'OK,' said Scoop, 'here's the story. Our passengers want to wake up in the morning and have a newspaper waiting outside their door, just like at home. So that's what I do – I write, edit, design and print a daily newspaper. It's a mix of news from the countries the passengers come from – mostly America – and stories about the ship, interesting passengers, profiles of the crew, that kind of thing. It's only small – eight, twelve, sometimes sixteen pages – but it's important; helps people feel that they're not entirely cut off from the outside world.'

'Can't they just switch the telly on?'

'We're in the middle of the ocean, there's no signal. The telly plays tapes we bring with us, mostly old TV shows, and documentaries about the islands the cruise visits. If they want news, it comes from me. Been doing it on different Stanford cruise ships for twenty-five years, son. Ever since I lost these.' He tapped his – well, no legs.

'It wasn't Pedroza, then.'

'I lost them in the first Gulf War. Do you remember that?'

'Before my time.'

'The *Daily Express* managed to get me a place on an aircraft carrier. It was to be my first time as a war correspondent. I was so excited when they told me, I was planning to run all the way home to tell my wife. Except I got knocked down by a taxi on the way. It smashed my legs up so badly I had to have them amputated.'

Jimmy didn't know what to say to *that*. He was actually struggling not to laugh. Sometimes you just can't help yourself. He tried to cover it by nodding at the boxes and saying, 'So what's the deal with this lot?'

'You know anything about computers?'

'Some.'

'Used a screwdriver before?'

'Now and again.'

'Ever wired a plug?'

'Sure.'

'All right then! I need these boxes opened and everything set up. It's a pain in the arse trying to do it from a chair. So you can start by sorting this lot out for me.'

Jimmy looked at the boxes, then back to Scoop. 'I'm not some kind of unpaid slave, you know.'

Scoop thought about that for a moment, and then said, 'Yes you are.'

Jimmy was disruptive, unruly and disrespectful. He didn't like being told what to do. But if he was interested in something, he gave it everything. He was also good with his hands – had to be, really, as there was never much money around at home. So if he wanted something, he built it himself. He'd created a motorcycle out of parts other people had thrown away and he'd built a tree house that was more like a fortress, complete with electric lights and a fridge. He could do things if you left him alone to get on with them and didn't breathe down his neck, particularly if he saw some value in it. Working for Scoop in exchange for a free cruise made sense to him.

Scoop himself wasn't entirely convinced, so he positioned himself at the end of the corridor to make sure Jimmy didn't slip out and lose himself in the depths of the ship again. But the office door remained closed, and when he re-entered after an hour he was genuinely surprised to find that all the work had been completed. Two desks were up, each with a computer and scanner on top, both switched on and apparently fully functioning; the printer was set up, there was a column of printer paper sitting beside it; a filing cabinet was screwed to the wall; and all of the packaging had been folded and neatly stacked in one corner, awaiting removal. Jimmy was sitting at one of the computers, installing a program.

'I didn't think you'd even have the boxes open,' said Scoop. Jimmy shrugged. 'This is *fantastic*.'

'So what now?' Jimmy asked. 'There's no passengers on board yet, so do you just sit on your arse until we arrive in Miami?' He said it without really thinking. 'I mean, you've no alternative but to sit on your arse, but is this all your work done?'

Scoop exploded in laughter. 'Hardly started, son, hardly started! What we have to do now is make sure it's all working, start making up a few dummy papers, print them up, pass them around, get feedback. Each ship has its own design, you see, its own character, and that has to be reflected in the newspaper, so the sooner we . . .'

Jimmy held up a hand. 'You keep saying *we*. Who exactly are you talking about?'

'Well, you and me.'

'I opened the boxes, I set up your gear. I thought that was it.'

'Well – I thought you might want to help with putting the paper together.'

'*Why?*'

Scoop folded his hands in his lap. He looked towards the balcony, and the grey sea beyond. 'Because I can't do it myself. You see, lad—'

There was a sudden sharp rap on the door. Scoop, seeing the panic in Jimmy's eyes, held up a calming hand. 'It's all right,' he said quietly. 'I ordered some food for you. Still – best if you slip into the bathroom until the coast is clear.'

Jimmy hid himself, but kept the door open just a fraction.

Scoop positioned himself at one of the desks, with his back to the door. 'Enter!' As the door opened he said, 'If you just put it down over . . .' but as he glanced around he saw what Jimmy had already seen: Claire, the surly teenager with the pink laces. Her black hair hung down over one eye and she was chewing gum. She hardly even looked at Scoop as she spoke, preferring instead to study her bright pink fingernails.

'Dad ordered me to come down to give you a hand unpack— oh.' She had looked up, finally. 'It's done.'

'Yes, Claire, all finished.'

'You did all this?'

'No. I had a team of elves to help me. Am I right in thinking your dad ordered you to come down *yesterday* to help me?'

'Yeah, well, I was busy.'

'I'm sure you were.'

'That it then?'

'Yes, Claire.'

'All right. See you.'

She shrugged and turned out of the cabin. Scoop

waited until he was sure she was gone, then called Jimmy out of the bathroom. 'Sorry about that. The owner's daughter.' He shook his head and sighed. 'And to think that one day she'll inherit all of this . . .' Scoop waved vaguely. 'She'll probably paint it pink.'

Jimmy sat on the edge of one of the desks and folded his arms. He wasn't the slightest bit interested in hearing about Claire Stanford. 'So why can't you put the paper together yourself?'

'Well. It's like this, Jimmy – this is my final trip for the company, my job is just to set up the newspaper here on the *Titanic* like I have on every other ship the Stanfords own, then hand over the reins to the new man when we arrive in Miami. There's a nice big company pension waiting for me if I can get through this trip, as I'll have completed my twenty-five years of service. But if for any reason I don't complete the voyage, then I'll get nothing. It's just the way big companies run. Anyway, the thing is, I don't know if I can do it. I'm just not well, son. It's not the legs, I'm used to them being gone, it's the other stuff – my blood pressure's bad, Jimmy, I've a real shake in my hands, and my eyes go all cloudy and I can't concentrate for more than . . . anyway, the truth is, I lied to the doctors before we set off. I told them I was fine, but I'm not. If you don't help me do this then I won't have a leg to stand on.' He thought about that for a moment. 'Or two, for that matter. Jimmy, I want you to help me run the paper. You'll do a bit of everything – find stories, write them up, design the pages, print it. Will you do it, Jimmy, will you help me?'

'No.'

'Aw Jimmy – why not? You could do it, easy.'

'Look, I'm sorry, all right? I'd be . . . useless, you know?'

'But how do you know?'

Jimmy shrugged. 'I just know. All right?'

Scoop rolled a little closer. His voice softened. 'You got expelled, didn't you?'

'How'd . . .?'

'It was on the report they sent with the photo. What'd you get expelled for?'

'For being stupid.'

'Ah, nonsense!' erupted Scoop. 'You're not stupid, Jimmy! Not stupid *thick* anyway. Stupid *headstrong* probably; stupid *I always know best* maybe.'

Jimmy gave the smallest shrug.

'Jimmy, son, that's the kind of stupid that gets things done, that changes things. They call people stupid when they just don't understand them. Guy that came up with the wheel, they probably called him stupid. Guy that invented aspirin, they probably told him he was thick. Photography, there's a stupid mistake, if ever there was one, and where would we be without it? Do you understand what I'm saying? You can do this, Jimmy, I know you can. It's your chance to prove to yourself that you're not the sort of kid they say you are. So are you on, Jimmy? Will we do this together?'

'No,' said Jimmy.

'I'll pay you,' said Scoop.

'OK,' said Jimmy.

Earthquake

Thousands of miles away from the *Titanic* a small earthquake shook the city of San Diego in California. One person was killed, twenty-seven injured, and a dozen buildings collapsed.

'You see,' said Scoop, 'that isn't particularly massive news – but if you were to check with our passenger list, you might find that dozens of them come from San Diego, and you can be sure it'll be big news for them. They'll be worried about relatives, their businesses – do you know what I mean?'

Jimmy had found the story on a newspaper website. Now he proceeded to copy it into the cruise ship newspaper they'd begun to put together that morning. Scoop stopped him. 'No, Jimmy – you can't just copy it. You have to make up your own story, based upon what you've read here.'

'Why?'

'Because those words, in that order, belong to that website. You have to take the facts that are there, and rewrite them.'

'So I can steal their facts?'

Scoop sighed. 'Up to a point. You should look at this story on perhaps a dozen different news sites, because each one is going to have their own version of it. One will know the name of the man who died, another will have an interview with the leading expert on earthquakes, yet another might know how long it will take to repair the damaged buildings. Do you see what I'm getting at?'

He did, kind of.

'Any story you write has to answer the five basic rules of journalism, and they're quite simple: you ask *who*, *what*, *where*, *when*, *how*. All right?'

'Who, what, where, when, how,' Jimmy repeated.

'That's it – *who* is who was killed, *what* is what caused him to die, *where* is obviously San Diego, *when* is clearly when did it happen, and *how* is what caused the earthquake.'

'Who, what, where, when and how,' Jimmy repeated again.

'Exactly.'

'So *who* is going to get me my lunch? Is that what you mean?' Jimmy asked.

'Well I . . .'

'*What* are you going to get me? And *where* are you going to get it from?'

'Jimmy, it's only eleven . . .'

'*When* are you going to get it then? And *how* are you going to get it before I starve to death?'

'That's very funny, Jimmy,' Scoop commented dryly.

'It's not funny. I'm starving. Being a journalist is hard work.'

Scoop took a deep breath. 'All right Jimmy, even though we've hardly started, I'll go and get you something.' He turned his wheelchair towards the door. 'Although if you weren't a wanted criminal it would most certainly be the other way around.'

Jimmy was a bit concerned about the design end of things, but Scoop quickly reassured him:

'Don't worry, Jimmy – there's software for that. A monkey could do it!'

'Are you calling me a monkey?'

Scoop gave him a long look. And then: 'There's some very bright monkeys around, you know.'

In the late afternoon Scoop said: 'I'm just going to stretch my legs, as it were.'

When he'd gone Jimmy returned to surfing the Internet for the latest news, and it was while doing this that his thoughts returned to home. His parents would be tearing their hair out (and his dad didn't have much to spare). He had the opportunity now to send them an e-mail – if only they had an e-mail address, access to the Internet, or, indeed, a computer. Well, they could just wait a few days. Maybe it would teach them to appreciate him a little more. There was nothing to stop him sending a message to them via his school, of course. It had a website.

School – he was actually missing it, a tiny little bit. Not the work, obviously, but his friends. Messing around. If he could have changed anything about the past few days it would have been to bring Gary Higgins with him on this adventure. They would have had a cracking time together.

Thinking about Gary reminded him of his expulsion. What choice had his headmaster had? None at all. He'd been reckless and disruptive and had almost destroyed a school bus. He should e-mail Mr McCartney and apologize for his actions.

Jimmy logged on to the school website, and clicked on Mr McCartney's e-mail address.

He wrote, *Dear Mr McCartney*.

Then he hesitated. He knew what he *should* write. He knew what he *ought* to write. But he was Jimmy Armstrong, and there was really very little doubt about what he *would* write.

> *Dear Mr McCartney. How're you doing you scabby-faced baldy-headed vulture? Do you know that your secretary looks like a hamster? Does she keep nuts in her cheeks? Does she have an exercise wheel? Are you having an affair with her? If you are your children will be scabby-faced baldy-headed vultures too, but with the added attraction of big teeth and cheeks for nuts. Yours sincerely, Jimmy Armstrong.*

Jimmy's finger hesitated over the 'send' button – but

only for a couple of seconds. He was finished with school. He was on the high seas now, he had a job and he was getting paid for it. *So stuff you, McCartney!*

He sent it.

Jimmy was a journalist now. He typed a headline: *Small Earthquake in San Diego – Not Many Dead.*

It was true, there weren't many dead. But what he couldn't know, not yet anyway, was that the earthquake would set off a chain of events that would lead to the end of civilization as we know it.

Really.

San Diego

It is a universal truth that teenage boys, given the choice of either throwing a bottle they have recently found high into the air and watching it smash or setting it gently out of harm's way, will almost certainly choose to throw it.

Given the opportunity to throw *two* bottles, they are unlikely to compromise by smashing one and saving the other.

The boys in question were called Cameron Rodriguez and Patrick Hernandez, a fact which we are only aware of because just a few days after throwing the bottles they were both dead.

They lived in a housing project in San Diego, California. It was a rough area, and dangerous. Often, when they wished to play undisturbed by the local gangs the boys wandered out of the project and squeezed under a high wire fence on to a stretch of lush grass surrounding a laboratory owned by a company called Boris Bio Tech. On the morning of the San Diego earthquake the lab's entire staff were taking part in a softball tournament several miles away.

They felt the earthquake, but didn't for one moment think that it might affect their laboratory or indeed, lead to the end of civilization as we know it. Why would they? They were enjoying beer and hotdogs, while back at the lab the vibrations caused a faulty latch on a cupboard to give way. As a result approximately thirty bottles fell from their shelves. Of these, all but two landed harmlessly on the carpeted floor. The two that didn't bounced off a desk and through an open window. It was a ground-floor lab, so they didn't have a great distance to travel before landing, perfectly intact, on the soft lawn outside.

They might have remained there until staff discovered them the next day, and the world would not have been ruined, but for the inquisitiveness of Cameron Rodriguez and Patrick Hernandez. They were just having fun. They could not know that Boris Bio Tech's main work was top secret or that it developed poison gases for use in chemical warfare. Not to attack other countries, you understand, but to defend against other countries that might attack using their own poison gases. One bottle contained a very, very deadly poison gas. The other also contained a very, very deadly poison gas, although slightly different. But what Cameron and Patrick achieved by throwing these bottles into the air and smashing them was something the scientists at Boris Bio Tech had never even dared attempt. They mixed the contents of the two bottles.

* * *

Back on the *Titanic*, meanwhile, the earthquake remained just a small item in a newspaper almost entirely compiled by Jimmy Armstrong. When Scoop finally returned, later that afternoon, he wasn't looking well at all. His eyes were red, his skin blotchy and his brow damp. Jimmy had surprised himself by how much he'd enjoyed rewriting the stories and then slotting them into the newspaper, and he was anxious to show the nearly finished product to Scoop, but Scoop was too miserable to even look. He said, 'I'm sure it's fine . . . I'll look at it later . . . have to lie down.'

The suite where the paper was produced had a small bedroom at the rear, and it was into this that Scoop rolled.

'What . . . what do you want me to do?' Jimmy asked from the doorway.

'Whatever you like . . .'

'Do you want me to get a doctor?'

'No . . . sleep . . .' Scoop hauled himself out of the chair and on to the bed. 'Tired . . . Oh, they found your uniform . . . so be . . . careful. Captain gave me this . . . thought there might be a story in it . . .' Scoop pulled something small out of his shirt pocket and tossed it towards him. 'Catch . . .' Jimmy caught it. His lucky penny. 'You can . . . tell me . . . all about it. Later . . .'

Scoop's head fell to one side and he immediately

began to snore. Jimmy turned the coin over in his hand. He'd forgotten all about it and its stupid history. Well – with Scoop sleeping and his work on the paper finished, now was as good a time as any to get rid of it. He would go to the tallest point on the ship – the climbing wall on the top deck – and chuck it into the sea from there. Jimmy didn't believe for one moment that it was unlucky or cursed, but he would do it for his granda, who clearly did.

As he turned to leave the room he was surprised to see two prosthetic legs standing in the corner behind him. He smiled to himself. Maybe these were the legs Scoop had intended stretching earlier. He wondered why the old man preferred to use a wheelchair. Still – *none of my business*. He gently closed the door.

His intention was to get rid of the coin, but there were, of course, distractions along the way. On the twelfth floor he discovered an amusement arcade which he hadn't noticed on the floor plans. He spent an hour playing pinball. He played a one-sided game of air hockey. There was a vintage *Star Wars* game which involved an attack on the *Death Star*. He played that nine times in a row, slapping the machine in frustration each time he was burned to a crisp. When he climbed out of the machine, Claire Stanford was standing there, with her arms folded.

'Oh,' said Jimmy.

'So you're the little twerp who ran away to sea.'

'So you're the owner's stuck-up daughter.'

'How dare you!'

'*How dare you!*'

'You're in *so* much trouble!'

'*You're in* so *much trouble!*'

'Stop that!'

'*Stop that!*'

'You . . .'

'*You . . .*'

'You are—'

'*You are . . .*'

'You are not funny!'

'Oh yeah?'

'Aha – didn't copy me that time!'

'*Aha – didn't copy me that time!*'

'My dad's going to toss you . . .'

'*My dad's going to toss you . . .*'

'. . . in a cell and throw away the key.'

'He'll have to catch me first.'

Claire glared at him. '*I've* caught you.'

Jimmy laughed. 'I think not.'

'Yes I have. You're my prisoner.'

'Uhuh. Right up to the point where I walk past you and escape.'

'I won't let you.'

'Uhuh.'

Jimmy took a step towards her.

'I have a black belt in judo,' said Claire, raising her hands.

'And I have a black belt at home. It keeps my trousers up.'

Jimmy went to move past her. He kept his right shoulder down, meaning to give her a good shove on the way. But just as he leaned into her, Claire grabbed his arm, twisted it up, brought it down over her own shoulder, put her entire weight under him and heaved up. Jimmy was lifted off his feet and thrown. He landed in a heap in the corner, and for good measure banged his head on the *Star Wars* game.

He looked at her somewhat groggily. Then he shook himself. 'Lucky,' he said.

'I don't think so.'

Jimmy got to his feet. She was certainly stronger than she looked. But she was a girl, and he was a rough, tough product of the back streets of Belfast. He wasn't going to hurt her, but he was going to teach her a lesson she wouldn't forget.

Ten seconds later Jimmy lay in another heap. Claire stood over him, bouncing from left to right. 'Do you want some more? Do you? Not copying me now, are you? Are you?'

'What do you want,' Jimmy snapped, 'a *Blue Peter* badge? So you know a few tricks. I bet *Daddy* paid for judo lessons.'

'So *what*?'

'Well we aren't even then, are we? So Daddy's little rich girl has a black belt. Big deal. I bet you have a pony as well.'

Claire folded her arms and gave him a disdainful look. 'You can say whatever you like. Makes no difference. You're my prisoner.'

Jimmy looked quickly around him. There were two exits within striking distance. She might be good at judo, but he was fast on his feet. There was no shame in running away. Surviving was more important.

As if she could hear what he was thinking she said, 'And don't even think about running for it. I'm a sprinter. I have medals for it; I've represented my school at national level.'

'*Oooooooooooooh*,' said Jimmy, 'aren't we great?'

'Just get up. I'm taking you to the Captain.'

Jimmy got to his feet. 'What about a fair fight?'

'That *was* fair. You're just a pathetic fighter.'

'I mean, using something in here, something neither of us has had any training on. That would be fair. Like the air hockey.'

Claire looked at the table. 'I can beat you at anything,' she said.

'If I win, you let me go.'

'And what if I win?'

'You won't, but if by some miracle you do, I'm your prisoner, I'll go quietly, and as a bonus I'll never again repeat what you say.'

'Is that a promise?'

'*Is that a promise?*'

She almost laughed. She managed to turn it into a grunt and nodded at the table. 'You're on,' she said.

* * *

Claire might have had a rich father and judo lessons from an expensive coach, but Jimmy was an amusement arcade veteran. When he wasn't in school he virtually lived in one. He rarely had money to play the machines, but he hustled it by challenging other kids. He rarely lost. There was no official competition or title, but if you asked anyone in Jimmy's school, they would have confirmed that he deserved to be crowned the Air Hockey Champion of East Belfast.

They agreed it would be best of five games. He let her win the first one, just to see the cocky, condescending look on her face. He let her win the second, and he loved the way she gloated over every victorious stroke.

And then he let her have it.

He whipped her ass.

Her face coloured up, sweat rolled down her brow, her mouth tightened in anger and as the final, winning goal shot in she let out a yell of frustration.

'That's not fair!' she shouted.

'*That's not fair!*' mimicked Jimmy.

'You've played this before!'

'*You've played this before!*'

Jimmy raised his hands in mock apology.

'You – you – you – you . . .'

'Won,' said Jimmy. 'And now I'm off – free as a bird.' He gave a little bird whistle as he sauntered past. But then he stopped and extended his hand. 'Listen, no hard feelings, eh?'

It was an unexpectedly civilized thing to do, and much more in keeping with the circles Claire usually moved in. She might have been spoiled, but she was well brought up. So, albeit reluctantly, she clasped his hand.

Jimmy smiled in a friendly manner, then suddenly twisted her arm and spun her round before giving her a hefty shove in the bum with his left foot. Claire shot across the arcade, crashed into the *Star Wars* game and crumpled to the floor.

'Sucker,' laughed Jimmy. He jogged happily out of the arcade.

He was exhilarated: first the air hockey, then the humiliating *coup de grâce*. It was in both his nature and nurture to extract victory by either fair means or foul and he saw nothing wrong with it. Whether it was on the tough streets of his city or in the more luxurious surroundings of the *Titanic*, it was all about survival. Attack was the best form of defence, and if God sees fit to give you an advantage, you grab it with both hands.

In hindsight, he should perhaps have chosen to lie low for a while, but Jimmy still had a mountain to climb. Or at least a climbing wall. He rode up to the top deck and began to work his way up the artificial cliff face. It was growing dark now and a cool breeze was blowing hard against him. Usually crew members provided safety harnesses for passengers attempting the wall, but even if there'd been one available, Jimmy wouldn't have needed it. In just a few minutes he was straddling the top of the the wall, barely out of breath. He stared out to sea. America was somewhere ahead of him. While trawling for news on the Internet earlier on he had done a little research into how long a ship might take to cross the Atlantic, and while it depended on speed and size, he reckoned that they were now approaching the halfway mark. By tomorrow there would be no turning back.

Jimmy thrust his hands into his overall pockets – and found the lucky penny. He held on to the wall with one arm, then pulled his other arm back to throw it . . .

'YOU BOY!'

Jimmy peered down. Captain Smith and three other officers were looking up at him.

'GET DOWN HERE NOW!'

Jimmy looked about him, then back down. 'Are you talking to me?'

'GET DOWN HERE!'

Jimmy took a deep breath. Unless he suddenly developed the ability to fly, or to swim huge distances, there was no escape this time. He slipped the lucky penny into his pocket, then began to climb down.

When he finally reached the deck, having taken his time, he was grabbed, held in a tight arm-lock and quickly marched away. As he moved along the deck

Claire Stanford stepped out of the shadows. 'Who's the sucker now?' she hissed. Then, following on behind the prisoner and his escort she added, 'As a matter of fact I *don't* have a pony. I have *three*.'

Captain Smith

He wasn't on trial, but it felt like it.

Jimmy was hauled into Captain Smith's quarters on Deck Twelve and ordered to stand in the middle of the floor while the Captain and First Officer Simon Jeffers sat looking at him from behind a desk. After a few moments Mr Stanford – designer of the ship and owner of the cruise company – also joined them. Claire Stanford sat behind him. Each time Jimmy scowled at her an annoying smirk appeared on her face.

'Well?' the Captain asked.

'Well as can be expected,' said Jimmy.

The Captain's eyes flashed angrily. 'I *mean*, well, what have you got to say for yourself?'

Jimmy shrugged.

'Have you any idea of the trouble you have caused?'

'Sort of, yeah.'

'And?'

'And what?'

'Have you anything to say?'

Jimmy thought about it for a moment. 'Nice ship.'

Mr Stanford jumped to his feet. 'How dare you!' he shouted. 'Do you think this is funny?'

Jimmy shrugged.

'Have you any idea of the worry you have caused at home? The man-hours we have had to devote to finding you? The expense we will incur if we have to return to port? Have you?'

'Sort of.'

'Again, what have you got to say for yourself?'

Jimmy looked across at the three men. Two were in uniform, one was in a grey suit. They all looked extremely angry.

Jimmy shrugged.

Mr Stanford's fist hit the table. 'I've a good mind to toss him overboard!' He sighed loudly, then sat down again.

First Officer Jeffers leaned towards the ship's owner and spoke in a quiet, controlled voice. 'Actually, Mr Stanford, we haven't yet reported to Belfast that he's been found. We *could* throw him overboard, and no one would be any the wiser.'

Captain Smith nodded as he lit his pipe. 'Good point,' he said. 'We *are* the only witnesses. Apart from Claire, of course. What do you say, Claire? Chuck him overboard?'

'Absolutely,' said Claire.

Jimmy swallowed. He *knew* they wouldn't throw him overboard. Or he *thought* he knew. But he'd also heard that strange things happened at sea. He also still had his lucky penny in his pocket, which was like a kiss of death. Still . . . still . . . even though he *knew* there was only an infinitesimal possibility of him being thrown into the sea, he thought a little backtracking might be in order. A little fake humility.

'Sorry,' Jimmy mumbled.

'What was that?' asked the Captain.

'*Sorry*.'

'For what?'

'For whatever I've done wrong.'

'Do you *know* what you've done wrong?'

'Yes.'

'Why don't you tell us, then?' asked Mr Stanford.

Jimmy shook his head.

'So you *don't* know?'

Jimmy took a deep breath. Now he was trying to hold on to his temper. Stanford was just like McCartney. He always had to keep pushing. Jimmy had never really apologized for anything in his life, but now that he'd made the effort apparently it wasn't good enough – Stanford was intent on making him spell out every last detail of his supposed indiscretions. 'Look,' he said, 'I'm sorry, all right? I sneaked on to the boat and I shouldn't have. I fell asleep. I didn't mean to stow away or whatever you call it. I don't *want* to be here . . .'

'Then why didn't you give yourself up as soon as you realized?'

'Well would you?' Jimmy snapped.

First Officer Jeffers almost laughed at that. A vague hint of a smile appeared on Smith's face. But Stanford's eyes blazed.

The Captain puffed on his pipe. 'Well,' he said, 'there's nothing can be done now. And much as we would *like* to throw you to the sharks we would only end up getting ourselves in trouble, and we can't have that. Now, thanks to the astonishing speed at which we are travelling – and you can thank Mr Stanford for that, she really is an amazing ship – we will very shortly reach the halfway point in our voyage to Miami, which I'm afraid makes it impractical for us to turn back to Belfast. So you will have to continue with us until we reach port. There you will be handed over to the authorities and they will do with you as they see fit. However, Master Armstrong, that doesn't mean you get free passage. You will be put to work.'

'What sort of work?' Jimmy asked.

'Whatever we decide!' Mr Stanford exploded.

Captain Smith raised a calming hand, then nodded across the cabin. 'Claire, if you could ask Scoop to step— *roll* into the room?'

Claire slipped out. A few moments later Scoop, who'd obviously been waiting outside, appeared in the doorway. He didn't look at Jimmy as he manoeuvred through the opening and pulled up beside him.

'Captain,' he said. 'Mr Stanford.' He nodded at Jeffers.

'Scoop – you've asked to have the boy work for you on the paper.'

'Yes, Captain. I gather he's supposed to be at school. Well I've a hundred and one things I could have him doing. I'll work him into the ground.'

Captain Smith nodded at Jimmy. 'Well? Can I trust you to work on the paper and not get into any more bother?'

Jimmy sighed. Then he nodded.

'Very well. And Claire?' Claire had retaken her seat, but now the Captain waved her forward. She stood on Scoop's other side. 'We should thank you for leading us to our young stowaway.' Claire beamed widely. 'However, you may not be aware that your encounter with young Mr Armstrong in the amusement arcade was actually caught on camera.'

The smile faltered. 'What do you mean—?'

'Be quiet, Claire, and listen,' her father snapped.

'Daddy, don't speak to—'

'Claire!'

She fell silent.

The Captain nodded at Mr Stanford before continuing. 'Yes, Claire. Obviously with an amusement arcade it's important for us to monitor what goes on there. Parents like to know that their children aren't getting up to any mischief or that they're not being bullied. First Officer Jeffers here happened to spot your little altercation with Jimmy, didn't you, Jeffers?'

'Yes, sir. Just caught the end of it.' He smiled at Claire. 'The judo lessons seem to be paying off.'

Claire couldn't manage a smile this time.

'In fact,' said the Captain, 'once alerted to the situation, we all came and watched. We all listened. Yes, Claire, it's a state-of-the-art system and we could hear every word. So you will understand that we were a little distressed to hear you promise to let the lad go if he beat you at air hockey, and then immediately renege on the deal by following him to the climbing wall and informing us.'

'Because he *kicked* me!' Claire exploded.

'And that's not to be condoned; but nevertheless, a deal is a deal. It's a terrible thing not to be able to trust someone.'

Claire looked hopefully to her father. 'Daddy . . .'

'The Captain's right, Claire. I was very disappointed. And more than that, your mother and I have both been very upset by your behaviour recently.'

'*What?*'

'You've been bad tempered, disobedient, you never have a pleasant word . . .'

'Daddy *please*, not in front of—!'

'. . . for anyone, you sulk all day and you *do* nothing . . .'

'Daddy!'

'No, Claire, we've had quite enough of your behaviour. The reason we bring it up now is that the Captain has a solution.'

'He *what*?'

'Claire, you were allowed to come on this trip because it was important to me to have my family with me; it was supposed to be a very special time for us. But you've come very close to ruining the voyage for all of us.'

'I—'

'Be quiet!' Tears sprang into his daughter's eyes. 'Now – Captain?'

'Claire – your birthday was just last week, wasn't it?'

'What?' She was now looking very confused.

'Tell me, what did your parents get you?'

She started to shrug, but then blurted out: 'A camera.'

'What sort of a camera?'

'I don't know.'

'That's because it's still sitting in its box,' said Mr Stanford. 'It's a state-of-the-art digital camera. Professional photographers would give their eye teeth for one, and I don't have to tell you it cost a small fortune. But she hardly looked at it.'

'I didn't *ask* for a camera,' Claire snapped.

Stanford shook his head sadly, then looked at the Captain and raised an eyebrow. 'You see what I'm up against?'

Captain Smith nodded. 'Claire – your parents have decided that you need to learn a thing or two, not just about honesty, but to appreciate what a very privileged life you lead. They've come to the end of their tether with you, quite frankly, and at least as far as the remainder of this trip is concerned, they are prepared to hand matters of discipline over to me.'

'*Discipline?*' She looked in disbelief at her father, who was now sitting back in his chair, arms folded. 'You can't do that . . .!'

'Well he has, Claire. And what I've decided . . .'

'You can't *do* that!' Claire repeated, only louder.

'Be quiet, Claire!' her father ordered.

Claire stood shaking her head, tears rolling down her cheeks.

'. . . what I've decided is that you take your new camera, you work out how to use it, and you work alongside Scoop and Jimmy on the newspaper. Isn't that right, Scoop?'

Scoop nodded. 'It'll be a great help.'

Jimmy looked aghast.

'Well, Claire?' asked the Captain.

'I won't do it. You can't make me.'

'Very well.' The Captain turned and nodded at Mr Stanford, who shook his head regretfully.

Claire followed this exchange. 'What . . . what?'

'Claire, if you can't do this simple thing we're asking then we'll have no alternative. I know how much you were looking forward to shopping in Miami and touring the Caribbean with us, but I'm afraid you'll be catching the first plane back to school instead.'

Claire looked horrified. 'You can't do that – I'm your *daughter*!'

'Sometimes I wonder,' said Mr Stanford.

* * *

In the end she agreed. She had no choice. Scoop rolled out of the cabin first, with Jimmy and Claire following behind.

'I *hate* you,' Claire hissed at Jimmy.

'Not as much as I hate you,' Jimmy hissed back.

'And I hate the both of you,' hissed Scoop, 'but I still have to work with you. Now shut your pie holes and get a move on.'

Fighting and Dying

Jimmy and Claire fought and bickered and swore and hurled insults, names and anything that wasn't tied down at each other on the way to Scoop's office. They went on and on and on and . . . eventually Scoop's wheelchair screeched to a halt. He spun around and yelled: 'ENOUGH!'

Jimmy let go of Claire's hair.

Claire released Jimmy's foot.

'There's no need to shout,' said Jimmy.

'I'm not deaf,' said Claire.

'Well then just . . . *stop* it. *Please*.' He opened the door and led them in. 'You'll be working together whether you like each other or not, so get used to it. But believe you me, it'll be an awful lot easier if you just learn to get on. All right?'

Jimmy shrugged. Claire looked at her nails.

'OK. Now, Jimmy, I want you to explain to Claire about the *who*, *what*, *where*, *when*, *how* . . .'

'The *what*?' Claire demanded.

'How to write a story,' said Jimmy.

Claire snorted. 'I know how to write a story.'

'This is different, Claire,' said Scoop. 'It's journalism.'

'Not fairytales about your little ponies,' said Jimmy.

'Shut your trap!'

'Kids, *please*!'

'I was editor of the school newspaper,' said Claire.

'*I was editor of the school newspaper*,' mimicked Jimmy. 'What was it, the *Pony Express*?'

They continued with the bickering until gradually they became aware that Scoop was just sitting there, watching, not bothering to tell them off. After a few more exchanges, they fell silent.

'All right,' Scoop said quietly, 'we're clearly not going to get anywhere with this tonight. And I've had enough of it. I want you to go to your rooms, and I want you both to have a long think. Captain Smith has spelled out to each of you what will happen if you don't work with me on this. So either come in bright and fresh and friendly in the morning, or don't come in at all and deal with the consequences.'

Jimmy shrugged. Claire examined her nails again.

'Right. Off with you then.'

They walked out together. They moved up the corridor side by side, in silence. When they came to the elevators at the end, they both stepped in. Claire pressed for the fourteenth floor. Jimmy pressed for the ninth. They travelled upwards without speaking or looking at each other.

When the doors opened Jimmy stepped out.

'Brain dead,' said Claire.

The doors began to close.

'Fat arse,' said Jimmy.

As they lay sleeping that night, lost in their own dreams and nightmares, the virus was spreading rapidly through the city of San Diego. TV news programmes were calling it 'The Plague' or 'The Red Death'. In St Mary's Hospital, where the two dying boys had been brought, the doctors were utterly unable to identify the cause of their illness, and weren't even aware that they themselves had been infected. By the time a well-practised quarantine procedure was finally introduced it was far too late. The virus was too strong. Thousands were falling ill. First there was a high fever, then came huge pulsating sores. Finally lungs filled with yellow poison, drowning the victims.

The city was dying – the state, the country, and the entire world was under a death sentence.

'We can use this, can't we?' Jimmy asked the next morning, nodding at a news story he'd pulled up on his computer screen. Scoop rolled up alongside and studied it. The Governor of California had declared a state of emergency in San Diego, and was being urged to do the same in Los Angeles. All flights to and from those cities had been grounded, and the roads closed. Scientists were battling to identify the source of the outbreak and to produce a cure High doses of antibiotics were being administered to patients but with little success. The President said his prayers were with the people of California. The first case was reported in Washington DC shortly after the President issued his statement.

'Well,' said Scoop, 'in this case we have several options. As a journalist, of course you want to use it; it's a huge story, it has everything you want – drama, tragedy, death . . . but you have to remember you're on a cruise ship, and you don't want to cause panic amongst your passengers. And if half of California is in quarantine then the passengers we were expecting from San Diego or Los Angeles probably aren't going to make it to the ship in time, so we don't have to write *for* them. What we do is practise responsible journalism – report the news in a calm, matter-of-fact way, don't sensationalize.'

Jimmy said: 'Damn. I was going to write the headline, *We're All Going to Die*.'

Scoop laughed. 'This is California we're talking about – Hollywood. They exaggerate *everything*. In a few days we'll find out that it's nothing more than bad flu.'

'What about – *Californians Should Stop Whining and Go Back to Work*?'

'No.'

Half an hour later the door opened and Claire appeared, yawning.

Scoop looked at his watch. 'Jimmy's been here since eight-thirty. It is now ten-fifteen.'

'I had a swim. Then I had to get my nails done.'

'We start at eight-thirty.'

'Relax, would you? It's not like it's a real job.'

Scoop took this as a direct attack on his profession. 'If you're late tomorrow you will be sacked,' he snapped. 'Then your father will take the appropriate action.'

Claire rolled her eyes. 'All right, all right, keep your hair on. I'm here now, aren't I?' She took a seat beside Jimmy. He hadn't looked at her, or said a word. He continued to study the screen. 'Good morning, James.'

'It's Jimmy.'

'Isn't that short for James? I much prefer James. Kings were called James. Jimmy is someone who comes round and fixes your drains.'

'It's Jimmy.'

'Please yourself.' She looked at Scoop. 'Well? What do you want me to do?'

Jimmy couldn't believe it. His first proper assignment was to go down to the kitchens and interview Pedroza, the chef. Claire was to go with him to take photographs.

He had protested immediately. 'But you told me he was as mad as a bag of spiders.'

'That's what you want in an interview, someone with a bit of personality.'

'But what if he goes mental on me?'

'Even better.'

Jimmy looked at Claire. 'What are you smirking at?'

'Nothing, James.'

They found Pedroza sitting over a coffee and reading an old newspaper at a table on a small section of the deck outside the kitchens reserved for catering staff. The floor was littered with cigarette butts.

Jimmy hesitantly approached. Scoop had told him that Pedroza was expecting him, but he certainly didn't look like he was. His black eyes burned into Jimmy. 'Ah . . . hello . . . I'm . . . from . . . the *newspaper* . . .' Jimmy began, pointing down at the paper. 'I'm here . . . to . . . *interview* . . . you . . .'

Pedroza looked at him blankly.

'You sound like you're talking to an old deaf person,' said Claire.

'Shut up,' snapped Jimmy. Turning back to Pedroza, he continued, 'Do . . . you . . . speak . . . *English*? Have . . . you . . . worked . . . on . . . a . . . ship . . .' and he waved vaguely around him, '. . . like . . . this . . . before?'

Pedroza's brow furrowed, then he spat something short and sharp in a language Jimmy didn't recognize.

'Where . . . do . . . *you* . . . come . . . from?' Then he pointed out to sea. 'Far . . . away?'

Pedroza thought for a moment, then he brightened suddenly and pointed at the water. 'Fish,' he said.

'Nice one,' said Claire.

'Will you shut up?' Jimmy exploded. 'I'd like to see you do any better!'

Claire smiled sarcastically, then sat down in the chair opposite Pedroza and began to address him in fluent Portuguese. Jimmy's mouth dropped open. A few moments later a torrent of words issued from the chef, all accompanied by enthusiastic hand gestures. Claire turned to Jimmy. 'He's from Africa originally, but has settled in Lisbon in Portugal, he's married with six children, he's been a chef with White Star for fifteen years, he only gets back to see his family twice a year and he misses them very much. Are you going to write any of this down?'

Jimmy fumbled for his pen. 'Ye-yeah – hold on . . .' He began to write as quickly as he could. 'Lisbon . . . six children . . . only gets back . . .' Then he glanced up. 'Why didn't you say you spoke Portuguese?'

'You didn't ask.' Before Jimmy could respond Claire returned her attention to the chef, and began firing questions at him. As soon as Pedroza responded, she translated in the same animated fashion, and Jimmy quickly jotted down the details. One hundred and five thousand meals prepared every week . . . three hundred thousand desserts . . . one and a half thousand pounds of coffee . . . eight thousand gallons of ice cream . . . When he'd filled seven pages with facts and figures, and they all seemed a lot more relaxed, Jimmy said: 'Ask him how come he screams at anyone who drops food on the carpet, or tries to smuggle it out of the restaurant.'

Claire repeated the question. Pedroza got out of his chair and poked Jimmy in the chest. He barked something. Then he poked him again. Jimmy took a step backwards. Pedroza snarled something else. As Jimmy moved backwards Pedroza went with him. Claire translated in staccato fashion as she followed them across the deck.

'He says . . . messy people drive him mad . . . he slaves over food but because it is free people don't care if they drop it . . . they don't pick it up . . . they grind it into the carpet . . . they fill their plates . . . and only eat a little bit . . . and throw the rest out . . . then try something else . . . they are greedy and lazy . . . and the food they leave . . . would feed his village in Africa for many years.'

Pedroza had Jimmy backed right up against the railings now and was still jabbering away.

Jimmy looked to Claire for help. 'Claire, please – tell him to back off!'

Claire spoke rapidly in Portuguese.

'And,' Jimmy added, 'why don't you tell him he's mad as a bag of spiders, and if he spits in my face one more time I'll twist his ears off and stick them up his nose.'

'Why don't you tell me yourself?' Pedroza asked, this time in perfect English.

'I . . . I . . . I . . . I . . . I . . . I . . .'

Pedroza laughed suddenly, prodded Jimmy once

more in the chest, then turned away. He retook his seat and lifted his newspaper.

Claire stared down at him in disbelief. 'You can speak . . .'

Pedroza's eyes narrowed. 'Sometimes it is good to have secrets.' He glanced across at Jimmy without any attempt to conceal his contempt. 'And sometimes it is good to know when to keep your mouth shut.'

Jimmy felt a shiver run down his spine.

'Did you notice,' Jimmy asked on the way back to the newspaper office, 'that in every single photo you took of him he had some kind of knife in his hand?'

'He's a chef, of course he had.'

'He creeps me out.'

'*You* creep *me* out.'

Jimmy made a face.

'These are really neat,' Claire said, clicking through the photos on the camera as they approached the office.

'Yeah, *right*,' said Jimmy.

When they re-entered the office they were surprised to find Scoop *standing* by the window, looking out. He rapped a fist on his legs, making a hollow, metallic sound. 'Thought I'd give them a spin,' he said, smiling. 'Land ahoy and all that. Never going to win an Olympic medal for sprinting, but they're not bad. Now then, how was our chef?'

'Mad as a . . .' Jimmy began, already sitting down at his desk and beginning to type.

'Fine . . .' said Claire at the same time.

Scoop looked from one to the other. 'OK, let's get a look at those pictures then.'

Claire began to push buttons on the back of her camera. 'If I can just hook it up to a monitor we can . . .' But then she stopped. She pushed some more buttons. Then she looked up, her face now rather pale. 'I've erased them.'

'What?' said Scoop.

'I was trying to get rid of the ones I didn't like, but I've erased them all.'

'Let me see.'

Scoop took hold of the camera. After a while he let out a long sigh. 'Did you by any chance read the instructions before you started pushing buttons?'

Claire examined her nails.

'Brain dead,' said Jimmy.

Claire's eyes snapped up. 'You—'

'Stop!' Scoop waved a warning finger at her. Claire held her tongue. 'All right, Claire, they're gone, it happens. It's not the end of the world. However, I want to put this paper together this afternoon, print up some copies, let the Captain take a look. But I can't run Jimmy's feature without a picture. If you race down to the kitchen now and smile nicely at him you might just persuade him to pose for you again.'

'All right. I'm really sorry.' Claire took her camera back and turned for the door. As she passed behind Jimmy she glanced at his screen. 'There's only one f in chef,' she hissed.

As she hurried through the door Jimmy shouted after her: 'And there's only one t in idiot!'

Life in the Freezer

Scoop was angry. An hour after hurrying off to retake Pedroza's picture Claire had still not returned. The paper was all ready to print but for the space left for her picture of the Portuguese chef. Jimmy knew it was only a dummy edition of the newspaper, a practice run that would only be seen by the Captain and a few crew members, but he still felt oddly excited about it: his article was inside. Scoop had read it over, removed a couple of paragraphs, moved several others around, but then pronounced himself more than happy with it. 'Jim lad,' he said, 'I think you've a talent for this.'

Jimmy shrugged and said, 'Yeah, right.' In two years at East Belfast High nobody had ever suggested that he had a talent for anything. Apart from causing trouble.

'Now where is that girl?'

'Off doing her nails,' suggested Jimmy. 'Or counting her money.'

Scoop ignored him. 'Do me a favour, will you, Jimmy? Take a run down to the kitchens and see if she's still down there. Maybe she's trying to do something arty with her camera – just tell her I haven't time for any of that nonsense, I've a paper to produce. Get her back up here pronto.'

At home, if anyone had asked him for a favour he would have told them where to go, or demanded payment in advance and then probably not done it anyway, but this felt different. He wanted to see his work in print. And his name. He wanted to read *by Jimmy Armstrong*. But it wasn't going to happen unless Claire showed up with her photos.

There was no sign of her in the kitchens. Pedroza snapped that she'd been and gone, and ordered Jimmy out because he was busy. Jimmy then travelled up to her family's penthouse suite on the tenth floor. The cabin door was open. Jimmy could see Claire's mother standing on the balcony. He knocked anyway, but when he got no response he stepped into the cabin. Her mum had an easel set up and was painting the setting sun, but the rush of the wind prevented her hearing him approach, so that when he did say hello she nearly jumped out of her skin.

'Sorry,' said Jimmy. 'I was looking for Claire.'

'Have you never heard of knocking?' said Mrs Stanford.

'I did knock.'

She looked him up and down, rather suspiciously. 'You're the stowaway, aren't you?' Jimmy shrugged. 'Tell me, what are you running away from?'

'Nothing.'

'You must be running away from something. If not, why stow away?'

'It was an accident.'

'I think I can admire a boy who ran away for a reason. I'm not sure I can admire one who ran away by mistake.'

Jimmy blinked at her. 'Have you seen Claire?'

'Oh, she was here a few minutes ago – stormed in and stormed out.'

'Do you know where she went?'

'How would I know that? I'm the last person she tells anything to. And a word of warning, young man. She's bad enough as she is – don't you be leading her any further astray. I know your sort.'

Jimmy just stood there. He was pretty sure that she didn't know his 'sort' at all, and she certainly didn't know him. He nodded at her painting. 'Have you been painting for long?'

'All of my life, child, all of my life.'

'Well, you'd think with all that practice you'd be a bit better at it.'

Jimmy hurriedly removed himself from the cabin.

He found Claire twenty minutes later, standing on the very top deck, staring out to sea. Her camera sat on a sunbed beside her. He came up behind her and snapped: 'What are you playing at, you lazy cow?'

Just like her mother, she hadn't heard him approach – but instead of looking mildly annoyed Claire looked absolutely terrified. Her eyes were red-rimmed from crying. There was obviously something going on with her. But it was none of his business. She pointed at the camera. 'There it is, take it.'

'You took the photos, right?'

'Yes, I took your stupid photos.'

'Then you have to come down and put them on to the computer and help pick out the right one.'

'I don't *have* to do anything. You take it if you want. It's only a silly pretend newspaper.'

'Right.' Jimmy lifted the camera and was about to walk off. But then he decided he wasn't going to let her off so easily. He stood with his hands on his hips. 'Can't stick with anything for more than five minutes before you go crying to Daddy, can you? You're a complete waste of space.'

He turned away – but he hadn't gone more than a few steps before she let out a cry, threw herself down on to one of the sunbeds and buried her face in her hands. This only made Jimmy angrier. He stomped back to the sunbed. 'What's wrong? Did your gold credit card fall overboard? Did you chip your nail polish?'

'Go away!'

'OK.' He turned again.

'No, wait!'

Jimmy sighed loudly. '*What?*'

Claire's face was still pressed against the sunbed's wooden slats. 'Why do you hate me?' she asked weakly.

Jimmy didn't even have to think about that one. 'It's a mix of your appearance and personality.'

She was quiet for a moment, then slowly turned and wiped at her eyes. 'I hate you too,' she said, 'but I'm scared and I have to tell someone.'

'Scared of what?'

'Do you swear to God you won't tell anyone?'

'No.'

'*Please*.' She said it with so much feeling that Jimmy was forced to deliver one of his better shrugs. Then he sat down on a sunbed. Not beside her, but three removed.

'What, then?'

Claire took a deep breath and held her hand against her chest while she tried to settle herself. When she spoke she didn't look at Jimmy but at the deck, and her voice was kind of vague, as if she was describing a dream she only half remembered.

'I . . . went down to take the photos . . . to the kitchens . . . but there was no one about so I walked straight through to the freezers. Have you seen them? They're huge and there's about a dozen of them . . . and I heard voices coming from inside one of them . . . and the door was open just a fraction . . . All I wanted was the stupid photo, you know? Anyway, I looked in and there were . . . like . . . these *people* in there . . . and they weren't crew they were like a family, men and women and children . . . just sitting there talking . . . The fridge wasn't even switched on so it wasn't cold, there were sunbeds on the floor and clothes scattered all over the place and it smelled terrible . . . and one of them looked up and saw me and I just froze . . . then he shouted something and I moved backwards . . . but straight into Pedroza, and he started screaming at me . . . but not even in Portuguese or English – in some . . . I don't know, African tongue or something. I told him I just wanted to take his picture again, and he calmed down and smiled and . . . that was even scarier. He led me back to the kitchen and he took out this huge knife and stood holding it up and I took my picture and just as I took it he said: "If you tell anyone what you saw in there I will use this knife to cut your head off. And after that I will cut your mother's head off. And then your father's. Do you understand?" And then he just smiled and walked away.'

She looked up for the first time, straight at Jimmy.

Jimmy nodded to himself for several moments. 'So how did the photo turn out?'

'Jimmy! Please! I'm serious.'

'Well, they're stowaways, aren't they? And Pedroza threatened to kill you because your record with stowaways isn't very good, is it?'

'That's not fair!'

'Isn't it?'

'No. You're . . . *different*. There's a whole family living in a freezer! They could be anything. What if they're terrorists?'

'Did they look like terrorists?'

'What do terrorists look like?'

'I've no idea.'

'Jimmy – please! They shouldn't be there! But Pedroza's going to kill me if I tell anyone!'

Jimmy nodded. Then he raised a finger, as if he'd had a sudden brainwave. 'I know what's going on . . .'

'*What?*'

'It's all a figment of your imagination.'

'My . . .?'

'You made all this up just to add a bit of excitement to your life, or to get a lot of people panicked or worried because . . . well, because that's what you're like. You like being the centre of attention.'

'You . . . you!' Claire suddenly reached across and snapped her camera out of his hands. 'Right! I'll *prove* it to you! I'm going down now to get a picture of them. And if you were any sort of a journalist at all, you'd want to come as well, to get the story, but you're obviously not. You can't even spell!'

She snorted dismissively and stomped off towards the elevators.

'Let me know if he cuts your head off!' Jimmy shouted after her.

If you mix anger with fear, you quite often get adrenaline. Now it buzzed through Claire like electricity. She was *determined* to prove that Pedroza's mysterious family existed. She only needed a second to take a photo and then she would make Jimmy Armstrong eat his words.

The first person she saw when she reached the kitchens was Pedroza himself. She almost turned back right there and then. But he was too busy overseeing dinner preparation to notice her and she was able to duck in low behind a counter and run, half doubled-over towards the freezers.

OK, so far so good.

Six massive doors lined either side of the freezer room. Five were closed, but the sixth, where she'd seen the family earlier, was still tantalizingly open. Claire swung the camera off her shoulder, set it the way Scoop had shown her, then cautiously ventured forward. There was no light on inside the freezer, so she would have to use flash. It would immediately alert those hiding inside, but she had no choice.

Hit and run. Hit and run!

Claire stood to one side of the door. All she could hear was a dull hum from the other freezers, the buzz of the fluorescent lights above and the thundering of her own heart. She checked her camera once more. She would only have one chance. She wasn't going to get them to say cheese.

Deep breath!

She counted to three, then she stepped into the gap, raised the camera and took her shot. She was already turning away as it flashed, but she stopped immediately. There was no need to flee. The freezer was completely empty.

Claire stared into it. Not only were the people gone, so were all of their belongings. The shabby suitcases, the rubbish on the floor, even the sunbed. She glanced to her left and right, trying to decide if somehow she'd targeted the wrong freezer.

No. I'm certain.

It was only an hour since her frightening encounter with Pedroza – long enough to move them elsewhere. As Jimmy had shown, it was easy enough to hide yourself on a ship as big as the *Titanic*. But she couldn't go back and tell him that. He would be doubly convinced she'd made it all up. There *had* to be some evidence.

Claire stepped into the freezer.

Although it wasn't switched on it was still cool inside. And clean. It was *just* a freezer.

Claire jumped at a sudden knock on the freezer door. Her heart threatened to burst out of her chest as she turned, fully expecting to see Pedroza with a carving knife. But it was Jimmy, grinning in.

'Why don't you introduce me to the family?' he asked smugly.

'Jimmy,' Claire hissed, 'what are you doing here?'

'Writing a story. At first it was going to be about a mysterious group of stowaways, now it's going to be about a little rich kid who makes up all kinds of crap.'

'They *were* here, I swear . . .'

Jimmy stepped into the freezer. The metallic floor, walls and ceiling were spotless. 'Come out and show yourselves!' Jimmy cried.

'Shhhh! Don't . . .'

And then she saw it.

Jimmy had moved to her left, blocking the light from outside for just a moment, but as the light bounced off the wall in front of her again she saw . . . she wasn't certain . . . she moved closer – it *was* . . .

'*Look*, Jimmy!'

Jimmy moved up to her shoulder. At first he saw nothing.

'I don't . . .'

'You're blocking the light again.'

Jimmy moved and looked again.

'I still don't . . .'

Then he saw it. A tiny hand-print on the wall. A child's hand.

Claire smiled triumphantly. 'They must have been here, how else could—'

It wasn't a *sound* that made them both turn together, it was a change in the light. Not sudden and swift, like a light being switched off, but just a gradual dimming.

The freezer door was closing!

They had the briefest glimpse of Pedroza's laughing face before they were plunged into utter darkness.

'No!' Claire yelled.

They charged blindly across the room together, but only in time to hear a lock being turned.

They hammered on the door. They demanded to be let out, they screamed and threatened and, after a while, begged. Yet, already, somewhere within themselves, they knew it was useless; that the doors were too thick; that all their banging and shouting could not be heard outside.

'Claire . . .'

'Please! Let us out! Please!'

'Claire!'

'*What?*'

'Listen.'

A loud hum.

'Oh no,' said Claire. 'Oh no!'

The freezer had been switched on.

They started their hammering on the door again.

'*Please . . . let us out! Please!*'

Ice

It was pitch black. This was a good thing in some ways, because they couldn't see the cold mist of their breath or the ice forming on their hair and eyebrows. They weren't aware of the look of raw fear in each other's eyes. There was just the hum of the freezer and the chattering of their teeth. It had been an hour. They were freezing.

They had agreed not to panic.

Then they had panicked.

They had yelled and hammered. They had jogged on the spot, trying to keep warm. But the cold penetrated everything astonishingly quickly. Of the two, Jimmy was better off. He was still wearing the overalls he had swiped from the crew locker room. Claire was in a T-shirt and jeans.

'How . . . could he . . . do this?' Jimmy whispered through frozen lips.

'If you'd . . . just believed me . . . then I wouldn't . . . have come . . . down here again . . .'

'So . . . it's *my* . . . fault?'

'Yes . . . everything . . . is your fault . . .'

Despite this, they hugged each other, trying to keep warm.

'I can't . . . feel my feet . . .' said Jimmy.

'My nose . . . is so *sore* . . .'

'I hate . . . this boat . . .'

'It's . . . a . . . ship . . .'

'Shut . . . *up* . . .'

'*You* . . . shut . . . up . . .' Claire squeezed tight against him. 'Why . . . do you . . . hate me . . . Jimmy?'

'I . . . don't know . . . I just . . . do.'

'If we get . . . out . . . we should . . . try and get along . . . better.'

'Why?'

'Oh . . . *Jimmy* . . .'

They were quiet then for a long while. Jimmy's mind wandered back home to the endless cacophony of life in the Armstrong house, to his mum who'd shout at him day and night, but defend him to her dying breath, then back further, back to his namesake, the first Lucky Jimmy Armstrong. How ironic – he had died in the icy seas with his beloved *Titanic*, and now here *he* was, freezing to death as well. And all for the sake of a photograph for a dummy newspaper not more than two or three people would ever have seen.

The camera!

Jimmy suddenly shook Claire. She had been drifting off as well.

'What . . . what . . .?'

'Claire . . . where's the camera . . . your camera, where is it?'

'What . . . camera . . . oh . . . I don't . . . I mean, I . . . I dropped it . . . when we were banging on . . . why?'

'We need to find it . . . come on . . . down on your hands and knees . . . move out that way . . .'

Claire got down and began feeling around her blindly. 'Why . . . Jimmy? What's the point . . .?'

Jimmy was already working his way across to the door. 'It's just . . . an idea . . . but if we can just . . .'

'Got it!'

Jimmy slid across the floor in Claire's direction. Their heads cracked together in the dark.

'Aaaaow!' Claire shouted. 'Watch where you're . . .'

'OK! Sorry! Just . . . can you . . . switch it on . . . in the dark?'

'I think . . .' Her numb fingers felt along the back of the camera.

'Scoop said . . . that with modern cameras . . . news photographers can send their pictures . . . directly to their newspapers . . . They have . . . built in . . . modems . . . the Internet . . .'

There was a sudden glow in the darkness as Claire found the switch.

'The menu . . . find the menu . . .'

They peered at the illuminated symbols.

'There . . .' An Internet icon. 'OK . . . now . . . listen to me . . . what if . . . we write something . . . on the wall, then we take our photo . . . beside it . . . send it . . . to Scoop . . .?'

'Jimmy . . . no . . . there wouldn't be . . . signal . . . not in here . . .'

'Do you . . . have a . . . better . . . idea?'

'No . . . I just . . .'

'Then let's try it!'

Jimmy felt his way across to the wall, which was now covered in a thin film of ice. He felt in his overall pocket and removed the lucky penny. Of some use at last! Jimmy had some difficulty with his own frozen fingers, but he finally got the coin into the right position and began to scrape letters into the wall.

'What . . . are . . . you . . . writing . . .?'

H . . . E . . . L . . . P . . . It was hard work. His fingers were so numb he kept dropping the coin. STUCK IN FREEZER.

They were odd-looking, spindly letters, and he'd no idea if they'd show up in a photo, but then he had no idea if the photo would ever make its way out of the freezer anyway.

'OK . . .' Jimmy said, 'now you . . . stand . . . in front . . . I'll take . . . your picture . . .'

'Me? Why . . . not . . . you . . .?'

'Because . . . they're going . . . to come . . . running an . . . awful lot faster . . . for the . . . owner's daughter . . . than for some . . . stowaway . . .'

'No . . .' said Claire. 'Both . . . of . . . us . . .'

She grabbed the arm of his overall and pulled him beside her. Her own fingers were shaking like crazy, but she still managed to set the timer. Then she held it out in front of them and took the picture. They immediately huddled around the little screen on the back and examined the image. They looked white-faced and slightly bug-eyed – and the letters behind them read: TUCK IN FREE.

Despite their horrible situation, they couldn't help but laugh.

'Come on . . . let's do . . . it . . . again . . .' Claire set the timer again, but this time laid the camera on the ground. Jimmy took the lucky penny and lodged it underneath so that the lens was pointing up.

Then they huddled together.

'Say cheese . . .' said Jimmy.

But neither of them did. The camera flashed. They checked the image again, and this time their written cry for help was perfectly clear. Claire called the menu up and they pressed the Internet icon.

Jimmy spelled out the newspaper's e-mail address, and Claire slowly typed it in. The keyboard was so tiny and her fingers so lacking in feeling it was difficult to get right. It took more than five minutes of pushing, then deleting, pushing, then deleting, before she succeeded.

Then it was ready to go.

'Fingers . . . crossed,' said Claire.

'I can't . . .' said Jimmy. 'They'll . . . snap off . . . if I . . . try . . .'

Claire pushed the 'send' button.

Scoop was sitting at his desk in the newspaper office when Captain Smith and Mr Stanford arrived together.

'Ah – gentlemen,' he said. 'Thanks for coming. I wanted to show you something.'

The captain and the owner pulled up a couple of chairs. Captain Smith nodded around the office. 'So what have you done with them?'

'They've disappeared on me.'

Mr Stanford shook his head. 'Never underestimate the ability of kids to make themselves scarce when there's work to be done. I don't know what I'm going to do with that child.'

Captain Smith smiled sympathetically. He had children of his own in London. 'Newspaper shaping up OK?' he asked.

'Finishing touches, Captain – but that's not what I want to show you. Actually, young Jimmy noticed it first, but it's much worse now, spreading like wildfire. Have you heard about this virus, this plague?'

Scoop nodded at his computer screen. There was a map of the United States showing that only three out of fifty states were now free of what they were calling the Red Death. California had the worst figures, with five hundred people already reported dead and tens of thousands infected. Scoop scrolled on down the page to a news report. A curfew had been imposed in Los Angeles. A number of people had been shot while trying to flee the city under the cover of darkness. Scientists were working around the clock to try to come up with an antidote.

Mr Stanford shook his head in disbelief. 'I'd heard there was something, but I'd no idea it was that bad. This could have a catastrophic effect on our profits.' Captain Smith exchanged a brief smile with Scoop. Stanford was a businessman, first and foremost. His first consideration would always be money. The ship owner peered more closely at the map. 'But the figures for Miami – they're not so bad. We might be fine yet.'

Scoop nodded. 'They'll come up with something, they always do. There's always a lot of panic with these things, anyway – everything gets exaggerated.'

'Well, let's hope so,' said Captain Smith. 'Still, let's keep an eye on it.'

At that moment a small box appeared on the screen and a soothing voice said, '*You have mail*'.

Scoop immediately clicked on to his in-coming mail box, then tutted.

'What's wrong?' asked the Captain.

'It's a photo, but I don't recognize the address. I don't like opening strange e-mails in case there's a virus. It's happened before – remember the cruise through the Panama canal, Mr Stanford? I opened that file and it crashed all our computers. We were nearly home again before we got it fixed.'

'If it's not one sort of virus, it's another,' huffed the ship owner. 'Play safe and delete it, Scoop. I suspect we're going to have enough problems when we arrive in Miami without our computers going down as well.'

Scoop nodded. 'I suppose you're right.'

After they'd left Scoop put the finishing touches to his newspaper – he found a passport-sized photograph of Pedroza in the ship's personnel files which slotted nicely into the story Jimmy had written. Jimmy wasn't a bad kid, he thought. A bit rough round the edges, but he had worked hard – at least, earlier in the day he had – and the articles he'd written were really quite good. Claire was another matter. A total waste of time.

As he worked, Scoop found his eyes occasionally flitting back to the e-mail message. He still hadn't deleted it, despite knowing it was the right thing to do. The very last thing he needed was an infected computer.

And yet.

He was a journalist, and the teaching words of *who*, *what*, *where*, *when* and *how* could also be combined into one single word – *curiosity*. Part of him was absolutely *dying* to know what was contained in the e-mail.

He stared at it.

He stared at it some more.

No. He didn't need the hassle.

Delete it.

A Question of Belief

They had been trapped in the freezer for four hours. They no longer expected to be rescued. They were going to die.

Jimmy asked Claire if she wanted to leave a farewell message. He would scrape it into the freezer wall with his lucky coin, but she would have to be quick because the meagre light they had from her camera was fading fast. 'To your parents . . . you could tell them you . . . love them . . . or hate them . . .'

Claire shook her head. 'Just write – *Pedroza . . . did it.*'

Jimmy wrote it. Then he slumped back down beside her.

'I just . . . want to sleep now,' she said.

Claire nodded against him. He gave her a gentle shake. 'Don't . . . try and stay awake.'

To try and keep her focussed Jimmy told her as best he could – his words slow and deliberate and taking long pauses for difficult, icy breaths – about the penny and the story of Lucky Jimmy Armstrong and the first *Titanic*, and then how he himself had come to be a stowaway in the first place, with the driver falling into the water and the e-mail he'd sent to his former headmaster.

Claire giggled.

But then she grew quiet.

Jimmy said, 'Are you . . . all right?'

'I was . . . just thinking . . . you said . . . I had . . . a big arse.'

'You said . . . I was brain dead.'

'Do . . . I have . . . a big . . . bum?'

'To tell you . . . the truth . . . I've never really . . . studied it. Am I . . . brain . . . dead?'

'Yes . . . you must be . . . to follow me . . . in here . . .'

'I was . . . following . . . your big . . . arse.'

Jimmy laughed. And she laughed against him.

'I don't want . . . to die,' said Claire.

The camera had given its last light. Jimmy closed his eyes. He just wanted it to end now. He tried as best he could to think nice thoughts about home and causing mayhem. Of coming home with a certain look on his face and his mum having a certain look on *her* face which said, 'What have you done *now*?' He had heard, or read, or been told that when you die you move towards a brilliant white light, and he was aware of one now, glimmering at the edges of his vision. He knew he should fight it, he should hold on to life for as long as he possibly could, but he felt so weak, so desperately cold, he just wanted to give in, just needed to embrace the light – it would be warm and comforting. Jimmy felt his whole body relax. Dying wasn't that hard, he thought, just like going to sl . . .

Jimmy blinked. A pristine room. Blink. Six beds. Blink. Warm.

His throat was sore and his head ached. But this was nice. The crossover hadn't been too bad. Heaven smelled of antiseptic.

It was a relief. He hadn't held out any great hope of getting into heaven. Hell – much more likely. But this certainly wasn't hell, unless it was some kind of waiting room the Devil used to lull you into a false sense of security.

No, it *had* to be heaven.

At least until a familiar voice said: 'The sleeper awakes.'

Jimmy twisted his head to his immediate left and saw Scoop sitting in his wheelchair. 'Who . . . what . . .?' he stammered.

'Where and when,' Scoop laughed. 'Welcome back to the land of the living, young man.'

'I don't under . . .'

'Got your e-mail. Took me a while to open it. Just in time, it seems. Another half an hour and you would have been gonners.'

'Claire?'

'Better powers of recovery. But then anger can often spur you on to great physical feats.'

'I don't under . . .'

'This thing about Pedroza.'

'What about . . .?'

'Her father doesn't believe her, so she's been up screaming and crying at him for the past hour. Pedroza denies it all of course . . .'

Jimmy pulled himself up into a sitting position. 'He locked us in!'

'He doesn't deny *that*. He says he saw the freezer door open when it shouldn't have been, so he locked it.'

'He switched it on!'

'He was *supposed* to. It has to be ready for food when we dock.'

'He looked directly at us, he *smiled*!'

'He denies it. And I must admit, I've never known him to smile.'

'*You* don't believe us either?'

Scoop took a deep breath. 'Well, son, it's not a question of my believing you. I'm a journalist, I just look at the facts. And I'll be perfectly honest here – you're a stowaway with a history of trouble-making and Claire's a rich kid with a habit of making things up: and Pedroza's been with the White Star Line for fifteen years and despite having a bit of a temper has never been in trouble once. Plus, there's certainly no evidence of this phantom family Claire claims to have seen.'

'She saw it.'

'How do you know?'

'She . . . told me . . . and there was a child's hand-print on . . .'

'Yes, she claimed that as well. I checked myself. No sign of it.'

'That doesn't mean . . .' Jimmy sighed. 'That's just . . . so typical!' He folded his arms and glared at the floor. It was good to be alive. But it would have been so much better to have been alive *and* believed. 'We nearly *died* in there!'

'Yes, you did.' But it wasn't Scoop, it was another officer, standing in the doorway, smiling in. 'Jimmy, isn't it?'

The officer crossed to him and extended his hand. Jimmy took it somewhat warily. 'I'm Doctor Hill. Frank. Frank Hill. I saved your life. No need to thank me, but if you ever strike it rich a nice cheque would be appreciated.'

He was warm and sunny. Jimmy was feeling exactly the opposite of warm and sunny.

'Pedroza tried to kill us,' he said.

'He's been trying to kill us for years,' laughed Dr Hill. 'Have you tried his scrambled eggs?'

'This isn't funny!' Jimmy exploded.

Dr Hill nodded thoughtfully. 'No – you're right. It's not funny. Scrambled eggs are a serious business.' He laughed again, put a hand on Jimmy's brow, checked his pulse, then made a brief note on a chart at the foot of his bed. 'Not too much damage done, Jimmy – no missing fingers or toes due to frostbite, but I'd still like you to stay in bed for the rest of the day.' Then he gave Jimmy a wink, replaced the chart and left the room, humming.

'I *hate* this!' Jimmy roared. 'Why does nobody believe us?'

He thumped the bed in frustration.

Scoop reached down beside his chair and picked up a sheaf of papers. 'Well – maybe you won't hate *this*.' He held up a copy of the first dummy edition of the ship's newspaper, the *Titanic Times*. Jimmy saw the main headline, *Mysterious Virus Affects California*, in big bold letters, but his attention was focussed on the line beneath: *by James Armstrong*.

'James?' he asked.

'It sounded more professional than Jimmy. Your interview with Pedroza is inside.'

Scoop rolled across and set several copies of the *Times* on Jimmy's bed. 'I'll leave you to have a read through, Jimmy.' He paused as he was about to turn away again. 'Son – you've done a good job, and you show a real talent for writing. You should give some thought to maybe doing this for a living. But don't be led astray. Claire's a bit of a wild one and she nearly got you both killed today. Never forget, though – her family is super rich. If she gets into trouble they will always look after her and sort her out and smooth over any hiccups. But they won't do the same for you. Will you remember that for me?'

Jimmy looked at him.

Then he shrugged.

13 Scoop's Secret

Now that he was safe, and alive, Jimmy was confused on several different levels. He wasn't entirely sure now that Pedroza *had* intentionally locked them in the freezer. His explanation that he was merely closing the door and switching it on in preparation for use made sense. Scoop assured him that he'd seen it written on the day's rota. Who knew what the evil smile he'd displayed while closing the door really meant? Perhaps that was just his smile. Perhaps he had just been thinking happy thoughts and really hadn't noticed them in the darkened interior.

What then of Claire's story? What about the family she claimed to have seen? Why would she make it up? To get attention? Because she was evil to the core?

That evening, while Jimmy rested in bed, Captain Smith visited. He assured him that a thorough search of the ship had been carried out and that no group of stowaways had been found.

Jimmy maintained that *he'd* managed to stay hidden for a couple of days, so why not this lot?

'Claire was talking about nine or ten individuals,

with children – young children. Jimmy – it's simply not possible that he could keep them hidden.'

'We found a hand-print, a child's . . .'

'Perhaps you did. But we had a dozen different school tours over the past few months and they all came through the kitchens. Do you not think it more likely that some mucky schoolkid has left his mark?'

Jimmy sighed.

He didn't know what to make of Claire at all. They'd gotten off on the wrong foot, without a doubt, but their relationship had thawed somewhat – even while they were freezing. But maybe they'd gotten on in the freezer because they had to. Now that they were free again . . . well, she hadn't come to see him yet. Captain Smith, in his own way, was warning him off her, and Scoop certainly hadn't pulled any punches. Jimmy was pretty expert at getting *himself* into trouble. Did he really need to hang about with someone who was clearly much, *much* better at it? Despite all his high jinks in Belfast, he'd never come even close to getting seriously injured. A few hours working alongside Claire and he'd almost frozen to death.

What he did feel good about – and he'd positively glowed when the Captain himself had praised it – was his work for the newspaper. He knew it was only a little paper, but there was something special about seeing his name in print. There were only two days left until their arrival in Miami, and the plan was to produce a paper for each of those days. Jimmy was determined to get right back to work.

Dr Hill twice caught him trying to sneak out of the *Titanic*'s hospital. Jimmy finally accepted that he would have to spend the night there and settled into a fitful sleep. Next morning he was up bright and early, and as there was no one around to stop him he hurried straight along to the *Times* office. But as he was going in, Dr Hill was coming out. They were both surprised to see each other. Dr Hill immediately blocked his way.

'I'm better,' said Jimmy. 'Really, I'm fine.'

'It's not you, Jimmy. Scoop's not well . . .'

'Oh.'

'You'd better run along.'

'But I've work to do.'

'That may be, but he's not up to it. Now . . .'

'I know what I have to do, I don't need any help.'

Dr Hill blew air out of his cheeks. 'Jimmy – do you know what's wrong with Scoop?'

'Apart from the legs?' The doctor nodded patiently. 'Well – his eyes and his blood pressure and his balance and . . . well, no, not exactly.'

Dr Hill looked up and down the corridor, then ushered Jimmy back into the newspaper office and closed the door. 'Listen Jimmy, this is his last cruise. Do you know that?'

Jimmy nodded. 'Yeah, he said. But if you report he's sick then he won't get—'

'His pension. Yes. And I've been covering for him as best I can. But I have other duties. Do you know what they call what he has, Jimmy?'

Jimmy shrugged.

'Scoop is an alcoholic, son.'

'Oh. I thought it was like his heart or cancer or some other kind of disease.'

'Jimmy, son, that's exactly what it is – a disease. Just you don't get much sympathy if you have it. If you really do know how to put the newspaper together, then do it. Because he's in no state. The Captain is expecting tomorrow's paper to be ready this evening. Is that too much to ask?'

Jimmy shook his head, although he really didn't know. He'd written a news story for the front page of the *Times* and a feature for inside, but there were at least ten other pages to fill.

Dr Hill glanced towards the bedroom. 'He'll sleep now – hopefully right through – but if you really can do this for him, well, it would be marvellous. Can I depend on you?'

Nobody had ever depended on Jimmy to do anything in his life, or if they had, they had invariably been disappointed. With the best will in the world, and being perfectly honest with himself, the best Jimmy could muster in response was, 'Probably.'

* * *

In fact, his response should have been, 'No.'

It was just too big a job for one person. It wasn't that he couldn't do the work – he could write the stories, he could design the pages, he could even print the thing, but he simply couldn't do them all at the same time. Just to add to his problem, he deleted two stories by mistake and then he lost the Internet connection for an hour (although that wasn't his fault).

He needed help.

There was only one place to go.

He found her on the top deck, sunbathing. She was wearing a red bikini. They were getting close to America now and the temperature had warmed considerably in the past few days. The grey water of the Atlantic was gradually giving way to the turquoise hues of the Caribbean.

Jimmy sat down beside her. She didn't acknowledge him. 'I need your help.'

'Is that like *support*?' Claire snapped. 'Because I got none from you!'

'Claire . . .'

'You *know* it was Pedroza! You *know* there were people in there! You *know* I'm not making this up!'

'I never said you were.'

'They think I'm a liar, they think I'm just looking for attention, that's all they've ever said about me!' She jabbed an accusing finger at him. 'So why didn't you back me up?'

'I was still defrosting!'

'After!'

'Because!'

'Because why?'

'I don't know!'

'I told you what happened!'

'I know you did!'

'And I showed you the hand-print!'

'I know!'

'And we both saw him laughing!'

'I know that!'

'*So?*'

'It's not enough!'

'It's enough for me!'

She turned her face away. Jimmy stood and stared out across the water. He was a pale and freckled Irish boy who only saw the sun for a few days each year and he could already feel it starting to burn. He turned back to her. 'Look Claire – it doesn't matter if I believe you. It's what *they* think, it always is. I know what it's like, I've been up to my neck in trouble all my life, but I don't do half the things they think I do and I still get blamed. So unless we can absolutely prove that Pedroza's responsible, then they're never going to believe us. So if you want to try and do that, then let's do it.'

She thought about that.

'But in the meantime, I need your help.'

'Huh.'

'I'm serious. Scoop is sick.' He told her about the

urgency of getting the paper out, and the chance of the old reporter losing his pension. He didn't mention that Scoop was an alcoholic. It was something he did instinctively. He had spent a lot of time at home apologizing on behalf of his dad, who was always getting into drunken scrapes. 'He needs your help. I need you help. Please.'

Her eyes flitted up. 'And we can investigate Pedroza as we go?'

'Yes, of course.'

She thought about it some more.

'Another hour's sunbathing, then I'll come down.'

Jimmy folded his arms. 'No.'

'What do you mean, *no*?'

'There isn't time. We need to start *now*.'

'*God*. You are such hard work.'

Claire rolled off her bed, picked up her towel and marched off. Then she stopped and looked back at him. 'Well? Are you coming or not?'

Jimmy smiled and immediately started after her.

As she started walking again she glanced back. 'One comment about my bum,' she warned, 'and you're *dead*.'

Jonas Jones

While Scoop's snoring reverberated gently through from next door, Jimmy and Claire read in silence the worrying reports coming in from around the world. The 'Red Death' was mutating. People were dying in their thousands. Yet no two reports were the same. In London people were dead within hours of contracting the virus. In one village in China an entire school came down with it within an hour, but by the next day all of the children were back in class, apparently perfectly healthy. New York was going to work as usual. Contact had been lost with Oklahoma City: the telephones were no longer working and all of its television and radio stations had fallen silent. In Kentucky the town of Hopkirk was reported to have lost eighty-five per cent of its population. But in Rawlings, three miles away, there wasn't a single reported case. Scientists had believed it was passed on by human contact. Yet there were villages in parts of Russia that were so remote that they had had no visitors in weeks, but people were dying there as well. Scientists were now saying that it was carried on the air, and that your life might depend on which way the wind blew.

The American President addressed the nation and assured them that a cure was on the way, which was quite close to what he had promised last time. Leaders of China and India and Great Britain had also placed their faith in the great abilities of scientists to develop a cure, a vaccine or a pill.

America remained the worst-affected country. Understandably, people were starting to panic. As workers fell ill, food supplies were becoming erratic. There were reports of riots and looting. The National Guard – at least those members well enough to report for duty – had been called on to the streets of several cities.

'This is horrible,' said Claire.

'And we're sailing right into it.'

The only good thing that could possibly be said about all this was that it focussed their minds away from Pedroza. Suddenly the fact that he might be trying to smuggle a few people across the Atlantic seemed unimportant.

Jimmy remembered Scoop's advice about noting where the passengers would be coming from, and to be sure to give them information about their home states – but not so much that they panicked. To this end they made sure to include good news stories too. People being cured of the virus. A beached whale being successfully towed back to sea. A hundred-year-old woman who'd just gained her pilot's licence. Plenty of sports results (while not dwelling on the fact that many football and baseball matches had been cancelled).

In the early afternoon Jimmy and Claire travelled down to the vast engine room to meet the Chief Engineer, a heavily-muscled Welsh man called Jonas Jones.

'Should we call you JJ?' Claire asked.

'No, Jonas Jones is my name. When I was growing up it was always "give me your pocket money, Jonas Jones; what are you looking at, Jonas Jones; do you want a thick ear, Jonas Jones?" I was a skinny little thing, see. That's why I have all these muscles now, I went out and growed them. Now when I go home, it's all "hello, Mr Jones; how are you, Mr Jones?" And I say, my name is Jonas Jones, and I'm right proud of it.'

Jimmy thought Jonas Jones was all right, only he rattled on a bit. It was clear that he loved his ship. He enthusiastically described his responsibilities – looking after the massive engines, the air conditioning, the heating, plumbing, refrigeration, ventilation, the water de-salinization systems, the electrics and every aspect of technical repair.

'You see, each propeller is driven by a double-wound three-phase synchronous motor with four-bladed bronze propellers. The motors are mounted directly on the propeller shaft inside the pod, arranged so that the centre propeller is . . .' He waved his arms across the vast engine room as he excitedly explained the *Titanic*'s capabilities, but as he glanced back at the young reporters and saw their dumbfounded looks he hesitated and said, 'Do you follow?'

They both shook their heads.

'Once more,' said Jimmy, 'but this time in English.'

Jonas smiled. 'Well, this isn't only the most powerful *cruise* ship in the world, it's the most powerful ship. If only we had some big guns upstairs we could . . . Well, what I'm saying is . . .' and he smiled down at Claire, '. . . your daddy didn't waste any money here. We have the best of everything. Did I mention the fuel? We go through four thousand gallons an hour . . .'

He went on for ages. Jimmy was frankly worried that his article would end up reading more like an engineering manual than a chatty piece about the life of a chief engineer. When it came time to take the photos Jonas insisted on gathering his crew around him.

'We're a team,' he said. 'Can't do anything without my team.'

Claire posed them in half a dozen different ways, but it was difficult to take in the huge size of the engine room without making the engineers themselves look the size of ants.

Jonas watched his team disperse, then pointed to the epaulets on his white shirt. There were four gold stripes sewn on to a burgundy-coloured patch. 'It's the colour of blood,' he said, 'in memory of the engineers who went down with the first *Titanic*.' He shook his head sadly. 'No lifeboats for them. Battled the freezing water down below right to the end.'

The memory of that disaster quietened him for a moment.

'Mr Jones?' Jimmy asked.

'Jonas, please.'

'Is this *Titanic* unsinkable?'

Jonas shook his head. 'No ship is unsinkable. The sea is the mightiest power on this planet, if it wants to sink you, well, it damn well will. But I'll tell you this, it's not the sea that sinks most ships, it's men. Men sank the *Titanic*, men who thought they were smarter than the sea, men who tried to go too fast, who tried to cut corners. This *Titanic ought* to be unsinkable, the way it's built; but I never underestimate the capacity of human beings to make stupid decisions.'

'So can I put in the paper that the ship's great but the Captain might run us into a big rock?'

Jonas burst into laughter. 'Be the last voyage I ever make if you do!'

Jimmy and Claire hurried back to the *Times* office, doing poor impressions of the Welshman's accent. Now Jimmy had to turn all those facts and figures into something interesting and Claire had to work on her photos. There was only space for one picture – but a single shot of the engineering crew wouldn't convey the power and majesty of the ship they ran, while just a picture of the engines would be rather boring. However, there was a software program on Scoop's computer that might allow her to merge two different shots so that the engines remained impressive while the crew could still provide the human interest without looking either like ants or giants.

Jimmy entered the office first and surprised Claire, following in behind, by swearing out loud. But then she saw what he was upset about: the computers had been overturned and lay on their sides on the floor, which was covered in reams of torn and crumpled paper.

'Jimmy – it's him, it's Pedroza, he's . . .'

But then they heard a groan, and then a cough, and they hurried across the office and there was Scoop, lying face down but trying to get up on to his knees. He pulled himself halfway up, then collapsed down again and threw up.

'He's been attacked!' Claire cried. 'Pedroza's . . .'

But Jimmy had spotted something – what Scoop had been trying to get hold of. A bottle of vodka.

'He hasn't been attacked, Claire.'

Claire stared at Scoop. Her hands went to her face. 'The Red Death.' She took a step back.

'Nope,' said Jimmy. He picked up the bottle and turned the label to show her. Her eyes widened.

'Vodka . . .?'

'Yup.'

'You mean he's drunk?'

'Yes he is . . . and most of the time, apparently. He's an alcoholic. Dr Hill told me.'

Claire looked sadly down at the old reporter. He was snoring gently now. But her sympathy only lasted for a few moments. 'He's wrecked the place! All our work!'

Jimmy stood beside her, nodding. 'If we tell on him, your dad will sack him.'

'My dad wouldn't . . .' But then she stopped. 'Yes he would.'

'So what do we do?'

Claire thought for a moment. 'OK. You clean up the sick, I'll check the computers.'

'I don't think so.'

'OK. I'll get him back into his room, you clean up the sick.'

'I think not.'

'Well, someone has to do it. We'll call the cleaners.'

'And make them promise not to tell anyone? I don't think so.'

'Well what then?'

'We do it between us.'

'We . . .' She looked truly horrified. 'But . . .'

'Come *on*,' said Jimmy.

Through a combination of dragging, pushing, prodding and shouting – mostly at each other, because

Scoop remained out for the count – they managed to get him back into bed.

Then they cleaned up the sick.

They were nearly sick themselves.

They righted the computers and tried to switch them on, convinced that Scoop's frenzied assault on his own office – a crazy attempt to locate a hidden supply of alcohol – had sunk their attempt to produce the *Titanic Times* all by themselves.

And yet, amazingly, everything was working perfectly. The stories they had painstakingly written were just as they'd left them, saved, unharmed, on the computers. Claire's photos were still on file.

They got right back to work.

Jimmy wrote at speed, picking out the letters on the keyboard with increasing speed and occasional accuracy. Luckily there was a good spell check. Claire tried a dozen different variations of her merged engine-room photos before finally settling on one. When they were both finished they designed the feature page together before checking the rest of the pages one last time.

'It's a good read,' said Jimmy.

'And it looks good.'

'You couldn't tell the difference between our *Times* and Scoop's.'

'And that's the whole point. Let's print it.'

When the ship was fully functioning, three thousand copies would be required first thing every morning, seven days a week. But that wasn't their problem. They had done their job. Whoever came on board in Miami would inherit a fully functioning newspaper production office. And it would only smell slightly of vomit.

They had been given an eight p.m. deadline for providing finished copies of the *Titanic Times* for Captain Smith's approval. Once he gave the go-ahead the paper would be distributed to the skeleton crew. By the time they had finished printing it out they had just ten minutes to spare, and what with the size of the ship it took most of that time to get to the bridge. Claire, a regular visitor to this and many other bridges, was more than familiar with it, but it blew Jimmy's mind. He had always thought of ships' bridges as featuring – well, basically a big wheel, maybe a bell, with waves crashing against the window. And bluff men saying things like 'Ahoy there, Captain!' Perhaps, as a concession to the twenty-first century, there might be some electronic equipment. Like radar. Or a toaster for midnight snacks.

This was like mission control.

The place bristled with computer monitors.

Crewmen in short-sleeved shirts studied electronic charts and forecasts and maps and . . . well, he hadn't a clue what they were all doing or what half of the equipment was for. It was just incredibly impressive.

Captain Smith was seated behind a desk to the rear, examining a monitor with First Officer Jeffers on his left shoulder and Claire's father on his right. They were all looking very grave.

'We've brought the papers,' Claire said proudly. She wasn't supposed to say it proudly. It was, after all, supposed to be Scoop's paper, but she could hardly help herself.

Captain Smith barely looked up. 'Just leave them there.'

Claire set them down, but then took off the top copy and opened it to the centre pages. 'Look, Daddy,' she beamed. 'My photo.'

Mr Stanford sighed and took hold of the paper. He glanced at the photo, then quickly closed it over. 'Yes, very good.' He handed it back. 'Now run along, there's a good girl.'

But Claire stood her ground. 'You hardly even looked at it!'

'Yes I did, and I'm sure it's very good. Now if you don't mind—'

'No!' Claire exploded. 'You order me to do something useful and then when I do it you're not the slightest bit interested! I nearly froze to death and you hardly raised an eyebrow!'

'Claire, come on,' said Jimmy. He caught hold of her arm and tried to pull her away. He'd been arguing with his parents for years and knew how pointless it was. But she wasn't for moving.

'Claire, that's quite enough,' her father barked. 'We have more important things on our minds right now.'

'You always have!'

Captain Smith clasped his hands before him and said, 'Claire.'

She glared at him. 'It's not fair, I do my best and all—'

'Claire.'

She took a deep breath. 'What?'

'We've had some very bad news.'

Jimmy had thought the bridge was quiet for . . . well, a bridge. But now he realized it was more than that. It was as if a dank chill had settled over it.

Captain Smith gave a little shake of his head, as if he couldn't quite believe what he was about to say. 'Claire . . . Jimmy. The President of the United States – they were taking him to a safe location. But his plane has disappeared. They think he's dead. This damned virus is going to get us all.'

Miami

The next few days should have been triumphant. The *Titanic* was the greatest cruise liner ever built and its arrival at the Port of Miami to undertake its first proper voyage should have been accompanied by brass bands and ticker tape and the excited commentary of television reporters. Instead hardly anyone noticed.

The President was missing, and his country was descending into chaos.

Jimmy, who had followed the spread of the Red Death right from the start, had not really been affected by the mounting death toll. It was all happening somewhere else. He was safe on the *Titanic*. Just reading about it somehow kept it unreal. But with the President missing, probably dead, it brought home just how frightening and dangerous this plague was. The President *ought* to have been safe. He had repeatedly gone on national TV to reassure people that everything would be all right; he had such power, so many weapons and scientists and experts, so many people to look after him and defend him . . . but they'd still managed to lose him.

* * *

Scoop finally reappeared as the ship docked in Miami, smiling and joking and saying what a bad flu he'd had but predicting that the beautiful Florida sun would soon sort him out. If he had noticed that two editions of the *Titanic Times* had been produced in his absence, he didn't mention it. Many of the crew not directly involved in the docking were lining the deck, and Jimmy and Claire, who now felt very much as if they belonged to that crew, were right there with them. That's where Scoop found them. He rolled up behind them, clapped his hands together and said, 'Hey kids, how's it going?' They turned. 'Hey – look at the long faces. We made it, didn't we? Gonna catch me some rays!'

Jimmy, who had his overalls unbuttoned nearly to the waist because of the morning heat, removed a folded copy of their most recent *Times* from his inside pocket and handed it to the veteran reporter.

Scoop opened it up and examined the front page with a mixture of disbelief and confusion. The headline said it all – *President Missing – Hope Fades*. 'I . . . I don't remember . . . did I write this? Must have . . . Anyway, life goes on.' He handed it back. 'My pension's in the bank, and I'm all set for a new life on the beach! Could life *be* any better?'

'You're going ashore?' Jimmy asked.

'Of course I am. Why wouldn't I?'

'Because people are dying,' said Claire.

'Ah, sure people are always dying.'

'The President is missing!'

'Well, they'll find him. And if they don't, they'll elect a new one, they always do.'

'But thousands of other people are dying as well,' said Jimmy. 'Look at the paper, Scoop, it's happening everywhere.'

Scoop laughed. 'God, you're awful serious, aren't you? Look – I was a foreign correspondent before I lost these old pins . . .'

'You told me you lost your legs *before* you became a foreign correspondent. Running for a taxi.'

'Ah, I just made that up to make you feel better. Truth is, Jimmy, Claire, I've seen massive wars, famines, plagues, earthquakes, volcanoes, tsunamis – you name it, I've been there, and they're awful things, truly awful, but people recover, they rebuild. Sometimes it takes years, sometimes just a few days, but they survive, they always do. I know this Red Death thingy is bad. But it will pass.' He clapped his hands together. 'So, I'm going to find a nice little hotel along the beach, I'm going to sit by the pool, have a nice cocktail, and wait until this nonsense fades away to nothing.' He held his hand out to each of them. 'Thanks for your help. I couldn't have put the paper together without you.'

They shook, then watched him roll happily down the gangplank.

'He has no idea,' said Jimmy. 'About the paper . . . or the plague.'

'Completely clueless,' agreed Claire.

With their hectic work on the paper over the past few days, Jimmy had not really given much thought to what would happen once the ship docked in Miami. He was thinking about plagues and presidents, not his own immediate future, so it came as a shock when First Officer Jeffers told him arrangements had been made for him to go ashore in the next hour, in order to catch a flight back to Ireland.

Jimmy just said, 'Oh.'

'We've spoken to the port authorities and they've agreed to make sure you catch your plane.'

Claire, standing beside him, was momentarily lost for words. They'd had lots of fights and bickered endlessly, but they'd also laughed a lot. They had forged a good partnership in producing their *Titanic Times*.

'You can't just let him go . . .' she began. 'People are . . . *dying* out there . . .'

Jeffers nodded. 'Yes, Claire, there's a few cases – but the authorities tell me it's reasonably safe. We're starting to board passengers for the cruise shortly, Jimmy, so I think it's important to get you on shore before we get too busy, eh?'

Jimmy shrugged.

'That's a good lad. I'll give you ten minutes to say your goodbyes, then I expect to see you at the portside gangplank on Deck Three, all right?'

'All right.'

First Officer Jeffers nodded at them both and turned away.

Jimmy looked at the ground. 'Well,' he said.

Claire tutted. 'It isn't fair. You're much safer on board.'

'Not much I can do.'

They wandered in a desultory fashion towards Deck Three. They stopped by the gangplank and looked over the rails at the dock below. A queue of passengers waiting to board snaked back for several hundred metres. They were making slow progress. Dr Hill and a team of medical experts employed by White Star Line were examining everyone – including new crewmen – for indications of plague. Those allowed on board were being issued with antibiotics and painkillers, even though nothing had yet been proved to affect the onslaught of the virus.

'You should be taking photos of this,' Jimmy said.

'What's the point?'

'Aren't you going to keep working on the paper?'

'It was good fun with the two of us. Not with some new guy.'

Claire pointed suddenly to her right. Scoop was rolling away along the dock. A porter pushing a trolley piled high with cases was struggling to keep up. 'Look at him go!'

'He's happy to get his legs on dry land,' said Jimmy.

Claire looked at him, then they both burst out laughing.

It faded quickly. Claire looked thoughtful. 'If you could stay – would you?'

'The point is I *can't*.'

'But if you could? Are you that desperate to go home?'

Jimmy shrugged. He had been a *little* homesick. But these past few days had been such fun.

'Right. Then this isn't over yet. Come with me.'

They found Mrs Stanford on the top deck, in a bikini, lying on a sunbed. 'I thought I'd stake my claim to one now,' she said as her daughter approached. 'Once the passengers are on board there's a strict policy against reserving sunbeds. I quite agree with it of course, *generally* speaking – but we do *own* the ship, so I ought to have first choice of . . .'

'Mother.'

Mrs Stanford peered over the top of her sunglasses. 'What is it, dear?'

'I want Jimmy to stay.'

'What? Who?' Claire shifted her position so that her mother could see Jimmy, standing some way back. 'Oh. *Him*. Well I'm sorry, Claire, you can't keep him. Puppies and stowaways aren't just for Christmas, you know. I know what you're like, he'll be your best friend for five minutes and then you'll lose interest and it'll be me – or one of the servants – who has to do all the cleaning up after him.'

Claire sat down on the sunbed beside her. She

clasped her hands together. 'I want you to tell Daddy that it's not safe to put Jimmy off the ship when there's so much sickness around.'

'Nonsense. He'll be perfectly fine. This Red Death nonsense is just a . . . hiccup.'

'Mum – people are dropping like flies!'

Mrs Stanford laughed. 'Do you really think your father would allow all these people on board if there was any danger involved? It's like any illness, dear, it affects the old first, and those who are already unwell, but if you're fit and well you can shrug it off. I'm not the slightest bit worried about it.'

'Mum, I've read the news reports. That's not what's happening.'

Mrs Stanford sighed. She lifted a wide-rimmed cocktail glass and happily sucked her drink up through a straw. 'No, Claire, the answer is no. No, no, no, no, no.'

'Then I'm going to tell Daddy about Uncle Winston.'

Mrs Stanford almost choked. She set the glass down so suddenly that the blue liquid within splashed up and over the edge. 'Excuse me?'

'Five years ago I saw you kissing Uncle Winston. Tongues and all.'

'Claire! I did *not*—'

'I saw you!'

'You were mistaken. Uncle Winston is a very good friend of your father's and . . .'

'You were having an affair.'

'We were *not* having—'

'Fine, then it won't matter if I tell Daddy . . .'

Claire stood up and began to walk away. 'Come on, Jimmy,' she said.

They'd gone about twenty metres when Mrs Stanford shouted after them. 'Claire – come back here.'

Claire stopped. She winked at Jimmy, then crossed back to her mother and raised an enquiring eyebrow.

'This . . . nonsense about Uncle Winston, that's exactly what it is. Nonsense. But we are very good friends, and up to a certain point I can understand how it might look to a very young child. While I have nothing to hide, your father *is* under a lot of pressure at the moment and he really doesn't need some dreadful domestic hoo-haa right in the middle of it. And although I'm sure this . . . sickness . . . will fade just as quickly as it started, the boy *is* in our custody and I see now that it wouldn't be right to just set him on shore and expose him to . . . well, you know what I mean. So if you want me to put a word in with your father . . .'

Claire nodded.

'Just give me another hour or two in this wonderful sun and then I'll . . .'

'No, mother, it has to be now.'

'Now? But I've only just—'

'*Now*.'

Mrs Stanford gave her daughter a despairing look, then sighed and reached for her robe. She glanced sadly up at the sun, slipped into her sandals, then indicated for Claire and Jimmy to follow her. As she passed Claire she hissed: 'This is blackmail, you know.'

'I know,' said Claire.

However, their hopes were quickly dashed. Although Claire and Jimmy waited outside Mr Stanford's office, they were able to listen through an open window. They strained at first to pick up the words but very soon they had no trouble hearing at all.

'And I'm telling you absolutely no way, Catherine!'

'But it's not safe out there, George!'

'Don't you think I've enough to worry about? Dear God, Catherine, I'm missing nearly a thousand passengers, sick or dead or stuck in some godforsaken airport trying to get here! And they'll sue me if I leave without them! And I've fifteen hundred passengers coming on board, and Lord knows how many of them are infected! And they'll sue me if this ship doesn't sail on time! A third of my crew hasn't shown up, food and supplies are arriving in dribs and drabs and even Frankie Savoy, who I am personally paying one hundred thousand dollars to entertain the guests on this maiden voyage is missing four members of his band and is refusing to perform unless I double his salary and find him a trumpet player! Do you think I have time to worry about this damned stowaway of yours?'

'Exactly darling – you shouldn't have to worry.

So let him stay on board and forget about him!'

'I can't! There's a court order demanding his immediate return! There are two Port of Miami police waiting to take him into custody! If I let him sail I'll be charged with taking a minor across international borders and I'll be thrown in prison! The answer is no. No! No! No! No!'

Mrs Stanford emerged a couple of minutes later. 'He's thinking about it,' she said.

Claire folded her arms. 'Mother – we heard.'

'Well – if there's a chance of him losing money, your father's first instinct is always to say no. If you heard, then you'll know I've done my best. And if you still choose to tell him about Uncle Winston, well that's your choice, but quite frankly, Claire, if you told him right now that I'd had an affair with every single member of the Vienna Male Voice Choir, I don't think he'd bat an eyelid. He's just got too much on his mind. So if you don't mind I'm going right back to my sunbathing.' She nodded once at Jimmy and sashayed away towards a set of sliding doors. As she passed through them, First Officer Jeffers stepped out. He did not look happy.

Jimmy turned to Claire. 'What'll we do now?'

'Run!'

The Stowaway

Claire reported in shortly before lunch. 'There's a massive row going on down there. The cops are telling my dad he can't sail without handing you over and my dad's saying they've already delayed sailing by an hour and he'll have a mutiny on his hands if he doesn't get underway. They're telling him they have a court order and he's telling them he will sue the Port Authority for twenty million dollars if they don't release the ship. Jonas Jones came down and threatened to punch one of them because we're burning up fuel and going nowhere. The only thing everyone agrees on is that they hate you.'

'Even you?'

'*Especially* me.'

'Why would you hate me?'

'Because you're upsetting my dad.' Jimmy looked at her. Then they both burst into laughter. 'Do you get on with yours?'

Jimmy shrugged. 'I suppose. He's just kind of there. I suppose he—'

His words were suddenly drowned out by an earsplitting blast of noise from the funnel behind them. A moment later the whole ship began to vibrate.

Claire punched him on the arm. 'We're moving!'

Jimmy punched her back.

So they were off. He was a stowaway again, but this time it was deliberate. It also felt quite different. Even though a third of the passengers and crew hadn't turned up, there were still people everywhere. The cabins that weren't occupied already were kept firmly locked. Crew members patrolled constantly. It no longer felt like it was *his* ship. The *Titanic* had been a big, empty shell with a barely adequate skeleton crew. Now passengers filled the hallways and corridors, children screamed happily as they dived into the pool and old folks piled their plates high in the self-service restaurants. It was a living, breathing entity, ploughing through the waters of the Caribbean like a mighty behemoth.

He pointed this out to Claire. 'It's like a mighty behemoth.'

'A mighty what?'

'Behemoth. It's a—'

'You're mental,' said Claire. 'Now try these on.'

It was no longer safe for Jimmy to traverse the ship in his stolen overalls. He needed to blend in more. So she'd raided one of the family cabins and stolen a suitcase full of clothes. From this she'd selected half a dozen T-shirts and three pairs of shorts. She looked away while he struggled out of his overalls.

'Was there nothing . . . better?'

'Beggars can't be choosers.'

'OK, you can look now.'

She gave a sarcastic wolf whistle.

'Ha-ha,' he said.

They messed around the upper decks for a couple of hours. They ate in the buffet restaurant, stuffing themselves until they could hardly move. Jimmy had a New York Yankees baseball cap which he kept on at all times. No one paid any attention to them. The passengers were too busy enjoying themselves, and the crew were too busy looking after the passengers. There were a hundred and one things for Jimmy and Claire to do on the *Titanic* but somehow, after a while, they found themselves to be extremely bored.

They returned to the sundeck on the top level. Claire scored some Cokes at the bar, then they sat looking down one level to the swimming pool and the kids screaming down the slide and the grannies standing up to their waist exchanging gossip.

'They're way too happy,' Jimmy said.

'I know,' said Claire. 'Why aren't they worried about the plague? It's probably on board already.'

'Maybe the hospital's full. Maybe there's bodies everywhere.'

Claire nodded. 'And what about Pedroza's mysterious stowaways? I didn't see them get off. Where could he be hiding them now?'

Jimmy sighed and changed the subject. 'I enjoyed the paper.'

'I know. It was fun.'

'Hard.'

'But fun.'

They'd been run ragged. It had been exciting and thrilling and scary.

'I wonder what the new guy's like?' said Claire. 'I'll bet he's making a real mess of our paper.'

'I'll bet Scoop showed him nothing, he was so keen to get off. He'll be floundering around, clueless.'

This time Claire sighed. 'I wish we could go and see what he's doing . . .'

'Well we can't.'

'Or – *you* can't. You'd get caught, for sure; but there's nothing to stop me going down. Maybe I can volunteer to help, then you can help me in secret.'

Jimmy shook his head. 'It won't work. I'd get caught. And I'm not working as your damn helper anyway.'

'It wouldn't be like that, Jimmy.'

Jimmy shrugged. He stared down at the pool again. He was a little annoyed at the notion of Claire being able to work on the paper again. As he looked down he became aware of a tall, thin black boy staring up at him from the shallow end. Jimmy stared right back. After a few moments the boy slipped under the water and began to swim towards the far end. Jimmy watched him for a few more seconds, then turned back to Claire. He knew he was being stupid about the paper. 'All right,' he said, 'you go down and check it out.'

'Are you sure? He'll probably chase me away.'

'Go on.'

Claire smiled hesitantly at him and turned away.

She hadn't gone more than a few metres, however, before Jimmy called after her. 'Big arse!'

'Brain dead!'

The only difference was that this time, they were both grinning.

Jimmy sat in the movie theatre on Deck Four. It was some Disney effort that had been around for years, but the auditorium was cool and dark and a good place to hide. He'd had enough after about half an hour however. When he got up to leave he noticed that the boy who'd been watching him from the pool was seated three rows behind him.

As Jimmy pushed through the doors, the boy got up to follow. As Jimmy reached the elevator just down the corridor and stepped into it, the boy hurried forwards to join him. As the doors began to close the boy broke into a run. Jimmy could have held them, but he didn't.

He got out one floor short of his ultimate destination and hid himself behind an extravagant floral display which nevertheless gave him a good view of the elevator doors.

If he is following me, he'll have waited below to see what floor my elevator stopped at.

Sure enough, just a few moments later, the next elevator arrived, the doors opened, and the boy stepped out and peered cautiously about him. Failing to spot Jimmy immediately, he then hurried past the floral display towards a customer services lounge where passengers were already busy booking their *next* cruises.

Jimmy used the stairs to return to the top deck. He wondered if he should chance going for a swim. The water looked so inviting and cool – but it would be very difficult to escape from it if he was spotted. As he leaned on the rail, thinking about it, he noticed that his skin was getting sunburned. He was going to have to liberate some sunscreen from . . .

He was poked in the back.

The black kid.

Up close he was a full head taller than him. He poked Jimmy in the chest.

'You.'

'You *what*?'

'You.'

With the third poke, Jimmy poked him right back.

The boy grabbed a handful of Jimmy's T-shirt. 'I've been following you.'

'I know,' said Jimmy. 'Are you gay?'

'You're wearing my T-shirt.'

'Yeah, *sure*,' said Jimmy then gave him a hard

shove in the chest. Caught off guard, the boy stumbled backwards. Jimmy took off. The boy came right after him.

Jimmy had never done a day's training in his life, but he was naturally pretty quick.

This other kid was faster.

Jimmy just managed to keep ahead of him by leaping over sunbeds and ducking under umbrellas and pulling ice buckets and ashtray stands over in his wake. He charged inside and took the carpeted stairs six at a time, using the polished rails for support.

They moved down through four decks like that, Jimmy never more than a dozen steps ahead of his pursuer. They pushed through elderly couples. Toddlers were pulled hastily out of their way. Then the boy made his move, diving from the top of a flight of stairs and just catching Jimmy around the neck. They landed in a heap, with the other boy on top, his weight forcing the wind out of Jimmy. The boy straddled him and grabbed him by the throat.

'My T-shirt!

'Get off me, you big fruit!'

'That's my T-shirt, now get it off!'

'Kiss my arse!'

The boy punched him. It hurt. He tasted blood and saw distant stars.

'Get it off!' He raised his fist again, quite ready to inflict more damage.

Jimmy, to give himself time to come up with an

alternative escape plan, pretended to cave in. 'OK . . . all right! Relax, would you?'

'Get it off . . .!'

'There's obviously been some kind of misunderstanding . . .'

'Get it off!'

'All right . . . Just, there's thousands of T-shirts like this one . . . Honestly, you think they make just one T-shirt like this?' It was red, with the letters *APNJ* across the top with the picture of an eagle below. 'I swear to God! I got this in Belfast, where'd you get yours?'

The boy barely hesitated. As he spat out the words, he poked each of the letters on Jimmy's chest. 'Asbury . . . Park . . . New . . . Jersey.'

'See? They sell them all over the world!'

'This is my school T-shirt! I go to school in Asbury Park, New Jersey! The eagle represents my school team! My name is sewn into the inside of the collar!' He grabbed the neck of the shirt and twisted it round. 'See? Ty Warner! That's my name! Ty Warner! You stole it from my room! Now take it off or I will kill you.'

Jimmy blinked up at him, then suddenly wailed: 'I *can't*!'

Ty Warner looked surprised. 'Why not?'

Tears formed up in the corner of Jimmy's eyes. 'Because it's the only T-shirt I have! I'm *sorry*. I didn't mean to steal it. Just to borrow it. Please! I'm a stowaway. I don't have any other clothes.' Tears rolled down his cheeks. '*Please* don't hit me again.'

Jimmy was an expert at crying to order. When violence and trickery didn't work, tears were often used as a last resort. He wasn't particularly proud of it, but he *was* particularly good at it.

Ty's voice softened. 'What do you mean, you're a stowaway?'

'I snuck on board. I'd nowhere else to go. My parents died of the Red Death.'

This more than anything caused Ty to scurry backwards off Jimmy.

'It's OK, I'm probably not infected.' The boy kept his distance. Jimmy sat up, then faked a sneeze. He wiped his nose on the arm of the T-shirt. 'You can have it back if you really . . .'

The boy held his hands up. 'No . . . you keep it . . .'

Jimmy wiped at his eyes. 'Are you sure?'

'Sure I'm sure. Just . . . keep your distance. And . . . uh . . . sorry about hitting you . . .'

Jimmy got to his feet. 'Thanks, mate,' he said, then tramped slowly back up the flight of stairs. He stopped when he reached the landing and looked back down at the boy, who was still watching him with a look of genuine horror. 'Oh . . . Ty, is it?' The boy nodded. 'Ty . . . I just wanted to say – SUCKER!'

Jimmy laughed, and fled. This time there was no catching him.

17

The Editor of the *Titanic Times*

Jimmy sought refuge in a lifeboat on the top deck where he and Claire had hidden out earlier. Through a small gap in the covers he was able to keep an eye on Ty Warner, who was patrolling relentlessly. It had clearly gone beyond a stolen T-shirt now. Next time they met there'd be no tears or lies or calling anyone a sucker. There would be extreme violence.

He was just beginning to nod off when he was roused by an announcement over the PA system:

'*Could James Armstrong please report to the newspaper office.*'

Oh sure. Like I'm going to fall for that one.

Ten minutes later it was made again: but this time it was Claire's voice. And she added, '*Really, it's fine.*'

Oh yeah. Right. You're being forced to call me in. Blackmailed by your own dad. He wondered what she'd sold him out for. A shopping trip in Miami? Another new pony?

'*Would James Armstrong report to the newspaper office immediately . . .*'

Not more than three seconds later the covers of the

lifeboat were ripped back, and there was First Officer Jeffers glaring down at him.

She had given him up!

The little—

Jeffers grabbed him and hauled him out. He plonked him down on the deck. 'All right, Jimmy, let's go . . .'

Jimmy shuffled forward reluctantly. 'You never would have got me if she hadn't—'

'Just keep moving.'

As they walked towards the elevators Ty Warner stepped out of a doorway and followed along behind. 'He stole my T-shirt . . .' he started.

'He's done a lot of things,' said Jeffers.

'Want my T-shirt back.'

'Leave your name with Customer Services; I'll make sure you get it.'

'Want it now.'

'Well you can't have it now.'

Ty stood sullenly behind them while they waited for the elevator. When it arrived he waited until the doors started to close before stepping in after them. 'It's my favourite T-shirt.'

'What are you, six years old?' said Jimmy.

'Quiet, Jimmy!' said Jeffers.

'Is it like your blanky?'

'I said, *quiet*.'

'What're you going to do, arrest me?'

Jeffers sighed.

'I want my shirt,' said Ty.

'I've told you. Report it to Customer Services, you'll get it—'

'I think you are gay,' said Jimmy.

'I said *quiet*, and I won't say it again!'

Jimmy shrugged.

'I want my—' Ty began.

'You too!' bellowed Jeffers.

Ty looked genuinely shocked. 'You can't talk to me like that!'

The elevator doors opened and Jeffers pushed Jimmy out in front of him. They were on the same floor as the newspaper office. 'Where are we going?' Jimmy asked.

'Just keep moving.'

'What about my T-shirt?' Ty asked.

Jeffers ignored him. As they progressed on down the corridor, Ty gradually fell behind. 'I'm going to tell my mom on you!' he shouted after them.

'You're a big girl's blouse!' Jimmy shouted back, and got a shove in the back for his trouble.

Jeffers stopped him outside the newspaper office. 'In here,' he said, and pushed the door open.

There she was – the betrayer. Claire sat on the edge of one of the desks; she looked sheepishly at him. There was no sign of the editor.

'Thanks a lot,' spat Jimmy. 'I hope your ponies die in a horrific traffic accident.'

'Jimmy . . .'

'I'm not talking to you.' He turned to Jeffers. 'So?'

'The new editor of the *Titanic Times* wanted a look at you. He's in the bathroom. Go in and see him.'

'Yeah, *right*.'

Jimmy stood where he was.

'Jimmy, please . . .' said Claire.

'I told you, I'm not talking to you.'

Jimmy looked towards the bathroom. 'What's he doing, a poo?'

Ty was back, standing in the open doorway. 'I want my T-shirt.'

Jeffers rolled his eyes. 'Go *away*,' he said, and pushed the door shut. He turned back to Jimmy and nodded at the bathroom.

Jimmy tutted. 'Better than looking at you two.' He strode into the bathroom.

It was empty.

'Turn to your left,' Claire called.

'What?' There was only a mirror.

'You're looking at the new editor of the *Titanic Times*.'

Jimmy looked at his own reflection for a moment, then swiftly turned back out into the office. 'What the hell are you talking about?'

Jeffers was smiling. So was Claire. She clapped her hands together. 'Jimmy! We're serious! The new guy didn't get on in Miami! No one else knows how to put the paper together! The Captain says you have to do it until the end of the cruise or the end of the world, whichever comes first!'

Jimmy looked from one to the other. 'You've got to be joking!'

There was a knock on the door.

'I want my T-shirt!'

Ty

They weren't joking.

Jeffers pulled out a chair for Jimmy to sit down. 'Guy called Travers was supposed to be doing this. He did actually get on board, but then he got right off again, said his parents were sick and couldn't leave them. So we're stuck. Fact is, Jimmy, the passengers go nuts if they don't get their fix of news in the morning, especially with what's going on at home. So we want you to do it. With Claire's help.'

Jimmy nodded at Claire. 'Was this your idea?'

Claire smiled again. 'I came down here and he . . .' she nodded at Jeffers, ' . . . was trying to put a paper together, but he hadn't a clue.'

'It's harder than it looks,' agreed Jeffers.

'So I told him you were the only one who really knew how to do it.'

'It makes sense, Jimmy,' said Jeffers. 'I checked it with the Captain and he checked it with Mr Stanford, and they both agreed. It's yours if you want it, until the end of the cruise.'

Jimmy examined his fingernails. This was indeed a

surprising turnaround in his fortunes. And, as his granda had often told him, it was important to make hay while the sun shone. 'So,' he said, 'how much do I get paid?'

Jeffers burst out laughing. 'What? You're lucky we don't toss you in the brig and throw the key away!'

Jimmy smiled indulgently. 'No, really. How much?'

'Jimmy . . .' said Claire, 'they're letting you—'

'I may be a stowaway, Claire, but I'm not a slave. I'll expect to be paid whatever whatshisname, Travers, was going to be paid.'

'You're only a kid!' Jeffers bellowed.

'Then stop exploiting me and pay me a fair wage!'

Jeffers put his hands on his hips. 'You, sir, have a brass neck.'

'Yeah, I know,' said Jimmy.

Jeffers told them he'd have to check with the Captain, but in the meantime could they *please* get started on the newspaper. Jeffers pulled his cap down hard, and was just leaving the office when Jimmy said, 'And Claire will have to be paid as well.' Jeffers took a deep breath and left the room, closing the door firmly behind him.

Claire immediately burst into laughter. 'You have such a nerve, Jimmy Armstrong.'

'It's *James*, when I'm working.'

So they got to work. It had already grown dark

outside, on this the first day of the first proper cruise of the *Titanic.* They had to prepare a complete newspaper for the Captain's approval, then print up several thousand copies and, finally, organize its distribution to every single cabin on the ship.

It was a huge task.

The news from the outside world was not good. Hundreds of thousands, possibly *millions*, had been infected by the Red Death. Power supplies were failing. Food supplies weren't reaching supermarkets. Crops lay rotting in the fields. Those who weren't dying were sick, and those who weren't sick were starving and cold. Arguments led to fights, fights led to riots, riots led to murder and destruction. Cities were burning. It was happening *everywhere*.

Nearly every rich country has a cache of supplies – food, water, medical equipment, fuel – with which to see through an emergency. When there is an earthquake or a flood these are quickly transported to the area in question. But now there were simply too many areas suffering for everyone to get essential supplies. And the suspicion grew that those that were available were being hoarded by the powerful and the rich, and that led to more rioting.

It was horrible out there.

They broke the news down according to the geographical origins of their passengers. Most were from the United States, but there were significant numbers from the United Kingdom, South America and Russia. Things weren't any better in those countries. Jimmy was pleased that there weren't any other passengers from Belfast. That meant he didn't have to look up what was happening at home. He just didn't want to know.

Claire stared gloomily at their front page when they eventually put it together. 'It has to end soon, doesn't it?'

'Has to.'

'They'll find a cure or it'll just stop by itself. Any other virus or plague has always ended *some*time. Otherwise we'd all have died thousands of years ago. The body finds ways to defend itself eventually, doesn't it? It's the survival of the fittest.'

Jimmy nodded grimly. 'I suppose. Except – I read this report that said it might have come out of some lab in California. That it might have been created by scientists and in that case – well, they say because it isn't a natural thing, but a thing that was created in a laboratory, we might not be able to defend ourselves against it.'

'Don't say that!'

'I'm not. *They* are.'

Their coverage of the Red Death continued from page one right through to page eight. Then they borrowed their profile of Jonas from the dummy edition to fill out another four pages. They still had four pages to fill. Jimmy walked across the office and opened the door. Ty Warner was still standing there.

'Give me my T-shirt,' he said.

Jimmy turned to Claire. 'Take his picture.'

'Why?'

'He can be our *Passenger of the Day*. It'll fill our empty space.'

Claire lifted her camera and moved into the doorway. 'Do you want to be our *Passenger of the Day*?'

'No. I want my T-shirt back.'

Jimmy shook his head. 'You can be our *Whining Passenger of the Day*.'

'I'm not *whining*. My mom says I'm tenacious. I'm like a dog with a bone. I'm not going away until I get it back.'

Jimmy was starting to get annoyed. 'Well I've nothing else to wear,' he snapped, 'so you can have it back when I'm finished with it. And by the way, I work for the ship now. And *her* dad owns it. Between us we can probably have you chucked overboard, so shut up about your shirt and have your picture taken.'

Claire raised her camera.

'Does your dad really own the ship?'

Claire nodded. 'Smile.'

She took the picture. She took another.

'What're you doing in there anyway?'

'Running the ship newspaper. The *Titanic Times*.'

'But you're only kids.'

'I know,' said Jimmy. 'Aren't we great?'

* * *

Ty took a look at the front page. 'What about New Jersey?' he asked.

'Same as everywhere.'

'We left three days ago, drove down. There were abandoned cars everywhere. Dad had extra gas hidden in the back.'

'Why didn't you just stay where you were?'

'My daddy said we paid thousands for this vacation, we weren't going to waste it because some people had the flu.'

'It's worse than flu,' said Claire.

'Maybe. Daddy says the papers always exaggerate, to sell more copies.'

'*This* paper is free,' said Jimmy.

Ty shook his head. 'No it's not. You have to spend thousands of dollars coming on this cruise to get it. It's the most expensive paper in the world. Anyhow, Daddy says we're better off on a ship away from all the trouble. It'll all be over by the time we get home.'

They questioned him for their newly created *Passenger of the Day* piece. He told them his favourite movies and music and food. He told them about his dad working as a computer programmer and his mum as a nurse. He was an only child. His ambition was to be an astronaut.

'Don't you have to be smart for that?' Jimmy asked.

'I am smart.'

'Are you top of your class?'

'Yes I am.'

Jimmy typed this in. 'And how long have you known you were gay?' and then allowed his fingers to hover over the keyboard, ready to type some more.

Ty stiffened in his chair. 'What're you . . .?'

'Oh relax, would you?' Jimmy laughed. 'I'm only joking.'

Ty kept his eyes fixed on Jimmy. 'I want you to know, that my daddy sends me to karate twice a week. If I keep it up, I'll be the youngest black belt in New Jersey.'

Jimmy nodded, impressed, as he typed. 'And, in all seriousness, do you think that will make you somehow *less* gay?'

Ty erupted out of his chair. 'You . . .!'

Claire immediately stepped between them. 'Stop it, both of you!'

Ty looked amazed. '*I* haven't done anything! Tell *him* to stop calling me gay!'

'There's nothing wrong with being gay,' said Claire.

'But I'm not gay!'

'And we will make that clear in the article. The headline will be . . .' She looked at Jimmy for help.

'*Ty Warner Is Definitely Not Gay!*'

Ty looked from one to the other. 'You . . . you're both mad!' Then he spun on his heel and fled from the newspaper office.

The *Titanic Times*

'After you,' said Jimmy.

'No, after *you* . . .'

They were about to enter the bridge with the first copy of the first proper paper they had prepared for the passengers of the *Titanic*. They were exhausted, but happy with their efforts – the *Times* was stuffed full of news, the feature articles were interesting and the design and layout were eye-catching. It looked professional. It *was* professional. And, as Ty had said, they were just kids. They had every right to feel proud of themselves.

Claire went first, Jimmy followed. Captain Smith and First Officer Jeffers were talking to Dr Hill in hushed tones and they had to wait for the opportunity to hand over the paper. Eventually Jeffers noticed them, smiled and said, 'Here they are now. Well, all done?'

Jimmy said, 'What about payment?'

Jeffers glanced at the Captain. 'I told you . . .'

'First Officer Jeffers tells me you drive a hard bargain,' said Captain Smith.

'No, it was quite easy really.'

The Captain's eyes twinkled for a moment, then he clicked his fingers. 'Well, let's have a look.'

Jimmy handed him the paper, then winked at Claire. It was her cue. 'We'll have the printing finished in about an hour, but we're going to need help with the distribution. There's nearly two thousand copies to get out.'

'We're short-staffed as it is,' said Jeffers.

'That's what we were thinking. So we want permission to hire some kids to do it for us.'

'Pardon?'

Jimmy nodded beside her. 'Half a dozen kids, ten dollars each, and we'll have that paper through everyone's door in an hour.'

The Captain passed the newspaper to Dr Hill. 'What do you think, Doctor?'

As the doctor began to study it Jeffers said, 'This sounds like a money-making scheme.'

Jimmy folded his arms. 'It's a solution to a problem. If you don't get the paper to the passengers, what's the point in doing it?'

'And kids love earning money,' Claire pointed out. 'They'll do it five times faster than your people can because we'll select only those who're prepared to run everywhere.'

'It'll be like a club. They'll feel like part of the crew.'

'But they'll take their orders from us.'

They looked eagerly towards Captain Smith for

approval. They had agreed that if they got the money, they'd pay half to the kids they recruited and keep the rest for themselves. It was important to make a profit. Captain Smith turned slightly to the side, and conferred quietly with Dr Hill. Then he turned back and nodded thoughtfully. 'We can certainly find the money to pay for the distribution,' he said, 'even if we have to dip into your father's wallet.' Claire smiled, slightly embarrassed. 'You've clearly put a lot of work into the paper, both of you. However . . .'

Captain Smith held up the *Times*.

Then he tore it in two.

'. . . we won't be sending *this* out to anyone.'

'What're you doing?' Claire shrieked.

'We've been working on that all day!' cried Jimmy.

Captain Smith sighed. 'I'm sure you have. But it's just not good enough. Our passengers are here to enjoy themselves. They want to leave their troubles behind. If they read this – good God, there's nothing but death and horror – they'll throw themselves over the side of the ship.'

'But that's what's happening out there!'

'I realize that, Jimmy, and certainly you shouldn't ignore it, but you need to make it more positive.'

'How? People are dying!'

'That's not my job!' the Captain erupted. 'I'm just telling you I'm not sending it out like this – it's like a sixteen-page suicide note. Put some good news in it, for goodness' sake. Put in some sports . . .'

'They've all been cancelled!'

'Then make something up! But sort it out!'

Claire's mouth dropped open a little. 'You can't talk to us like that!'

'Yes I can. When you agreed to edit this newspaper, when you accepted a wage for doing it, you became employees of this ship. So listen very carefully. We need a newspaper ready for tomorrow morning and I don't care if you have to stay up all night to make it. Now scram!'

It was raining outside. Torrential. But it was warm rain, like Jimmy had never felt before. With all the work on the paper and the horrors he was writing about Jimmy had almost forgotten where he was. In the Caribbean. He had never even been on holiday with his family – had never left Ireland before, in fact.

Claire said, 'I hate him.'

'I hate him too.'

'Who does he think he is, tearing our paper up like that?'

'I'd like to set his beard on fire. And stick a firework up his arse.'

They stared out into the rain. They were quiet for nearly a minute.

'But he is right,' said Jimmy.

'I know,' said Claire.

★ ★ ★

They returned to the office and set to work on a new version of the paper. They did not ignore the Red Death. In fact, it still remained the main story on the front page. Thousands had died, there was no escaping that fact. But when they looked at the Internet again, they saw that there were positive stories. Many people were still working. Plenty of cities were not experiencing riots. Scientists were predicting that it would burn itself out. The facts were all the same, they were just examined from a different perspective.

Claire and Jimmy worked for three solid hours, then ran off another copy of the paper and took it to the bridge. This time they entered with a little more trepidation. Captain Smith immediately examined their work, his eyes flitting up to them from time to time as he read each article. Finally he finished and handed the paper back to Jimmy.

'Much better,' he said. 'Start printing immediately.'

Then he turned away.

Jimmy and Claire exchanged glances.

'Is that it?' said Claire. 'He might have said thank you.'

First Officer Jeffers came up behind them. 'He has other things on his mind right now,' he said. 'At lunchtime today we had our first cases of this . . . Red Death . . . reported. Three of them. I've just informed the Captain that we now have thirty-two. Dr Hill believes there may be one hundred by tomorrow. In that case we will no longer be a cruise ship. We will be a plague ship.'

Claire stared at him.

Jimmy stared at him.

'He could still have said thank you,' said Claire.

Dr Hill was wrong about the possibility of there being a hundred cases of the Red Death by morning.

There were one hundred and fifty.

Seven people were dead, all of them over the age of sixty.

Captain Smith declared that Level Five, on which the small hospital was situated, be quarantined. Passengers who had cabins on that level had to move.

Jimmy and Claire managed just a few hours' sleep – it had taken longer than they thought to distribute the papers, despite hiring six kids from the amusement arcade – and it was past two in the morning before they were finished. Then they had to be up early again to start work on the next edition. They didn't mind.

They met for breakfast in the buffet restaurant on Level Eleven, and it was there that Ty Warner found them. He stood rather sheepishly facing Jimmy. He unfolded a copy of the *Times* from a pocket on the leg of his shorts.

'You didn't call me gay,' he said.

'Nope,' said Jimmy.

'The photo turned out good.' Claire smiled round at him. He went on, 'About twenty people have said hello to me this morning. They all know I'm *Passenger of the Day*. My momma collected up all the copies she could find, she's gonna take them home to show the rest of the family. If she gets better. She has that thing. The bug.' Claire made room for him to sit down. 'Last night she was fine, but woke up early this morning real sick, throwing up, big red smudges on her arm. They took her upstairs. Won't let me see her. Won't let anyone up. Say the whole place is in quarantine. I'm real worried about her.'

They sat quietly for a little bit. Then Jimmy said, 'If you think I'm giving you your T-shirt back because I feel sorry for you, you've another thing coming.'

Ty looked a little confused. 'I didn't mention the T-shirt. You can keep the T-shirt.'

Claire put a hand on his arm. 'Don't worry about him, it's just his sense of humour. Besides, it doesn't need giving back, it needs a wash.'

'It's all I have,' Jimmy protested, sniffing at himself. 'And it's not that bad.'

Claire raised an eyebrow. 'Oh yeah?'

'I want to see my momma,' Ty said. 'I don't think putting all the sick people in one place is going to stop this thing spreading. Sure we all been mixing since we got on this boat.'

'It's not a boat,' said Jimmy.

'What?' asked Ty.

'It's a ship. Scoop says a boat's what you get on to when your ship is sinking.'

'Don't see that it matters,' said Ty. 'All I want to do is go see my momma.'

Claire gave his arm a squeeze. 'It's too dangerous.'

Ty shook his head. 'If I was going to get it, I would have it right now. I was with my momma all night, we breath in the same air, don't we? And I'm sitting here with you, so if I have it, maybe you have it, maybe we all have it, just some it hits, some it don't. I don't want her lying on some bed, nobody looking after her.'

'What about your dad?'

'He says he isn't going near her. They fight a lot. He says if she sees him she'll surely breathe all over him out of badness. So there's only me.'

Claire looked at Jimmy. 'He has a point, you know. We all breathe the same air. If we're going to get it, we're going to get it – nothing can be done. We should help him get to see his mum.'

'*We?*'

'This is my dad's ship, I know where all the service elevators are. We could possibly bypass whatever security they have on the main elevators. I'd like to try. And you stole his T-shirt, so you owe him.'

'You think that's equal to going up there? That's mental! They're all dying!' He suddenly realized what he'd said and looked apologetically across at Ty. 'I mean – I'm sure your mum will be fine . . . but still, you know what I mean. And anyway, we've a newspaper to run, and even if we found out anything useful up there, we wouldn't be allowed to use it, so what's the point?'

'You're just chicken,' said Claire.

'Absolutely,' said Jimmy.

They left him sitting there. He finished his bacon and got some more. He ate sausages and pancakes covered in maple syrup.

Chicken!

After what I've done?

He walked out of the restaurant and along to the newspaper office. But when he tried to go on-line to survey the morning's news the computer kept telling him that the line was busy. So he left that for a while and rifled through a large box of pamphlets and brochures Scoop had left behind, looking for some information on the *Titanic's* first port of call, the city of San Juan in Puerto Rico, which would have to be profiled in detail in that night's edition of the paper.

He found it quickly enough, then sat at his computer and began trying to compose an article.

Chicken!

Who did she think she was? What had *she* ever done that was brave? She hadn't stowed away – *twice*. Or outwitted all those search parties. And who came up with the idea of e-mailing a photo from her camera, thus saving their lives? And she was calling *him* chicken? All she'd ever done in her spoiled little life was huff.

Jimmy tried to concentrate on Puerto Rico. He wrote about it being discovered five hundred years ago by Christopher Columbus. How it became a Spanish colony, with the local Indian tribes either being wiped out or decimated. In the nineteenth century it had struggled for independence as its population grew and agriculture flourished, with the coffee bean becoming its most important product. After the Spanish American War and the Treaty of Paris was signed the island was ceded to the United States, with Puerto Ricans being granted American citizenship.

It was *extremely* boring.

Chicken!

Right – that was it. He wasn't prepared to just be a desk jockey. He was sure she wasn't the slightest bit concerned about Ty, she was just nosey. She always wanted precisely what she wasn't allowed. And it didn't matter if that meant putting her life and Ty's in danger by smuggling him into the plague zone. Jimmy pushed back from the desk. He was going to yank Claire out of there and tell her exactly how much of a fool she was being.

The smell got him first.

Jimmy had with him a small flannel soaked in water, which he held over his nose and mouth, but it didn't do much good. He had never seen a dead body, or smelled one, for that matter. But somehow he knew what the stench was.

It was . . . revolting.

The cabins on either side of the corridor were packed full of the sick and dying. Nurses were doing their best to cope, but it was clear that there were just too many. The hundred and fifty cases Ty had mentioned at breakfast seemed to have quadrupled.

'Jimmy!'

Dr Hill's hair was plastered to his head and his white doctor's coat was heavily stained.

'What're you doing here, Jimmy? It isn't safe!'

'Looking for Claire.'

Dr Hill rubbed at his brow, then looked about him. He appeared to be a little confused. 'She *was* here . . . with another boy – his mum died. And then his dad did as well.'

'His . . .?'

'Had some sort of convulsion. Don't know if it was the Red Death or not. Not sure where they went . . .' He shook his head and sighed. 'We don't know anything about this damn virus, Jimmy, I don't know whether I'm doing any good at all up here.'

Jimmy looked back along the corridor. 'How many are there?'

'I don't know. I don't even want to think about it. All I know is, it's getting worse, every hour. Now for goodness' sake, get out of here before you catch it as well.'

Jimmy didn't need to be told twice.

He found them on the fifteenth. Ty was leaning against the rail, staring out to sea. Claire sat on a sunbed behind him. She had tears in her eyes.

'Jimmy . . .'

'I heard.'

She glanced up at Ty, then lowered her voice. 'He came on a cruise with his mum and dad, and two days later they're both dead.'

'It's horrible,' said Jimmy, 'but what can we do?'

'Adopt him,' said Claire.

The Fleet

They gave Ty a job on the paper, thinking that if they kept him busy he wouldn't think about his parents so much. But when they got back to the office there was still no Internet access, so they immediately marched right up to the bridge to find out why. They were kept waiting at the door for ten minutes until a stressed-looking First Officer Jeffers finally appeared. He led them across to the rail so that he could get the maximum benefit of the breeze.

'Sorry,' he said, 'things are a bit hectic. We haven't been able to get a coherent response from the port authorities in San Juan. One minute they say everything is fine, come ahead, the next they're screaming down the phone. I think things are pretty bad there as well.' Then he nodded across at Ty, who was hanging well back. 'Who's your friend?' They told him quickly. 'That's incredibly sad,' said Jeffers, shaking his head.

'So are we still actually going to San Juan?' Jimmy asked.

'Have to. We need to top up our fuel and . . .' He

glanced towards Ty, then lowered his voice. 'We'll have to take the bodies off.'

Claire made a face. 'What's my daddy even thinking, allowing the cruise to continue when so many people are unwell? We should just turn around and go home.'

'Things are even worse at home, Claire.'

'We haven't been able to keep track,' said Jimmy. 'Our Internet connection is down. That's why we're here, is there—'

'Captain Smith has switched it off.'

'Why?' Jimmy asked. 'We promised not to use all the gory stuff in the paper.'

'I know that, but it's not just about your access, Jimmy, it's the entire ship. Captain Smith believes that if the passengers hear how bad things are getting there could be complete chaos. If fifteen hundred people make their minds up to do something, we'll be helpless. You have to play your part with the paper. We don't want people to panic. All right?'

Claire nodded. Jimmy looked at the ground.

'Jimmy?'

He gave a little shrug. 'It just doesn't seem right. People know there's a plague out there, and they know people are dying on this ship. Why can't we just tell them the truth? People don't like being lied to.'

'Because those are the Captain's orders.'

'And do you think he's right?'

Jeffers' eyes locked with Jimmy's. 'Those are the Captain's orders,' he repeated.

* * *

'What's wrong with you?' Claire asked. 'You're usually so enthusiastic.'

Jimmy shrugged. They were back in the office, working. His heart wasn't in it. He loved the paper, but he didn't like what he was writing. 'I just think it's wrong. Look at this – I'm writing about the fortress of San Cristobal and how wonderful it would be to visit and all the jewellery shops and . . . what's the point? There aren't going to be any tours of the island.'

'You don't know that, Jimmy.'

'Claire – the hospital is full of dead bodies; the Captain won't let us look at the Internet because it might be too horrific and they don't seem to be able to get any sense out of anyone in San Juan. Do you really think anyone at all is going to be interested in going sightseeing? Ty – have you any interest at all in visiting an old fort or buying cheap jewellery?'

Ty, who was replenishing paper supplies for the printer, nodded across. 'Yes, please,' he said.

Claire smiled.

'It can't be any worse than being here,' said Ty.

'Can't it? We're on a nice ship, we have lots of food, but who knows what it's like on the island? We don't know anything about this virus! For all we know anyone who dies from it turns into a blood-sucking zombie!' Jimmy cleared his throat. 'Although obviously your parents won't have . . .' Jimmy sighed. 'Look, my point is, we shouldn't be writing this crap. We should be writing the truth. We shouldn't be hiding things from people. We should be recording what's actually happening, not ignoring it or hiding it.'

'Like a proper newspaper,' said Claire.

'Exactly. We should have photographs of the conditions in the hospital, we should have interviews with the doctors, we should have reports from every city every passenger comes from. We should . . . tell the truth.'

'Captain Smith would never approve it. He'd just tear it up again.'

'Then we make two papers – one for him and one for the rest of the ship.'

Claire's eyes narrowed. '*What?*'

'Why not? We have all the equipment here. We can write it, print it up and distribute it around the ship, and hopefully enough passengers will get to read it before he catches on.'

'Jimmy – Mr Jeffers was worried about the *passengers* staging a mutiny. But *this* is a mutiny. And what if the passengers mutiny *because* of what we write?'

They debated it back and forth. One moment Claire was keen, the next she was frightened, then she felt disloyal, then she felt indignant that they were being made to mislead people

'Look Jimmy, it's all right for you, you've nothing to lose. But this is my dad's ship! I can't—'

'Do anything in case he doesn't buy you another pony?'

'That's not fair!'

'But true. I wouldn't worry about it, Claire, the ponies're probably all dead anyway.'

'Jimmy!'

'Oh yeah. Lying in a field just rotting away . . .'

Claire jumped to her feet. 'You . . . you . . . you're just *evil*, Jimmy Armstrong!'

She stormed out of the office.

Jimmy drummed his fingers on the table.

'That wasn't very clever,' said Ty.

Jimmy had a long history of annoying people. He wanted to say something smart and cutting back to Ty, but nothing smart and cutting would come. So he just said, 'Shut your cake hole,' and went after Claire.

He guessed right. She was going to see her parents. There is no accounting for the way the human mind works. The world was in the grip of a deadly plague, but for the moment she was more concerned about her ponies.

Jimmy caught up with her just as she was approaching their cabin.

'Claire!' She stopped and glared back at him. He came right up. 'I'm sorry.'

'For what?' Claire snapped back.

'For saying that.'

'For saying what?'

'Whatever I said.'

'You don't even know what you said.'

'Yes I do.'

'What, then?'

'All that stuff. Look, does it matter, I'm apologizing!'

Claire took a deep breath. She looked at the carpet. 'I'm sorry for running off. I'm just scared.'

'I'm sure the ponies are fine.'

'It's not just them. It's . . . everything.'

'I know. I'm the same. I'm too scared to even try and contact my parents in case I hear something I don't want to hear.'

'You *should* call them.' Claire turned to the door, but before she opened it she looked back at him. 'Come with me.'

'Are you sure?'

'Sure. If I start acting stupid, give me a kick.'

'With pleasure.'

Claire smiled and opened the door. She had the briefest glimpse of her father lying on the bed, fully clothed, his eyes wide and staring, before her mother hurried across and pushed her back out. Then she stepped out into the corridor and closed the door behind her.

'Is Daddy . . . is he . . . does he have the . . .?'

'No . . . of course not, Claire, he's just . . . resting.' She looked tearful. 'Walk with me, dear.'

If she even noticed Jimmy, she didn't say. He fell in behind them as they moved along the corridor.

'What's wrong, Mummy?' Claire asked.

'Daddy's worried about the fleet, that's all.'

Claire had patiently explained to Jimmy that her family didn't just own the *Titanic*, but a fleet of nine cruise ships, all of which operated out of Miami.

'Why, what's happened?'

Mrs Stanford refused to answer until they'd arrived at the champagne bar on Level Twelve. She ordered the most expensive bottle they had left. The waiter told them that passengers had been going mad for it. 'They're spending all their money in case . . . you know . . .' He trailed off when he saw Mrs Stanford's frosty look. He poured her a glass and brought it on a tray with the bottle and an ice bucket over to the only free table. Jimmy had been in bars before, either with his dad or trying to get his dad out of one, but this was the quietest one he'd ever been in. People were drunk, but miserable and silent.

Claire's mother took a long drink. 'Well,' she said, 'that's better. Life always seems better with a little glass of champagne.'

'Mum – the fleet.'

'The fleet. Well, Claire, as you know, the company decided to continue with the cruise schedule despite this . . . flu . . . in the hope that it would soon pass and everything would get back to normal. Six of the nine ships put to sea, but unfortunately we seem to have lost contact with four of them.'

'What do you mean, lost contact?'

'What I say, dear. They're gone. Disappeared. There are still three in port, of course – although one of them is on fire. Your father saw it on a news report on his computer. He's quite devastated. He says we're ruined. I prefer to look on it as a little hiccup.' She took another long sip of her champagne, draining the glass. She set it down. 'We're Stanfords, after all, we always bounce back.' She stood up, then lifted the champagne bottle out of the bucket. 'I'll just take this back to share with your father – the room service is so dreadfully slow.'

She started to walk away. She gave Jimmy a rather frosty smile as she passed.

'Mum!'

Mrs Stanford stopped. Claire came running up and gave her a hug.

'Oh! Dear, what was that for?'

'Just.'

'Well – that's nice.'

'Mum, can I ask you something?'

'Of course, dear.'

'If there's bad news, do you think it's better to tell someone straight, or to keep it from them so they won't feel miserable?'

'Well – I think you should always tell the truth. When you start to tell fibs it invariably makes matters worse. Why do you ask?'

'Oh – no reason. Love you, Mum.'

Mrs Stanford smiled. She started to turn again, then paused. 'That reminds me. I did tell you about the ponies, didn't I?'

'*Mum?*'

'There's just been so much going on. We had an e-mail to say they've escaped from the farm. I'm sure they're perfectly fine and they'll turn up soon enough, but I just thought you should know. See you later, darling.'

Mrs Stanford hurried away.

Claire returned to the table and sat down heavily. 'Don't you *dare* smile.'

'I'm not.' Although he was, he couldn't help it. He quickly changed the subject. 'So what are we going to do about the paper?'

Claire took a deep breath. 'All my life my parents have been trying to get me to behave in exactly the way they want. Well now I'm going to. If they say I should tell the truth, then I'm going to tell it. Let's do our newspaper. Let's do it properly.'

'Is this just because of the ponies?'

'No! It's because it's the right thing to do.'

'I agree. And I'm sure they'll turn up.'

Claire nodded.

'Unless someone eats them,' said Jimmy.

Dolphins

It was a team effort. Claire surprised her parents by insisting that they take her out for dinner; both of them were rather drunk, and so were inclined to interpret this as a sudden flowering of her love for them. She *did* love them, but this was a deliberate act of deception which allowed Jimmy to slip into their cabin and access Mr Stanford's Internet connection. They had guessed correctly that while the rest of the ship was denied access to the web, the owner would make sure he was still connected. Meanwhile Ty, under the pretence of visiting his parents' bodies, smuggled Claire's camera into the hospital wing and began recording the distressing plight of the infected passengers.

At ten minutes to eight Jimmy and Claire arrived on the bridge with their fake edition of the *Titanic Times*. The story on the front page said that the plague was still spreading but that medical experts were hopeful of making a breakthrough soon. It wasn't a lie. It just ignored the larger truth. Inside, it was packed with information about San Juan and duty-free shopping and snippets about activities on the ship. The *Passenger of the Day* was eighty-three-year-old Miss Kitty Calhoon who confessed to having another stowaway on board – Franklin, a small pink poodle. They were pictured together on the back page.

Captain Smith, his eyes red and the bags beneath them as thick as teabags, flicked through the paper, nodding with approval. 'This is much more like it . . .' But when he saw Kitty and Franklin his brow furrowed. 'What is this?' he demanded angrily. 'This woman has a dog on board?' He turned to First Officer Jeffers. 'How could this happen? How did she get it past security?'

'I . . . don't know . . . Captain.'

'I want her arrested immediately and the dog destroyed.'

'Captain?'

'You know as well as I do, Mr Jeffers, that this ship must abide by the many international agreements which prevent the transportation of livestock between nations without proper documentation and approvals. This is *exactly* how disease spreads.'

'With all due respect, Captain, I think a poodle is the least of our—'

'Mr Jeffers! I have given you an order, now please ensure that it is carried out immediately!'

'Yes, sir, right away.'

Jeffers hurried from the bridge. Captain Smith took another look at the photo on the back page, shook his head, then handed the paper back to Jimmy. 'Good job all round, permission to print granted.'

Outside, Jimmy said, 'That was a bit weird.'

'Did you see the look he gave Jeffers?'

'I know. What's he going to be like when he sees our *real* paper?'

Claire rolled her eyes. 'I intend not to be there for that one.' She stopped. 'Damn. Look, I've forgotten something – you head back and start printing, I'll be there in a couple of minutes.'

'Are you chickening out on me?'

'No!'

Claire arrived back twenty minutes later wearing a shoulder bag. Printing was progressing nicely. Jimmy gave her the thumbs up. They both knew how important it was to get the paper out to the passengers as quickly as possible, because Captain Smith would ban it the moment he saw it. To this end Ty had recruited twice the number of delivery boys and girls they'd used the previous night. They waited impatiently outside in the corridor. They didn't care what the paper contained, they just wanted the money.

As the fresh copies slid perfectly out of the printer Jimmy said, 'It's not too late for either of you to back out.'

'What do you mean?'

'I mean, it's your dad's ship, Claire. If you feel bad about doing this you can just go upstairs now and I'll say you had nothing to do with it. And you've got enough problems, Ty.'

Claire shook her head. 'We're in this together.' She nodded at Ty as he divided up the finished copies into even piles. 'All of us.'

'We're like . . . revolutionaries,' said Ty.

'All for one and one for all,' said Claire. '*The Three Musketeers*. Which reminds me – did you ever read that book at school?'

Ty shook his head.

'Saw the movie,' said Jimmy.

'So you'll know that there weren't really three musketeers in the story, there were four.'

Jimmy shrugged. 'So what?'

'Well, here's *our* fourth.'

Claire set the shoulder bag down on her desk. Ty looked at it. Jimmy looked at it. Then the bag moved. It *whimpered*.

'*Claire?*'

'I had to do something.'

'*Claire!*'

She opened the bag, and out popped a pink little poodle head. Franklin was huffing and puffing. Then he began to whine. He jumped down from the desk and began to sniff around the office floor.

'I hate yappy little rats,' said Jimmy.

'So do I,' said Claire, 'but I still keep *you* around.' It didn't raise a smile. 'Jimmy, I just couldn't . . . Kitty is such a sweet old lady and it would absolutely kill her if anything happened to Franklin. I promised her we'd look after him until the coast is clear.'

'How'd you manage to beat Jeffers and get to Franklin first?'

'Well I knew what cabin Kitty was in, he had to go and find out. But when I came out with Franklin in the bag Jeffers was standing at the rail, just looking out to sea. I started to walk past him and Franklin barked. Jeffers just said, "Evening, Claire," then went up to her door. He *knew*.'

'More than one way to follow orders,' said Jimmy. 'Just as there's more than one way to produce a newspap—'

He stopped. Franklin was peeing over one of the piles of newspapers.

'Claire!'

The distribution of two thousand *Titanic Times* – including thirty-seven slightly damp copies – was carried out with military efficiency between midnight and one a.m. There were small pigeonholes for mail outside each cabin, but the delivery team was under instruction to ignore these and slip the papers under each door so that they would physically be inside the room when their occupants woke in the morning. When it was finally completed and the delivery boys paid, Jimmy, Claire and Ty locked up the office and split up to go to their rooms.

But none of them did.

* * *

Ty returned to the hospital and sat with the bodies of his parents. Twice the nurses ordered him out for fear of him catching the Red Death, and twice he returned.

Claire sought out her father, and found him close to the bridge, standing smoking a cigar and staring down at the waves in the moonlight. She stood beside him for several minutes without speaking. She wasn't even sure he knew she was there, so intent was his gaze, but then he suddenly pointed at the water. 'Look, Claire – dolphins!'

And there they were, six of them, bouncing alongside the mighty ship.

'They're beautiful!' Claire cried. 'Aren't they, Daddy?'

He nodded slowly. 'They surely are.'

She gave his arm a little squeeze. 'Don't they say dolphins sometimes come to help people when they're in trouble? Do you think that's what they're doing?'

'I hope so, darling, I hope so.'

One deck below, Jimmy was also watching the dolphins. He had the lucky penny in his hand. He was wondering whether, if he threw it hard enough and with enough accuracy, he could hit one of them.

The Theatre

Jimmy's cabin on Level Ten was a mess. Stolen clothes and plates of half-eaten food littered the floor, sweet wrappers and half-full cans of soda covered every surface. Every morning a cleaner knocked on the door asking to come in, and every morning Jimmy told her to go away. This morning, she didn't knock. It might have been an oversight or she might have given up. But he suspected it was more than that. It was the *Times*. It was *out there*.

He was proud of what he'd done, but it wasn't in his nature to go and face the music. It was in his nature to hide. Or run away. Or to let someone else take the blame. Claire, in fact.

Jimmy phoned the Stanford suite, all ready to ask for Claire in an American accent in case her father answered, but it was Claire herself who picked up. 'What have you heard?' he asked.

'Mr Jeffers came to the door at about five this morning. I'm presuming he showed my dad the paper. I heard Daddy swear, then he told Mummy he had to go out. He hasn't been back since. Mummy spoke to him on the phone – they're all having a meeting in Captain Smith's quarters.'

'They're going to feed us to the sharks. Did your mum read it as well?'

'She did. She said, that's dreadful, I didn't realize, those poor people, there must be something we can do to help. Then she went to get her nails done.'

They were still discussing what to do when they were interrupted by an announcement over the PA. Jimmy recognized First Officer Jeffers' voice calling all passengers and crew to a public meeting in the theatre on Level Three in thirty minutes' time.

'Oh God,' said Claire. 'This is it then.'

It was a one-thousand-seat theatre which normally hosted celebrity guest speakers during the day and cabaret shows at night, but this morning there were well over two thousand people packed into it – mostly passengers but also a large number of crew. It was usually a place of laughter and music, but there was now an almost tangible air of fear and anger. As Jimmy squeezed through to the front row he noted that many people were clutching copies of the *Titanic Times*.

Claire hadn't managed to claim a seat, but instead sat cross-legged on the floor. Jimmy knelt down beside her. The stage was still clear, but there was a microphone set up with six chairs lined up behind it. From somewhere towards the back of the theatre a slow, impatient hand clapping began and then quickly spread until the entire place reverberated to the sound of thousands of sweaty palms coming together.

Less than a minute later Captain Smith appeared at the side of the stage, then walked slowly across it, followed by Mr Stanford, First Officer Jeffers, Chief Engineer Jonas Jones and Dr Hill. They were greeted with a chorus of boos. Captain Smith stood before the microphone and waited for the hubbub to subside, but it went on and on as questions were yelled along with insults.

Eventually, *eventually* the noise receded enough for Captain Smith to be heard. He began by thanking everyone for coming – and this was greeted with another chorus of boos.

'I'm here to apologize.' This surprised them. The noise subsided again. 'As you know, when we set sail, it was with the intention of making sure that you enjoyed a marvellous vacation. That is what you paid for. We set sail with the full expectation that this virus would quickly run its course both in America and around the world and that we would return you safely to a country that was already well on the way to recovery. However, as we continued to monitor the situation it became clear that – well, that *nothing* was clear. All the news we were getting from home was contradictory, misleading and confusing. For this reason I took the decision to limit the amount of news that you had access to. I didn't want to cause unrest or panic. We all have loved ones waiting for us and we are all naturally anxious to know what's going on. I accept now that this was wrong. I also knew it was inevitable that we would have some cases of this . . . Red Death . . . on board, but I have been truly shocked by the speed with which it has spread. The extent of this was also kept from you, and I apologize for this as well. Reviewing the situation last night, and taking on board advice from Mr Stanford and my senior crew, I decided that you all – passengers and crew alike – should be made aware of the true situation, both here on the ship and at home. I decided that the best way to do it would be through our ship newspaper so that you would have all the facts right in front of you . . .'

Jimmy looked at Claire in disbelief. 'He . . .'

'. . . and so that you could take the time to properly digest these facts before I summoned you to this meeting. They have been presented in the newspaper by my staff, who have exhausted every possible avenue to ensure their accuracy. I think you will find it is a fair depiction of the state of our two worlds at this moment in time – here, on the ship and, well, everywhere else.'

Captain Smith gave Jimmy and Claire the tiniest nod.

'Ladies and gentlemen, these are not good times. Forty passengers have now passed away . . .' the audience were stunned into silence by this, '. . . and three hundred more are infected. We have established a quarantine area on the hospital deck, but the truth is we just don't know how to stop the virus. Nobody does. Dr Hill . . .' he turned slightly and raised a hand towards him, '. . . and his staff have been working flat out. Two of his nurses died during the night.'

A man in a Hawaiian shirt stood up. 'Captain, sir, that's very sad, and we certainly appreciate everything the doctor and his staff are doing, but doesn't it make sense to turn the ship around now, and return to port?' This was greeted with applause from the audience. 'We all have people we're worried about, and we'd be really happy to go home and see them. Don't see the sense of staying cooped up on board with this Red Death running rampant. At least at home we might get the chance to outrun it.'

There was more applause and some cheering.

Captain Smith raised a hand for calm. 'Sir, we'd all like to go home, but the fact of the matter is that until we can establish exactly what's going on back there we're safer staying where we are.'

The man in the Hawaiian shirt gave a little laugh. 'Well why don't you just phone 'em up and ask?'

That brought a wave of laughter.

'Sir, at six o'clock this morning we lost contact with our home port of Miami. We have to assume that it is no longer functioning. Communication with anywhere is becoming very, very difficult.'

Another man shouted from the back. 'Just sail in, tie up and let us off!'

'Sir, in my opinion it is simply not safe to return to port right now. Until we can establish that it *is* safe it is my intention to continue with the cruise . . .'

Howls of protest erupted. Those who had seats jumped up and waved their fists and yelled and threw copies of the *Titanic Times* towards the stage. It took several minutes for them to calm down.

'Ladies and gentlemen,' Captain Smith eventually continued, 'we have no way of knowing exactly what the situation is at home, but certainly there has been rioting, and looting, and shortages of food. At least here on board we have supplies to see us through the remainder of the cruise; plus, at each of our three scheduled stops – later this morning at San Juan, then at the island of St Thomas and Cozumel in Mexico – we have dedicated fuel supplies. We are safe on the *Titanic*, and we *will* look after you.'

Most of the passengers were desperate to go home, but at least some of them were also beginning to see the sense of *not* going home.

An old woman spoke from halfway down the aisle. Jimmy glanced around and saw that it was Kitty Calhoon. She waved a walking stick towards the Captain as she spoke.

'Captain Smith! Do you think it might be all right, given the circumstances, for Franklin to come out of hiding now?'

The Captain looked genuinely perplexed. 'Franklin?' First Officer Jeffers stepped forward and quietly spoke in his ear. The Captain sighed. 'Mrs Calhoon, I think that will be fine.'

She smiled happily and sat. Another man just to her right, with his shirt open to his navel and a V of sunburned skin got to his feet.

'Captain Smith,' he said, 'we've paid good money for this trip and if it's going to be disrupted by this illness, if we're going to be unable to go on the excursions we were promised, then we're going to be entitled to some compensation.'

This brought applause. Captain Smith sighed again and turned to Mr Stanford. 'Perhaps, Mr Stanford . . .?'

Claire's dad got stiffly to his feet. He looked gaunt and pale as he approached the microphone. 'We – ah, at White Star . . . we pride ourselves on always . . . putting . . . our customers . . . first. But perhaps this . . . isn't the time to . . .'

'I didn't pay five grand for a cruise on a plague ship!'

More applause.

'We'll sue you for a million bucks!' an elderly man shouted.

'Please – there's no need for . . .'

'We want a full refund, we want compensation, we want—'

'Stop it!' Mr Stanford shouted suddenly, his eyes blazing. 'Don't you understand? Everything is going to hell out there! Money doesn't matter any more! It's all over . . .!'

Captain Smith quickly returned to the microphone

and gently nudged his employer to one side. 'If you can, I'd like you all just to go back upstairs and to do your best to enjoy the ship and all its facilities. Hopefully the news from home will start to—'

'Captain Smith!'

Jimmy turned to his left and saw that the chef Pedroza was standing in the aisle, with about twenty of his colleagues grouped around him.

'Yes, Mr Pedroza?'

Many of the passengers had already begun to vacate their seats, but they stopped now; it was something in the way Pedroza spoke, and the resignation in Captain Smith's voice in response.

'Captain Smith – what the boss says about the money, not mattering any more. Is he right?'

'I'm not sure what you mean, Mr Pedroza.'

'If everything is crazy out there, then money – it has no value, right?'

'What's your point, sir?'

'If money's worth nothing – what are we working for? Why should we do what you say?'

His colleagues murmured their support.

Captain Smith fixed Pedroza with a hard look. 'You will do what I say because you signed a contract agreeing to work! Any man who refuses to obey an order will be arrested and charged with mutin—!'

He stopped as Mr Stanford, who had been standing beside him, suddenly collapsed forward, just missing the audience below and landing in a crumpled heap at the very edge of the stage. Dr Hill and Jonas Jones rushed to help him and a moment later Claire climbed up to join them.

Dr Hill removed Mr Stanford's tie and was just unbuttoning his shirt to give him some air and to check his heart when Claire dropped to her knees beside her father.

'Please . . . is he . . .?' But then she saw what Dr Hill had already spotted.

Red blotches across her father's chest.

'Oh no . . .!' she cried. 'Please *no* . . .!'

The Fire

Mr Stanford, as befitted his position as owner of the White Star Line, was taken to a private cabin. Claire went up with him, holding his hand as he lay on the stretcher. Mrs Stanford was summoned from their suite. Both were advised to stay away because of the danger of them catching the Red Death as well, but they ignored this. They loved him. Also, it didn't seem to make any difference. Mr Stanford hadn't been anywhere near the hospital wing, but he'd still caught it.

Dr Hill was grey with fatigue and despair. Nothing he did seemed to help. In his darker moments he thought it might be simpler to scuttle the ship and end everyone's misery. Jonas Jones thought it was a miracle that the doctor himself hadn't caught it. Dr Hill said that when you first became a doctor you tended to catch everything within the first few months but that the body's immune system quickly built up its resistance, otherwise doctors would be off sick all the time. So he was pretty confident that he could fend off the Red Death, despite being exposed to it all day long. Jonas Jones didn't disbelieve him, but still kept his distance. They communicated by phone.

Acrid smoke hung over the city of San Juan as the *Titanic* approached its harbour. Those passengers who were well emerged on to the decks to watch, vainly hoping that the port might be bustling with people, waiting to greet them and sell them cheap jewellery or time shares or who might even try to steal their wallets – anything that would make the world seem normal again. Jimmy was with them on the top deck when a match was struck just to his left, and he turned to find Captain Smith lighting his pipe. They hadn't met since the Captain had made his claims about the newspaper. He took a puff and spoke without turning.

'Two hundred years ago you'd have been swinging from the yardarm for pulling a stunt like that. Mutiny, they'd call it.'

'Two hundred years ago there wouldn't have been a newspaper on a ship, or computers and printers to make it possible.'

'Two hundred years ago you'd have walked the plank for passing seditious rumour.'

'It wasn't rumour – it was all true.'

Captain Smith shook his head. 'Do you know something, Jimmy Armstrong? You'd make a terrible soldier, because you're absolutely dreadful at following orders.' Jimmy started to say something, but the Captain held up his hand. 'On the other hand I suspect you'd make a wonderful general, because once you make your mind up there's no compromise, you absolutely stick to your guns.'

Jimmy shrugged.

'Even great leaders make mistakes. You were right about the newspaper, I was wrong. However, you will also find that great leaders often take the credit for other people's bright ideas, as I did earlier. The point is, lad, that there's only room for one captain on this ship, one leader – particularly at times of crisis. In future, if my orders are disobeyed, I won't hesitate to put you off my ship. Do you understand?'

Jimmy nodded.

'OK. Do you know what they call *The Times* of London? They call it the *paper of record*. When historians want to know the truth about the big, important stories of, say, a hundred years ago, they go to the British Library or go on-line and look at *The Times*. Well, I don't think our *Times* should be any different. Tragic as it is, we are experiencing something truly extraordinary, Jimmy. A plague, a breakdown in civilization, who knows what else? It shouldn't go unrecorded. Your newspaper today showed me that. We have to record *our* story; the *Titanic Times* has to be *our* paper of record. That's what I want you to do from now on, Jimmy – and Claire, if she's willing – keep producing the paper, make a history of our voyage, the good bits, the bad bits, the *truth*. Do you think you can do that?'

Jimmy studied the Captain intently. 'Can I ask you something, first?'

'Yes, of course.'

'One day, will you take the *Titanic* home to Belfast?'

Captain Smith looked surprised. 'I thought you were going to ask for money.'

'I would have,' said Jimmy, 'but it appears to be worthless at the moment.'

The Captain smiled. He took Jimmy by the shoulders and looked into his eyes. 'One day, I promise, the *Titanic* will return to Belfast.'

Jimmy put out his hand. 'OK, as long as we have the freedom to write it as we see it, if we have unlimited access to every meeting, every decision, every event, then I'm happy to accept.'

Captain Smith hesitated. 'Why do I have the feeling I'm going to regret this?'

Jimmy gave an innocent shrug.

The Captain shook his head, then instead of offering his hand, saluted. Jimmy, somewhat awkwardly, followed suit.

As they emerged on to Deck Two Jimmy and Claire spotted the two small landing parties preparing to go ashore. One, led by Jonas Jones, would go straight to the fuel depot and attempt to replenish the ship's supplies. The other, led by First Officer Jeffers, had less specific instructions – just to find out the conditions in the city. Jeffers was passing out weapons to members of his eight-man squad when Jimmy and Claire lined up with them.

'And where do you think you're going?' he asked.

'Ashore, with you,' said Jimmy.

'Reporting,' said Claire, 'for the *Titanic Times*.' She held up her camera.

'We'll see about that.'

Jeffers lifted his radio and turned away. They couldn't quite make out what was said, but when he faced them a couple of minutes later he looked rather flushed.

'All right,' he said, 'but stay close, and if I tell you to do something, you damned well do it.'

A single gangplank was lowered on to the quayside. Jeffers' squad cautiously made its way off the ship first, with guns raised. When it had secured the immediate area, Jonas Jones' squad followed and was then escorted to the fuel depot. Once Jeffers was satisfied that there was no immediate threat Jones' group was left with a single guard to undertake the refuelling. The rest of Jeffers' squad commandeered two abandoned vehicles and drove towards the centre of the city.

Jimmy and Claire were in the rear of the second vehicle, a Jeep. Jimmy was *still* wearing Ty's T-shirt. Claire was looking altogether cooler in a red T-shirt with a long white skirt. As they roared along she took photos of smouldering shops and wrecked cars. The most remarkable thing here was the complete and utter lack of people. There was no noise, but for the occasional bark of a dog.

'Where is everyone?' Claire asked.

'Maybe they fled the city because of the plague. Or they're all dead.'

'There's one and a half million people live in San Juan. They can't *all* be dead.' She paused. 'Can they? There'd be bodies everywhere.'

The smoke was bitter and harsh on their throats. Everything smelled rotten.

Jeffers, driving the lead vehicle, led them along Calle Cruz towards City Hall. There they left two men to guard the vehicles and mounted the steps into what had been the seat of Government. Their footsteps echoed on the marble floor. Papers were littered everywhere. But still no sign of anyone. When they returned to their vehicles Jeffers took out a street map. 'The smoke . . . seems to be coming from . . . *here* . . .' The section of the map he was pointing to was marked as the historic fortress of San Cristobal, situated on high ground to the east of the city but invisible now because of the smoke. 'Perhaps it's some kind of a signal fire. We should check it out.'

Progress was slow because of the increasing number of abandoned vehicles on the road, and soon the smoke grew so dense that Claire gave up trying to take photographs and concentrated on holding the neck of her T-shirt up over her mouth. The crewman in the front passenger seat passed back a bottle of water for them to wash their stinging eyes.

As they wound up the road towards the fortress the wind at last began to change direction and they soon emerged from the turgid smoke into the summer sun. Jeffers stopped his Jeep in the shadow of a high wall at the rear of the fortress and the second vehicle pulled in behind. Even from the outside, they could feel the intense heat being given off by the fire within. Jimmy climbed out and put his hands against the wall, which appeared to be a metre or so thick, yet was hot to the touch.

Jeffers left two guards with the vehicles then led the rest of them up a set of stone steps to a metal gate which should have given them access to the fortress's central courtyard, but was bolted closed from the inside. Jeffers rattled the gate in frustration, then took a step back and looked along the wall for some other means of access.

Jimmy said, 'I'm the lightest. Give me a hand up and I'll get over and open it from the inside.'

'Actually, *I'm* the lightest,' said Claire.

Jeffers looked from one to the other. 'Let me see – the stowaway or the daughter of the owner of the ship. Mmmm. Let's go for the stowaway.'

Two of the squad gave Jimmy a lift up. The climb was easy enough, but was complicated by the barbed wire strung across the top. As he contemplated the best way to get through it, he tried to identify the source of the heat, but the breeze circulating within the walls was blowing smoke in every direction and for the moment he could see nothing. Jimmy pulled at several strands of the barbed wire and managed to prise them apart. He slipped one leg through the gap and followed with the rest of his body, then lowered himself part of the way down the other side of the wall while pulling his other leg through behind. He was almost cleanly over when his shoelace snagged and he found himself hanging in midair; he pulled once, twice, then on the third attempt ripped it free. The force of it caused him to fall hard on to the concrete rampart below, knocking the wind out of him, and forcing an involuntary cry from his lips.

'Jimmy – are you all right?' Jeffers called from the other side.

'Ugggggggghhhhhhhh . . . *yes*. I think so.'

He was sore, but nothing seemed to be broken.

'Open the door then!'

'All right – hold on to your . . .'

He stopped. The wind had changed direction again, clearing enough of the smoke to give Jimmy his first proper view of the inferno below. The base of the fire not only covered almost the entire circumference of the courtyard, it was also built up several metres high. A steady roar came from the blazing heap and there was a staccato popping and snapping as branches splintered and split.

Then he realized that they weren't branches.

They were bones.

Thousands of them, twisted and broken.

He saw skulls, with flames licking through hollow eye sockets.

White hands opening and closing in the heat. Fingers pointing . . . pointing at *him*.

'Oh my . . . oh my . . .' Jimmy whispered.

'Jimmy! Open the door!'

Still dazed by the horrific sight before him, Jimmy nodded vaguely and began to turn – and then his heart almost stopped.

A man stood before him, with a rifle raised and pointing at him. His skin was almost translucent, his eyes were red and raw, his hair matted. He wore a military uniform blackened with smoke and ripped and stained by unknown fluids.

'Who are you?' the soldier demanded, his voice raspy and jagged. 'What are you doing here?' He jabbed the gun at Jimmy.

Jimmy held his hands up. 'I . . . I . . . I . . .' He pointed vaguely towards the sea. 'The ship . . . I'm from the ship . . .'

The man didn't even look. He was mad with panic and fear. His finger was already curled around the trigger and his hand was shaking. *All* of him was shaking.

'This is . . . Government property! You are not . . . allowed here!'

'Jimmy!' Jeffers shouted from the other side. 'What's going on?'

The man's eyes rolled back in his head.

'Please,' said Jimmy, 'we're here to help, we can take you . . .'

The man opened his mouth to speak again, but no sound would come. He was racked by a sudden coughing fit; the force of it bent him over and he dropped the gun. He sank to his knees and toppled backwards, thumping into the back wall. Jimmy turned quickly and unbolted the gate. Jeffers, with his gun drawn, was the first through. He immediately pushed Jimmy to one side and covered the fallen guard with his weapon. Another crewman kicked the dropped rifle over the edge of the rampart into the flames below.

Claire came running up to Jimmy. 'Are you all right?'

Instead of speaking, Jimmy nodded towards the fire. The other squad members were noticing as well.

'Oh my God,' said Claire. 'There must be . . .'

'Take a photo,' said Jimmy.

'I can't . . . they . . .'

'You have to.'

Claire took a deep breath. She nodded. 'I'll climb . . . higher. A better angle . . .'

Jimmy helped her up on to the wall and held her shins as she steadied herself and began to take her pictures.

Jeffers knelt beside the sick man and gave him a drink of water. He gulped greedily from the plastic bottle then splashed some over his face. Jimmy had thought he was an old man, but as the ash and dirt washed away he realized that he probably wasn't much more than eighteen or nineteen.

'What happened here?' Jeffers asked gently.

'My commander, he orders . . . burn the dead . . . but they just . . . kept coming . . .!'

'Where is your commander now?'

'He . . . didn't come back . . .' The guard stared down at the inferno below. 'Ten thousand . . . I counted. Ten thousand . . .'

'Where have the rest of the people gone?'

The guard was started to drift away. Jeffers gave him a gentle shake. 'Where are they? Where did they go?'

The guard's burning eyes flicked up. 'They haven't gone . . . anywhere . . .'

He looked towards the fortress walls, then he was wracked by another coughing fit and slumped down again.

Claire had finished photographing the huge funeral pyre. She turned to look down over the city. The smoke was slowly drifting to the south, and as it thinned out over the harbour the *Titanic* began to emerge. Claire raised her camera and took a picture. She noticed some movement around the gangplank but couldn't quite identify it, so she increased the magnification. For a moment she didn't understand what she was seeing. The whole area around the dock seemed to be moving; then there were short flashes of light. She increased the magnification once more – and then she let out an involuntary cry.

'What – what is it?' Jimmy shouted up. But she could only stand and stare. Jimmy heaved himself up on to the top of the wall. Claire handed him the camera. All she could say was, 'The ship . . .'

Jimmy took just a moment to focus in. The ship . . . the gangplank . . . and hundreds . . . no *thousands* of people packed around it, trying to force their way on board. There were flashes of light – gunfire – both from the ship and from the quayside. Jimmy raked the camera right along the length of the dock and back towards the city . . . people were emerging from houses carrying suitcases and bags and pushing prams loaded with possessions, all of them moving as quickly as they could in the direction of the *Titanic*.

He swung back to the ship and saw the gangplank begin to move backwards, hurling a number of people into the water. As it was drawn fully on to the ship there were several more gun flashes . . . and then there was a mighty blast of the ship's horn that seemed to roll towards them across the city. First Officer Jeffers looked up from the rampart.

'What is it, Jimmy?'

'It's the *Titanic*! She's leaving!'

A Rum Situation

There was no doubt about it, the *Titanic* was *definitely* leaving. Her sleek white form was slowly making its way out of San Juan harbour, much to the distress of all those left behind on the dock – not to mention those watching from the ramparts of the fortress of San Cristobal.

'Do you think it was a trap?' Jimmy asked. 'They set the fire to lure us in, waited until we docked, then rushed the ship?'

First Officer Jeffers, who was watching the scene through a pair of binoculars, shook his head. He could see that thousands were still making their way through the streets of the city towards the dock. 'I would be surprised if it was that organized. I think they were all hiding out of fear of catching the plague: they've probably been without food or power or water: and maybe word spread that we'd come to rescue them and they couldn't help themselves.'

'Well *shouldn't* we be rescuing them?' Claire asked.

'I'm sure Captain Smith took the first few on board, but there's no way we could cope with *that* many – it would be a disaster. He's quite right to sail away – and we'd be with him if it wasn't for a certain *idiot*.' Jeffers turned and glared at a sheepish-looking Petty Officer Benson, who was supposed to have maintained contact with the ship, but had instead dropped the only radio and smashed it – and then hadn't confessed in the hope that they'd get back on board without anyone noticing. Jimmy was just relieved that for once he wasn't getting blamed for something.

'They're not just going to leave us, are they?' Claire asked.

'They might leave me,' said Jimmy, 'but they *definitely* won't leave you.'

They took a final look down at the massive funeral pyre, then Jeffers led them back out of the fortress to the vehicles. They took the emaciated guard, Miguel, with them. He kept saying *thank you, thank you, thank you*. Eventually one of the squad said, 'Thank us if we get back to the ship.'

'Thank you,' said Miguel.

Instead of heading for the docks, Jeffers, with a map folded out on his lap, led them out of the city and on to a road heading west towards a town called Dorado. The plan was to get to what would hopefully be a less crowded harbour there and commandeer a boat capable of getting them out to the *Titanic*.

They had travelled less than a mile when Benson said, 'Sir, we're being followed.'

Everyone looked back. There was no mistaking it. Three cars.

'Maybe they're just out for a drive,' said Jimmy.

A moment later the first gunshot *pinged* into the road just to their left.

'And may be they're not,' said Claire.

'Step on it,' said Jeffers.

The two Jeeps accelerated, and their pursuers followed suit. It became a race, twisting through abandoned vehicles and careering across sidewalks. Jimmy and Claire were glad that they'd swapped Jeeps, as their original vehicle, now at the back, seemed to be attracting most of the gunfire.

'What do they want?' Jimmy shouted.

Before Jeffers could respond he suddenly swung the Jeep to one side. The road ahead was blocked by several cars. At first this seemed like just another obstacle to get round – but then a shot shattered their windshield. Claire screamed and ducked down. So did Jimmy. They weren't abandoned vehicles – they'd been deliberately placed there!

The second Jeep braked too quickly – veering up on to two wheels and then toppling over on to its side. The four crewmen scrambled out and tugged Miguel after them before racing across towards Jeffers' jeep. But just as they reached it another shot rang out and one of them fell, clutching his leg. Jeffers stood up in his seat, drew his gun and fired three times towards the road block, then swivelled and fired twice at the small pursuing convoy as it bore down on them. The shot crewman was picked up by two of his comrades and helped on board. Then they sped off in the direction they'd come, hopelessly overcrowded now and heading straight for their pursuers. Jeffers kept his foot on the pedal, refusing to budge until the very last moment when he threw the Jeep to one side. It mounted the sidewalk with a heavy thud but kept going, passing by the line of pursuing vehicles at speed, with all of them doing their best to keep their heads down and limbs tucked in as gunshots peppered the vehicle.

Several hundred metres further along, and with their enemies, whoever they were, already turning their own vehicles to continue the pursuit, Jeffers steered them into a side road. He was hoping to find an alternative means of escape – but immediately they saw that it too was blocked, this time by a large truck, lying on its side, its cargo of hundreds of crates of bottles lying smashed around it. The entire area stank of alcohol. Nor was there any going back. The convoy in pursuit was just turning into the side road as well, and had spread out to cover both lanes. Jeffers remained admirably calm – he saw a large set of closed iron gates on his right, topped by a giant *Bacardi* sign and set into a wall at least two metres high which ran as far as they could see in either direction.

Jeffers aimed the Jeep and roared towards the gates. 'Hold on!' he shouted.

Jimmy felt his whole body jar as their vehicle crashed through the gates and then skidded to a halt.

'OK!' Jeffers shouted. 'Close them up quick! Prepare to repel!'

Two of the crewmen dashed for the gates even as the pursuing convoy raced towards them. The others took up shooting positions and began to fire at the onrushing vehicles. One immediately veered off and crashed into the overturned truck, another braked suddenly, causing two cars following behind to crash into each other and it.

With their immediate entrance blocked, the remaining vehicles came to a halt on the far side of the road. Drivers and passengers slipped out and took up more protected positions behind them. Jeffers drew his crewmen back from the gate to the Jeep, and they all crouched in behind it. Behind them there was a steep grass bank which boasted several thick bushes, and it was behind one of these that they laid the shot crewman. Claire ripped off part of his torn trouser leg and turned it into a rough bandage. Then, not forgetting her new job, took some photographs of her handiwork.

The private road they were on led back towards a large group of buildings, several hundred metres away. Jeffers was peering towards them, trying to decide if they might make a better hiding place, when Jimmy nudged his arm.

'It's where they make Bacardi rum,' he said. 'I wrote

about it for the paper. It's famous all over the world. It usually costs ten dollars to take a tour and you get two free drinks.'

'Thanks, Jimmy,' said Jeffers, 'you're a mine of useless information.'

'HEY!'

The voice came from beyond the gate. A man was approaching, with his hands raised.

Jeffers told his crewmen to keep him covered then walked forward to the gate. Claire tried to stand up to take a photo, but was hauled back down. The man on the other side was heavily built, with a short black beard, and he wore a T-shirt which had once been white. He nodded at Jeffers then snapped, 'We want the girl.'

'Why?'

'We know who she is. You give us the girl, we let you go. Otherwise, we come in and take her.'

'You can try.'

They locked eyes. 'OK, sailor boy, if you want. But I tell you this, we raided the city armoury. We have weapons here that will blow you to pieces, man.'

The man behind him nodded. Jeffers saw someone else step out from the cover of one of the cars carrying some kind of missile launcher. He wasn't really sure what type – he was First Officer on a *cruise* ship. There wasn't much demand for heavy weapons there.

Behind the Jeep, Jimmy glanced at Claire. She looked very pale indeed.

'How would they know who you are?' Jimmy whispered.

Claire shook her head.

Back at the gate, Jeffers asked the bearded man why they wanted Claire.

'Why you think? Her daddy owns the ship. We have her, they'll bring it back. You have food, you have medical supplies, you can take us somewhere that's not dying.'

Jeffers shook his head. 'We have the plague on board as well.'

'Anything's better than here. We want off this island. So you give her up now or we'll blast you.'

'If you fire that thing, you will kill her as well.'

The man shrugged. 'Then we're no worse off. So you hand her over, now.'

Jeffers glanced at his watch. 'We need to talk. Give us one hour.'

'Fifteen minutes.'

'Thirty.'

'This ain't no car showroom, man! No bargains. Fifteen, or we start shooting.' As he finished speaking, three more cars, full of heavily-armed men, drove up.

Jeffers looked at them warily, then slowly backed away.

Claire immediately said, 'Please don't give me up.'

'How did they know?' Jeffers asked.

Claire looked at the ground. Benson looked down as well.

'OK, let's have it. One of you.'

'It's my fault,' said Claire. 'When we were at the City Hall I asked Mr Benson if I could use the radio. He said not without permission. But I told him my daddy owned the ship, which meant that *I* had permission. So he let me. I just wanted to know how my daddy was, but the radio operator on board didn't want to check for me because he'd been told to keep the frequencies clear for emergency signals, so I had to explain to him just exactly how important I was and . . . well, I suppose those guys . . . maybe were listening for radio signals and . . . well . . .'

Jeffers sighed. Then he looked at Benson. 'Not having a real good day, are you, Benson?'

'No, sir.'

'And you know you're going to pay for it, don't you?'

'Yes, sir.' He cleared his throat. 'Ahm – how?'

Jeffers smiled.

The gunmen watched as the crew from the *Titanic* argued loudly amongst themselves. At one point they began to place bets as two sailors exchanged punches and wrestled each other to the ground. They didn't notice Jimmy dart from one bush to the next up the high bank, and then disappear down the other side. They weren't aware that he was running as fast as he could towards the rum factory, while crouched down, undercover.

He had less than ten minutes to find what he was looking for. He had been given clear instructions. It was a massive factory. It stank not only of fermenting alcohol, but also of death. He passed six bodies, horrendously bloated and blue. He charged along corridors, bursting through doors; through a museum, a tourist café, then across a courtyard.

Bingo!

A warehouse full of bottles of Bacardi.

OK. Now – in Jeffers' exact words: 'Choose a battlefield.'

First Officer Jeffers may not have been familiar with heavy weapons, but he knew a thing or two about strategy. This wasn't due to any military training. It was due to a misspent youth playing with toy soldiers and organizing war games amongst his friends. There was hardly a campaign in the history of warfare that he hadn't recreated in his garage at home, from the grandest battle involving hundreds of thousands of men to tiny exchanges involving guerrilla fighters.

So he had been able to explain to Jimmy very quickly and in precise detail exactly what was needed. They were only a small unit with few weapons, facing a heavily-armed, numerically superior force. They had to adapt. They needed the element of surprise, the advantage of high ground and the ability to lure their enemy into the trap.

Jimmy spotted what he thought would be the best place to make their stand. There was a narrow alley running between the museum and one of the warehouses, which led on to a courtyard. It was a dead end, with walls on three sides and first- and second-floor windows overlooking it.

Jimmy hurried to the end of the alley. The Jeep, with Claire and the crew still gathered behind it, was about three hundred metres away. He put his fingers to his lips and whistled. Jeffers heard it immediately and waved back.

The leader of the gunmen was called Mendoza. He had already lost three sisters and two nephews to the plague. Before you start feeling particularly sorry for him, though, you should realize that before the plague came to Puerto Rico he was a gangster and a drug dealer. That is not to say he deserved to lose family members he loved, just that he was not a particularly nice man to start with. Even before the plague, if there was profit in it, he would happily have held hostage the daughter of a wealthy ship owner. His idea of charity was to give the sailors sixteen minutes to give the girl up, rather than fifteen.

Just as the second hand on his expensive watch – stolen from the dead wrist of a plague victim – came round to complete the sixteenth minute, the Jeep behind the gates suddenly started up, the crew crowded on to it and it took off at speed towards the factory buildings.

Mendoza and his gang – now twenty strong – immediately fired off a fusillade of shots after it, but to no effect. They sprang towards their vehicles and crashed through the gates after them.

The Jeep was built for rough terrain, not for speed: while Mendoza had had the pick of the city's abandoned sports cars, so his expensive little convoy was soon gaining ground. The Jeep turned off to the right and disappeared down an alley between two of the factory buildings. Mendoza smiled. He lived nearby and was familiar with the layout of the complex. He knew that this was a dead end; that the Jeep was trapped.

Good. He would enjoy this.

Mendoza led his cars up the alley and out into the courtyard. He saw the Jeep straight ahead – abandoned. The men – *the cowards!* – had clearly run away, but the girl he was after was standing in front of the vehicle, her head bowed in submission, her face hidden by a baseball cap and her skirt blowing in the cool breeze.

The cars pulled up a dozen metres short of the girl and the gangsters piled out, bristling with weapons. Mendoza signalled for them to stay back.

'She is for me!' he shouted.

All around his followers clapped and wolf-whistled as he fixed his hair and licked his lips and pretended to wipe the worst of the dirt off his clothes. He tucked his gun into his belt and swaggered forward. He had heard her voice on the radio and found it sweet and attractive; then he had glimpsed her through the gates and thought how pretty she was. He had every intention of using her to bargain his way on to the mighty ship, but there was nothing to stop him having a little fun first.

'Hey, pretty rich girl,' he said huskily, reaching out to gently lift Claire's chin, 'what about a little kiss?'

Mendoza's mouth moved towards her as the brim of Claire's baseball cap came up – but it was not Claire's face. It was a man. With a moustache.

'Kiss *this*,' said Benson, producing a gun from behind his skirt.

For several moments the other gangsters didn't realize what was going on, so busy were they whooping and yelling as their boss went into action, but then Benson's baseball cap fell off and they saw something they couldn't quite believe.

'Drop your weapons or I'll blow his head off!' Benson shouted.

Then they realized.

But they didn't drop their guns.

'Drop them!' Benson shouted. Sweat cascaded down his brow. He was a radio operator. The most dangerous thing he'd done in his life before this was to wire a plug. 'Tell them!' he said.

Mendoza turned his head slightly. But he didn't – or couldn't – speak, not with a gun pointing at him.

And the others hesitated.

They were survivors of the plague and had banded together to increase their chances of surviving. They were teachers and bakers and tailors and civil servants. Most of them had never picked up a gun before. They had been drunk for most of the past four days. None of them particularly liked Mendoza. He was a bully, and mean, but he was also a leader and made decisions when all they could do was argue amongst themselves.

Behind, one of their vehicles suddenly exploded in a ball of fire and they cowered down.

They looked up and saw the sailors standing at windows on every side of them, brandishing bottles of Bacardi with a piece of torn cloth wrapped around the neck. Once lit and thrown, the glass would smash and the alcohol would ignite explosively. It was a lethal mix.

'Drop your weapons and get out of here!' Jeffers shouted from a window on the left of the square courtyard. 'Now!' He pulled his arm back, threatening to throw another bomb.

It was enough.

If they'd been anything other than a drunken mob they might have put up a fight – they had much superior weapons – but they were confused and suddenly in fear for their lives. One man dropped his weapon and backed away; then he started running. Another followed, and another, and soon they were all in flight.

Benson lowered the gun and whispered huskily in Mendoza's ear. 'Are you sure you don't want that kiss?'

Mendoza shook his head violently.

'Then get the hell out of here!'

Mendoza didn't need a second invitation.

As he fled down the alley the crewmen, together with Jimmy and Claire, stood in the windows on three sides of the square and cheered.

26 The Pizza Incident

The next issue of the *Titanic Times* included a thrilling account of their adventures on the island of Puerto Rico, but was noticeably short of photographs of Mr Benson in a skirt. There were other photographs however: the funeral pyre; official documents scattered around the deserted City Hall; the *Titanic*, three-quarters hidden by smoke; and finally the pleasure boat they had commandeered from the harbour at Dorado and piloted back to the ship.

Claire took the first copy off the printer up to her father in the hospital that evening, but they wouldn't let her in. He was too ill. Her mother was showing the first symptoms of the plague as well, and was now sharing a room with him. On her way out of the hospital she saw Ty lying on a bed. When she tried to speak to him she was chased away.

Jimmy was busy printing off two thousand copies, with the delivery team waiting impatiently out in the corridor, when Claire returned, glum-faced. She sat at her desk and began to turn her camera over in her hands.

'Not good?'

'Not good. Ty's there as well.' She kicked at a desk leg. 'Today was *incredible* and the paper's fantastic, but when it's all said and done we're still on a plague ship and we're all going to die.'

'Speak for yourself.' He lifted the first bundle of papers and went to the door. 'Deck Four,' he told the first boy in line, 'and this time knock on the door and make sure there's someone in. We're wasting too many copies on empty rooms. Leave the rest in the library.'

As Jimmy returned to the printer, Claire took his photograph. 'What's that for?'

'In case something happens to you, so I'll have a picture to put in the paper. Here, take one of me.'

She handed him the camera. He took a head and shoulders shot.

'It's funny,' said Jimmy. 'Scoop told me that every newspaper keeps a collection of photos of people, so that they'll have one handy if they need it. You know what they call it? The *morgue*. This whole bloody ship is a morgue.'

Claire shook her head sadly. 'They're all dying up there. They're screaming and burning with fever and they just want someone to put them out of their misery. Jimmy – if I catch it, I don't want to be hanging around for days. Will you just push me overboard or something, so I can drown, or the sharks can have me?'

'No,' said Jimmy.

'Why not?'

'Just because.'

'I'd push *you* overboard. Even if you weren't sick.'

Jimmy smiled at that. He lifted another stack of papers. 'Come on, give me a hand with these.'

The paper also contained interviews with several of the Puerto Ricans who'd been allowed on board by Captain Smith. There were forty of them in all. They had nervously approached Jonas Jones as he supervised the refuelling. They were starving and ragged, their children crying and wailing, and he couldn't help but feel sorry for them. But what had seemed like a simple act of charity had quickly gotten out of hand, with thousands streaming out of the city and trying to fight their way on board. Realizing that control of the ship could quickly be lost, Captain Smith had been forced to order Jonas Jones back on board before the refuelling was completed and the *Titanic* had sailed out under gunfire.

Dr Hill had examined the new arrivals and found none to be suffering from the Red Death. *Yet*. They were the lucky ones. Tens of thousands had died. Those few Government officials who were still alive had ordered the bodies to be taken to the fortress to be burned in an attempt to stop the plague spreading. Those who were left alive in the city had to fight for every scrap of food. The water was bad; the electricity was off; gangs roamed the streets, smashing and stealing and killing. To those who had made it on board, the

Titanic was like a mighty white angel arriving to take them to heaven.

The newspaper also contained information about the next port of call, the tiny island of St Thomas. It was just forty miles to the east of Puerto Rico and had a population of 56,000 – or at least it had before the plague. It had proved impossible to make radio contact with the island. They suspected the picture would be the same as in Puerto Rico, but Captain Smith was determined to stick to the itinerary, not least because he hoped they'd be able to complete the refuelling that had been interrupted in San Juan. The capital was called Charlotte Amalie, but Magens Bay on the opposite side of the island had been described by *National Geographic* magazine as having one of the world's ten most beautiful beaches. Jimmy had written optimistically that perhaps they could all stop off there for a swim.

It didn't seem very likely.

When the newspaper distribution was finished, Jimmy and Claire rounded up their delivery team and took them up to the twenty-four-hour buffet restaurant on Deck Eleven for a midnight feast. Although the team was still being paid, they too had begun to realize that their dollars were more or less worthless now and as a result they were becoming restless and less inclined to turn up for work. This was to be an attempt by Jimmy and Claire to build a team spirit. Jimmy had a speech all prepared about how important it was to keep a record of everything that happened, the role the paper played in keeping people informed and how they too could get involved in reporting stories and taking photos.

The speech was actually going down quite well, as they tore into pizza after pizza, and Jimmy was just getting to a rather more bloodthirsty version of what had happened at the fortress of San Cristobal when he was interrupted by Kitty Calhoon. She had Franklin in her arms and wanted to know if it was possible for dogs to catch the Red Death. Someone at the table said, 'Hope so,' and they all dissolved into hysterical laughter.

Miss Calhoon, who was partially deaf, didn't catch on. Jimmy, struggling to keep his face straight, was trying to put a coherent answer together when he was saved by a sudden crashing from behind. They all turned to see First Officer Jeffers getting involved in a shouting match between chef Pedroza and a group of the new Puerto Rican passengers. There were several smashed plates already on the floor. As they watched Pedroza picked up another and threw it down.

Jimmy sensed a story. Claire wordlessly lifted her camera and together they crossed the floor of the restaurant just in time to observe Pedroza jab a finger into Jeffers' chest.

'Touch me again, Mr Pedroza, and I will have you locked up.'

'Then you get them out of here!'

'They have as much right to be here as you have, sir.'

'No! They eat our food, there is less left for us. We don't know how long we'll be on this ship! We have no food to spare!'

He jabbed at the First Officer again.

'Mr Pedroza! I'm warning you!'

Dozens of other diners had gotten up from their tables and were now gathering around. One, an overweight man in a too-tight T-shirt, shouted: 'He's right! We paid for that food – it should be kept for us, not given to some refugees!'

Other passengers nodded in agreement.

'There is more than enough food to spare. You know that, Mr Pedroza.'

'Not for long! Not if we keep feeding these people!'

'Do you want us to starve them?'

'I want you to send them back where they came from!'

This drew a round of applause from some of the passengers.

'Mr Pedroza, this is a direct order from Captain Smith. These people are guests on this ship and are to be treated as such. Now, you *will* feed them!'

Pedroza glared at Jeffers, then turned on his heel and stormed back into the kitchens. Jeffers stared after him for a moment before addressing the other passengers. 'If you'll all just go back to your seats . . .'

Some of them did; others walked out of the

restaurant, muttering and casting filthy looks towards the nervous Puerto Ricans. Jeffers turned to the buffet table, lifted a slice of pizza, put it on a plate, then knelt down before one of the refugee kids. 'There you go, son,' he said.

'No like pizza,' said the boy.

Jimmy couldn't sleep. The incident in the restaurant had disturbed him. When they'd been stranded on Puerto Rico, getting back to the ship had been the most important thing because it represented safety, and home. Even though people were sick and dying on board there was something tremendously comforting about the *Titanic* – not just its size and the fact that it dominated everything; it was the way the crew and passengers looked upon it as their best hope in a ruined world. He had thought that after the public meeting in the theatre everything had been resolved, that they would face whatever problems there were together. The argument over the pizza had shown how wrong he was. People could turn on each other very quickly. The ship was just like Puerto Rico – it was an island, and once order was lost it could very quickly descend into anarchy.

If *he* couldn't sleep, well, there was no reason why his best friend should be allowed to either. And she *was* his best friend. He knew it, and she knew it. They came from different worlds, but they'd clicked. But *just* friends. Nothing more.

Jimmy took the elevator up to her suite. With both her parents in the hospital wing, she was by herself. She was sitting out on the veranda, wearing a long-sleeved sweatshirt with the hood pulled up against the breeze. Jimmy took a Diet Coke from her mini bar and sat down beside her. She had tears in her eyes.

'Your dad?'

'Don't think he'll last much longer. Mum's getting worse. Dr Hill's very nice, but he's not a very good liar.'

'Maybe he's *pretending* not to be a very good liar, so you'll get the message without him having to be hard on you.'

She thought about that. 'Maybe he's pretending to be pretending to be a not very good liar.'

'Does that make him a very good liar or not?'

Claire shrugged.

'If they die,' said Jimmy, 'and of course I hope they don't – but if they do, then this is your ship. You're the boss. You can say, take me to the Antarctic, or take me to Australia, and they'll have to.'

Claire shook her head.

'No you will, seriously – you can tell Mr Benson to wear your skirts all the time and you can get the Puerto Ricans to pelt Pedroza with three-day-old pizzas. You can . . .'

Jimmy stopped. Claire had rolled up her sleeve and was showing him her arm.

It was covered in red blotches.

'Oh God,' said Jimmy.

'A lot of use he is.'

'Oh Jesus.'

'Him as well.'

'Claire . . . when did . . .?'

'About the time of the pizza incident. I thought perhaps I was just allergic to Pedroza, but I guess not. Jimmy – you can leave now, if you want. I wouldn't want you to . . .'

'If I get it, I get it.'

'That's nice, but stupid.'

Jimmy shrugged. 'Can I get you a Coke or something?'

'I can get my own Coke. I'm not an invalid. Not yet I just thought I wouldn't get it. I'm . . .'

'Rich.'

'. . . never sick. I haven't had a cold *ever*. And now I'm going to . . .'

'Don't say that . . .'

'. . . die.'

'Claire.'

'It's the truth. These blotches will get bigger and bigger and then I'll get a fever and start throwing up, then there'll be the convulsions and I'll scream and beg to die and eventually I'll fall into a coma and that'll be that.'

Jimmy sighed. 'It's a pity you're not older.'

'Why?'

'Well, I could marry you then and when you died all the ships would belong to me. I'd be *loaded*.'

'And what makes you think I'd marry *you*?'

'Claire, for goodness' sake, who else would ask you? You're a nightmare.'

She thought about that for a moment. 'I'm sorry to disappoint you, Jimmy, but I'd rather marry Pedroza.'

He smiled.

She smiled.

They fell silent.

Ten minutes later Claire said, 'I don't want to go into the hospital.'

'They have the best—'

'They can't do anything. I want to stay here. I want to . . .'

'Don't say it.'

'. . . die here . . .' she adopted a haughtier version of her own quite haughty voice, '. . . in the style to which I've become accustomed.'

'I'll stay with you then.'

'No, I might take ages. And you've a job to do.'

'Stuff the job.'

'No, Jimmy – it's important. You know it is. I want you to go to St Thomas tomorrow, take my camera and go to that beach . . .'

'Magens Bay'

'Yes . . . Magens Bay. You said it was one of the ten best in the world . . .'

'I didn't, some magazine did. They probably paid

them to say it. It's probably crap. It's probably covered in cigarette butts.'

'No, it's not. Take a photo of it, Jimmy, and bring it back to me. I love beaches.'

'OK,' said Jimmy.

'And make sure it's not out of focus.'

'All right.'

'And use a wide-angle lens . . .'

'I will . . .'

'And try to—'

'Claire. I know you're dying, but you're still very annoying. I know how to take a photograph.'

'Then prove it.'

The Beach

The *Titanic*'s visit to San Juan had shown how easily control of the ship could be lost. If they hadn't removed the gangplank in the nick of time the crew would very quickly have been overwhelmed. Captain Smith wasn't going to take that chance again in St Thomas – particularly as the island had a long history of sheltering pirates. Cut-throats like Captain Kidd and Blackbeard had caroused there. Sir Francis Drake had launched his attacks on Spanish galleons laden with New World gold from the island. Granted, that was all very far in the past, but traditions have a habit of being handed down in small communities. So instead of sailing into the main port of Charlotte Amalie where fuel supplies were theoretically waiting, the Captain chose instead to sail around the island and drop anchor off Magens Bay. From there he would dispatch a patrol ashore to approach the capital from the rear. If it appeared calm, and the docks could be secured, the ship would then enter to refuel.

Once again, First Officer Jeffers objected to Jimmy being included in the shore party. Once again he was overruled. Nevertheless, Jeffers poked a finger at him and issued a stern warning: 'Don't get in the way; don't cause trouble; don't wander off.'

Jimmy shrugged. He sat in the back of a small inflatable as it was slowly winched down the side of the *Titanic*. He held Claire's camera in his lap. He had stayed with her all night. Less than an hour before, with her in the grip of the fever and having lost all lucidity, he had reluctantly called Dr Hill and he had ordered her immediate removal to the hospital wing. Jimmy knew it was the right thing to do, but he also felt sad about letting her down. He would take as many photos of Magens Bay as he could, and he would make sure they were fantastic. But deep down he knew she would never see them. People didn't get better from the Red Death, even rich people.

They glided along – Jeffers, Benson, Jonas Jones, two crewmen and Jimmy – on perfectly calm, brilliantly turquoise water towards the beach. As they drew closer Jimmy began to understand why it was so highly rated – there was almost a mile of brilliantly white sand, backing on to palm trees which rapidly gave way to heavily-forested mountains. It all looked absolutely stunning. Jimmy knew that no matter how good his photographs were, they could never do justice to this. He took several panoramic shots anyway, but then he lowered his camera.

'What's that sound?' he asked.

They were still several hundred metres away

from the beach, but others on the little craft could hear it as well.

Music.

'It's . . . Bob Marley!' said Benson.

And it was – reggae music, drifting across the water towards them. As they drew closer still they saw that the sunbeds, set at intervals along the entire length of the beach, were nearly all occupied.

Sunbathers!

'My God,' said Jeffers. 'It's passed them by.'

They were all smiles now. This was as unexpected as it was incredible. They ran the boat right up on to the sand. Bob Marley was singing 'One Love'; the smell of French fries and onions assaulted them (in a nice way). Jeffers jumped out first and dashed up towards the first set of sunbeds.

Then he stopped suddenly.

Jimmy and the others crowded up behind him.

Three sunbeds. Three bloated, putrid bodies, swarming with flies.

Jeffers turned immediately to his left and threw up.

Jimmy stared down at them, horrified.

Jonas hurried along to the next set of beds. They were dead there too – and as far as he could see along the beach.

'I don't understand,' said Jimmy. 'If they had the plague, how come they're all still here, as if they're sunbathing?'

'We know there's different strains of it,' said Jonas.

'Looks like this one killed them instantly. No bad thing, maybe.'

Jimmy couldn't bring himself to lift his camera. How could he take a photo of *this* back to Claire?

'OK,' said Jeffers, 'let's remember why we're here. There's a car park over there, let's see if we can find some keys or jump-start something that can carry us all. Jimmy – see if you can turn that music off, maybe get us something to drink.'

Jeffers pointed towards a bar about a hundred metres along the beach, which seemed to be the source of the music.

'See if you can mix me up a nice cocktail while you're there,' said Jeffers.

Jimmy hurried away along the sand. He forced himself to take several pictures – not for Claire, but for the paper. That was his role in life now. He was the official chronicler of the *Titanic*. A journalist and historian. He shouldn't think about Claire, dying on board, or those poor sunbathers, drinking their cold beers and playing with their children one minute, and the next, rotting and stinking. He had to edit it out. He had to focus on his job.

There were a dozen dead people in the bar. Some had clearly been sitting at stools when the virus struck and just toppled off on to the floor. Others were at tables with plates of food before them, slumped down as if they'd decided to take an afternoon nap. The smell wasn't too bad because the air conditioning was on. A glass-fronted cooler behind the bar was still lit, and of course there was the music, which was so much louder up close. Clearly the bar had its own private generator which had continued working ever since death had paid its nightmare visit. Jimmy hunted around for a few minutes, and finally found it outside, around the back. He pushed a lever up, and Bob Marley slowly ground to a halt. Now all that could be heard was the buzzing of tens of thousands of flies around the bodies.

Jimmy re-entered the bar and opened the fridge. He took out a can of Diet Coke, popped the lid, and took a long drink.

From behind, a voice said, 'That's one dollar.'

Jimmy laughed and turned, expecting to see one of his companions, but it wasn't. There was a bare-chested man in khaki shorts with a shotgun raised and pointed at him.

'One dollar,' he repeated.

'I don't have one dollar,' said Jimmy.

'You better have. It comes out of my wages if you don't.'

Jimmy swallowed. 'I really don't have it.'

The man opened fire. As Jimmy threw himself to the ground the CD jukebox behind him exploded.

'One dollar!'

Jimmy raised his hands in a calming fashion and slowly got back to his feet. 'Won't . . . *that* come out of your wages?'

'No! I'm not responsible for the jukebox! Just the bar!'

'OK . . . all right . . .'

Thundering footsteps sounded along the wooden walkway outside the bar, and a moment later Jonas Jones and Benson appeared in the doorway. The man with the shotgun immediately swung towards them. They raised their hands.

'Is it a drink from the bar you want?' the man asked. 'Or are you here for something to eat?'

Jonas and Benson exchanged glances.

'A drink would be nice,' said Benson. 'And then if we could look at a menu.'

'Take a seat,' said the man, indicating one of the vacated bar stools. 'I'll be with you in a minute.' He jabbed the shotgun towards Jimmy again. 'Well?'

'I . . . uh . . . left my wallet . . . on the beach . . .'

The man studied him suspiciously for a moment, then snapped: 'Well go and get it. If you're not back in two minutes I'll come looking for you.'

Jimmy backed out of the bar.

Outside he immediately ran into Jeffers and the remaining crew. He quickly explained that there was a crazy man with a gun inside, and that Jonas and Benson were nevertheless ordering drinks.

'They're *what*?' Jeffers demanded.

Jimmy explained again. 'Now – do any of you have a dollar?'

They checked their pockets, but none of them did. There was no need to carry money on the *Titanic* at the best of times, and now that these were the worst of times, there was even less point. As Pedroza had realized, dollars were now completely and utterly worthless. Jeffers nodded back down the beach. 'If you want dollars, that's where you'll get them.'

It was a disgusting notion – but he was determined to go back to the bar. The man with the gun was terrifying in his madness, but also kind of fascinating. Jimmy darted along the sand, found a woman's handbag and searched through it, all the time keeping his eyes averted from her swollen corpse and, in particular, her two feet, right beside the bag, which rats had partially gnawed away. He found thirty dollars.

When he got back to the bar Jeffers was peering into it through the half open shutters. The man had set the gun down and was mixing a cocktail for Benson. He'd already poured a glass of beer for Jonas. Neither of them looked particularly uncomfortable. Jimmy moved towards the doors.

'*Jimmy!*' Jeffers hissed. 'What are you doing?'

'I owe him a dollar.'

'Stay where you are, that's an or—'

Jimmy ignored him. He stepped into the bar, holding the dollars up before him and grinning at the man behind the bar. 'The drinks are on me!' he cried. The man waved him in. Jimmy, in turn, looked back at Jeffers and waved *him* in. Jeffers hesitated, then shook his head and reluctantly holstered his gun.

A minute later they were *all* sitting on bar stools,

sipping drinks, the floor behind them littered with mouldering corpses.

It was very surreal.

They talked about the weather. They talked about sports. And music. There had been a wide-eyed look about the man from the start, but as they sat there it gradually diminished. He said his name was Nick Tabarrok and he'd worked as assistant manager of the beach bar for the past seven years. A week previously the manager had suddenly resigned following a row with his wife, packed his bags and caught the ferry to a neighbouring island, leaving Nick in charge for the first time. He was determined to prove that he was up to the job. Everything went perfectly for the first day. On the second, everyone died. But he was absolutely set on keeping the bar working and the books balanced until its owners returned.

'Don't you think,' Benson hesitantly suggested, 'it would have been a good idea to move the bodies out of the bar?'

Nick peered at them, almost as if he was seeing them for the first time. 'Yeah. Suppose. Health inspectors won't be too keen on that . . .' He laughed, but just for a moment. His brow furrowed and he shook his head. 'I . . . *should* have . . .'

Jonas finished his beer and set his glass down. 'Set us up another one there, Nick.'

Jeffers glanced at his watch and gave Jonas a hard look.

Jonas ignored him. As Nick poured him another drink he said, 'So, Nick, how come you didn't . . . you know . . . with the rest of them?'

Nick set the glass down before the Chief Engineer. 'But I did.'

Jonas laughed. 'What are you, a ghost, then?'

'No, I mean, I flopped down just like the others, most of them were gone in ten minutes, but then Mamma Joss appeared and gave me her medicine and when I woke up the next day, I was fine.'

'Mamma Joss?'

'Mamma Joss. She's my granny . . . or auntie . . . or something. She lives up on the mountain. She's . . . about a hundred and twenty years old. She's . . . a doctor. Not got certificates, but . . . knows all the old cures.'

'And she cured you?' Jeffers asked, his voice heavy with doubt.

'Oh yeah,' said Nick. 'I was always her favourite.'

'And what about all those guys out there, she didn't help them?'

Nick shook his head. 'Course not. She doesn't like tourists. We don't see her down here much, she stays clear. Good thing she came down that day, though.'

'Where is she now?' Jimmy asked.

'She went home, I guess. She has chickens. A goat. Need to be fed.'

Jeffers drained his glass, then tapped his watch. 'OK lads, we've work to do.'

Jonas picked up his newly poured beer and sank it in one. Nick lifted their glasses and began to wash them. Jimmy left money on the counter for the drinks, and told a grateful Nick to keep the change.

Back in the car park Jeffers took only a couple of minutes to select a people carrier capable of carrying them all to Charlotte Amalie and to usher them on board. But as the others climbed in Jimmy stayed where he was. Jeffers wound down a window. 'C'mon Jimmy,' he snapped impatiently, 'we're already running . . .'

Jimmy shook his head. 'We can't go.'

'What?'

'The old woman. Mamma Joss. We have to find her.'

'Jimmy, what're you talking about? We have to get moving, *now* . . .'

'No – didn't you hear what he said? She has a cure.'

Jeffers laughed. '*Jimmy* – you didn't believe all that, did you? He's barking mad! There is no magic cure.'

'Then how do you explain that every single one of those people out there is dead and he's alive?'

'That doesn't prove anything! *We're* alive, aren't we? Now get in the car!'

'No.'

'Jimmy . . .'

'Just . . . just *wait* a minute. Look – if there's even a tiny chance she has a cure, isn't it worth finding out?

Hundreds of people are dying on the ship, so why not take a chance and find out if there's anything in this?'

Jeffers drummed his fingers on the side of the car. 'You, Jimmy Armstrong, are a pain in the arse.'

'I know that.'

'We have to get to Charlotte Amalie. The ship needs to refuel.'

'I know that.'

He drummed his fingers again.

'Right.' Jeffers turned in his seat. 'Benson?'

'Sir?'

'Get another car, get hold of the mad barman, then take him and Jimmy up into the mountains and see if you can find this woman.'

'Sir? Why me, sir?'

'Do you really have to ask, Mr Benson?'

'No, sir.'

'Right then. Get on with it.' Benson reluctantly climbed out. 'And try not to drop your radio this time.'

'Yes, sir.'

Jeffers nodded at Jimmy. 'Good luck,' he said.

'Thank you.'

'See you back on the ship with your magic cure.'

He laughed to himself, then put his foot down hard on the pedal and the vehicle roared off in a cloud of dust, leaving Jimmy and Benson with dozens of rotting bodies and a mad barman for company.

Mamma Joss

It was little more than a shack nestling amongst the trees. A small dog barked at them as they drove into a rubbish-strewn yard. Benson was the first out of the car. Instead of facing the house, he looked back down the mountain and out across the bay.

'Would you just look at that,' he said.

Jimmy stood beside him. It was one of the most beautiful views you could ever see, with the trees sweeping down to the azure sea below, the tourists on the beach merely dots in an astonishing vista and even the *Titanic*, sitting five miles off shore, reduced to the size of a toy ship floating serenely in a warm, freshly run bath.

'Stunning,' agreed Jimmy. 'If you forget about the dead people on their sunbeds.'

Nick, who must have seen the view thousands of times, didn't even look. The dog rushed towards him, wagging a stubby tail, but he pushed past it and continued on towards the front door, calling out: 'Mamma Joss! Mamma Joss! It's Nick! Don't shoot!'

Benson, who'd been issued with a pistol, eased a hand towards his holster.

The door was already half open. Nick stepped inside, followed somewhat warily by Benson, and then Jimmy. It was cool and dark, but it also smelled – Jimmy wasn't exactly sure what it smelled *of*, but the closest he could get to it was when his granny used to make soup at home. Not from a tin, but from scratch.

'Mamma Joss . . . Mamma Joss?' Nick called again.

It was a tiny little place with a bed in one corner, a wicker chair with a pile of blankets on it in another. There was an ancient black stove and a big old battery radio. There was an oil lamp sitting on a rickety table, which Nick lit. As the single room brightened Jimmy let out a sudden yell – there was a pair of feet sticking out from beneath the blankets. They were bony and filthy and the nails on them were yellow and curled.

'Mamma . . .!' Nick strode to the chair and pulled the blankets back. 'Mamma?'

The dead woman was tiny and shrivelled and the surprise of the blankets being whipped away caused a spider to scurry back up her left nostril.

'*Mamma* . . .' said Nick, bending towards her. He took her cold, brittle, birdy hand in his and rubbed it. 'Mamma . . .'

'Sorry,' said Jimmy.

Benson shook his head sympathetically before turning for the door; he signalled for Jimmy to join him outside. When he emerged into the brightness once more, Benson had moved back across the yard and was looking out over the bay again.

'Well,' he said. 'That was a total waste of time.'

'No it wasn't,' Jimmy countered.

'Of course it was! If the old bat couldn't even protect herself from the plague, how could she have saved Nick or anyone else? Come on, let's get out of here.'

He began to move towards the car, but Jimmy stepped into his path. 'No, wait. Mr Benson – you didn't look at her properly.'

'Yes I did, Jimmy. She's definitely dead.'

'Yes – but no. There's none of the blotches, none of the signs. She's dead because she's about a hundred and twenty years old, not from the plague.'

Benson was already halfway towards disagreeing when he stopped himself. You could almost see the cogs in his brain working it out. Finally he nodded. 'You know something – there's none of the typical signs of plague on that woman. I think she might just have died of old age. C'mon Jimmy, let's check this out . . .'

Benson brushed past Jimmy and hurried back towards the shack. Jimmy shook his head in disbelief, then followed. Inside, Nick was still holding the old woman's hand. He glanced up at them.

'She delivered me,' he said. 'And my mother . . . and my mother's mother.'

'Well,' said Benson, 'perhaps she can deliver *us*. This medicine you're talking about, what was it like? Can you find it for us?'

Nick patted Mamma Joss's hand and replaced it under the blankets, which he then pulled up over her. He turned to the little gas-fired stove. There were two pots sitting on it. He peered into one, and then the other. 'I think one is the medicine,' he said, 'and the other is probably soup.'

'So which is which?' Jimmy asked.

'I don't know. I was unconscious when she gave it to me.'

They took it in turns to lean over the pots and smell, but although each had a distinct aroma, they still had no idea which was a nice savoury soup and which could potentially save the lives of thousands of people.

'Well, we'll just have to take them both,' said Jimmy.

They searched for lids for both pots, but could only find one.

'You'll have to guard it with your life,' said Benson, handing the one without the lid to Jimmy.

As they were carrying them out to the car, Nick called them back.

'If you're taking the medicine,' he said, 'in return you must help me bury Mamma Joss. We cannot leave her like this.'

Nick had not been worried about the dead bodies littering his bar and the beach, but Mamma Joss was different. They were tourists, she was family. They set the pots down and set about digging a grave behind the shack. There were only some small trowels with which to work on the sun-dried earth, so it took them more than forty minutes in the boiling sun. Benson tried to get away with just a shallow trench, but Nick insisted on going deeper and deeper, saying he didn't want wild animals to come and dig the body up. Eventually he called a halt, and between them they carried Mamma Joss, wrapped in blankets, out and set her gently down into her final resting place.

They bowed their heads for a moment. Nick said a short prayer. He glanced down at the little dog, sitting beside him now, and said, 'Just you and me now, Barney.'

Barney let out a single bark and trotted out of sight.

While Jimmy and Benson shovelled the soil back on top of her, Nick fashioned a small cross from two fallen branches tied with an odd bit of string and dug it into one end of the little mound of soil they had created.

When they returned to the front of the shack, tired and sweaty, the first thing they saw was the small dog, lying panting contentedly beside the pots.

'Oh God *no* . . .!' Jimmy shouted as he dashed across, causing the dog to rear up and scurry out of the way. 'No . . .!'

But the damage had been done. The pot without the lid had been completely licked clean. The other was untouched.

'What'll we do?' Jimmy asked, looking up at Benson

in despair. 'What if that was the one, what if . . .?'

Benson lowered his voice. He glanced around at Nick, who was some distance away, securing the shack's front door. 'We'll have to bring the dog.'

'*What?*'

Nick was walking slowly back towards them.

'Just leave it to me,' Benson whispered.

Nick stopped beside them. 'I'll miss her,' he said quietly.

'I know you will,' said Benson, patting him gently on the shoulder. 'Anyway – you and Barney, you'll be coming back to the ship with us now. Do with a good man like you on board. And dog.'

Nick shook his head. 'Nice offer, man, but no way. Have to get the bar ready, for when the tourists come back.'

Benson glanced at Jimmy, then back to Nick. 'I'm sorry, Nick – but I don't think they will be coming back. It's not just this island got sick, it's the whole world. There aren't any more tourists.'

Nick laughed. 'They'll be back. They always come back. Till then, me and Barney going to sort this place out, that right?' He made a clicking sound with his tongue, and Barney appeared from behind a bush and scampered up to him. Nick knelt down and ruffled the dog's fur.

Benson looked exasperated. 'Nick – to tell you the truth, we really need Barney to help us out. He may have eaten our medicine. We need to analyse what it is, and we can only do that if we take him to the ship.'

Nick looked horrified. 'You mean you'll have to cut him open?'

'No – not . . . necessarily. It will probably . . . come out naturally. But it's really vitally important. If there's any chance at all that this medicine works, then it could save hundreds, thousands, may be millions of lives if we can reproduce it. So we really have to take the dog.'

Nick thought about it for a few moments.

'And you really think the tourists aren't coming back?'

'I know they're not.'

Nick scratched behind the dog's ears before looking up. 'OK then. You can have the pot for free. But you'll have to pay for Barney.'

'*What . . .?*'

'You'll have to pay.'

'Nick.' Benson's voice became grave and important. 'This is for the good of all mankind.'

Nick nodded. 'I realize that. But if the tourists don't come back, then I don't get any tips. And that's where I make most of my money – I have to make a living. If Barney really can save the world, then that's got to be worth quite a lot. I mean, all these drugs companies, they make huge amounts, don't they?'

Benson shook his head. 'Nick, we can't . . .'

It was time for Jimmy to contribute something. He'd been listening with mounting incredulity as

Benson tried to strike a deal with a man who was not only mourning the loss of a loved one, but was also either on the verge of madness or completely barking. Jimmy put a hand on Benson's arm, and at the same time gave him a surreptitious wink. 'Mr Benson,' he said, 'I think Nick has a point. He should be paid.' Benson looked confused. Jimmy nodded at Nick. 'How much were you thinking of?'

Nick did a quick mental calculation. Then another.

'Fourteen million dollars.'

Benson rolled his eyes. Then he patted his pockets. 'I'm afraid I don't have that much on me at the moment,' he said.

Jimmy gave him a hard look. 'Mr Benson – you know what we do in these cases.'

'Do I? . . . I mean, yes, of course, we . . .'

'We write him an IOU.'

Benson's mouth dropped open a fraction. 'An . . .?'

Jimmy nodded. 'An IOU, for fourteen million dollars. That'll be OK with you, won't it, Nick? You just present it at the British Consulate, and they'll make sure you get the fourteen million dollars.'

Nick studied Jimmy for several long moments. But then he nodded. 'Fine with me,' he said. 'Although to tell you the truth, I'd prefer to keep the dog.'

They used a folded copy of the *Titanic Times* Jimmy had in his back pocket to write the IOU on.

Nick examined it happily before folding it into his

shirt pocket. He picked Barney up and carried him to the car. He set him down in the back seat and patted his head one last time. 'To think,' he said sadly, 'that the fate of the world might depend on what comes out of your ass.'

They left Nick up on the mountain. On the way back down to the beach Benson radioed Jeffers to see how he was getting on at Charlotte Amalie. He grimly reported that the plague seemed to have wiped out the port's entire population. Although this meant that it was therefore safe for the *Titanic* to dock, they were having difficulty establishing contact with the ship. He asked Benson to try from his side of the mountain, but he couldn't get through either.

'It could be anything,' Benson observed. 'Atmospheric conditions, most likely. Maybe there's a storm coming. Or some kind of breakdown on the ship.'

Jimmy added his opinion. 'The plague may have killed everyone on board who knows how to operate a radio.'

'Thanks for that cheery thought,' said Jeffers. Then he ordered Benson to take the inflatable back to the ship to pass on the message that it was now safe to dock.

As they shot out across the water Jimmy cradled the pot in his lap, leaning down on the lid with his elbow while holding tight on to Barney. He was thinking about Claire and Ty and trying not to get his hopes up too far. After all, they were gambling on the word of a madman.

What if Claire was already— *No!* He wouldn't even think it.

Dead!

He couldn't help himself. He'd been gone for hours.

The team responsible for winching them back on board was waiting on the third deck. Benson brought the inflatable expertly alongside, and with the sea so calm was easily able to attach the required cables. Barney began to bark excitedly as the boat was slowly lifted out of the water. Jimmy patted him to try and keep him calm.

Benson waved his radio up at the crew above. 'We tried to call!'

Despite the fact that he got the thumbs-up sign in response Benson muttered darkly: 'How much do you bet I get blamed anyway?'

'Fourteen million dollars,' said Jimmy.

The inflatable finally came level with the deck and was guided in. Barney, sensing dry land, immediately wriggled out of Jimmy's grip, leaped from the rubber craft on to the deck and tried to dash away. Benson shouted at the crew to catch him, and added, 'For goodness' sake don't let him poo anywhere! He may have vital . . .'

But he stopped then, because what he had taken to be a colleague, standing in a crisp white shirt and baseball cap, was not, in fact. It was Pedroza, and he was aiming a gun at them. He wasn't alone. There were at least a dozen others standing watching them, all armed with pistols or knives.

Jimmy didn't have to be told what had happened.

They had seized control of the ship.

Mutineers

They had been gone from the ship for four hours. In that time a second row over the feeding of the San Juan refugees had quickly escalated into a riot which led to Captain Smith and the senior officers who had remained on board being overwhelmed. Pedroza and his comrades seized control of the bridge, disarmed the crew and locked the Captain, together with anyone who was not 'with' Pedroza, into the theatre under armed guard. These numbered almost five hundred people. Jimmy, still clutching his pot but minus Barney, was now amongst them.

Arguments raged amongst the prisoners. Some believed that Captain Smith should have immediately returned the *Titanic* to Miami once the seriousness of the plague both on the ship and on dry land became apparent – they were anxious about their relatives and their homes, their pets and their bank accounts. Others thought that all of the infected on board should have immediately been put on shore in order to safeguard everyone else. Many argued that the San Juan refugees should have been left to fend for themselves on the island. Others believed the ship should pick up as many survivors as it could – it was their duty as good Christians. Or Muslims. Or Hindus. Or just as good human beings. The only thing they *all* seemed to agree on was that they were better off with a Captain who knew how to sail, than a master chef who could rustle up a tender steak and a perfect cheesecake but didn't know stern from aft. As it was, the *Titanic* remained at anchor five miles off St Thomas, slowly burning through its remaining fuel.

Jimmy, once he got over the shock of being made a prisoner, immediately secured the pot of Mamma Joss's soup – or life-saving medicine – in a small locker by the side of the stage. His main concern after that was how to get to the hospital to check on Claire. Almost as soon as he set about to achieve this, he was surprised to find Dr Hill and his nursing staff occupying a row of seats near the back of the theatre. They all looked quite miserable.

As Jimmy hurried up to ask about Claire, the doctor was just in the act of reaching up to scratch his head. The movement pushed the sleeve of his uniform up far enough to reveal a series of red blotches on his lower arm. The doctor saw that Jimmy had spotted the fatal marks and quickly pushed his sleeve back down. He put a finger to his lips before glancing anxiously about him.

'I'm sorry . . .' Jimmy whispered as he lowered himself into a stall beside him.

Dr Hill shook his head. 'Can't be helped,' he quietly replied. 'But keep it under your hat, Jimmy – not good for morale if people see that even their doctor has it.'

'What . . . what about Claire?'

'I'm afraid she's not too well, son. And that was a few hours ago. They forced my entire staff out, so none of my patients are getting water or pain relief or—'

'I have a cure,' Jimmy said simply.

Dr Hill nodded, but there was a tiredness about the gesture, as if it was a learned reaction. Patients and passengers must have suggested a hundred different remedies to him over the past few days, each one of them as useless as the last. However, he noted the serious look on Jimmy's face, and decided to indulge him. What harm could it do at this late stage, with the end so near? 'What do you mean, son?' he asked, forcing a note of interest into his voice.

Encouraged, Jimmy quickly described what they'd found on the island: the bodies on the beach, Nick's bar, Mamma Joss's medicine and Barney helping himself to a free lunch. Yet in the telling it somehow didn't seem quite so likely to Jimmy that there really was any hope. He had allowed his hopes to build, but now that he was actually voicing them it suddenly felt as if he was vainly clutching at straws. That it was ridiculous to pin the hopes of mankind's survival on a pot of soup and a mangy old mutt.

Despite his doubts, Jimmy was surprised to see Dr Hill was looking quite thoughtful.

'They were all dead on their sunbeds?' the doctor asked.

'Apart from Nick. And Mamma Joss – for a while, anyway. Why?'

Dr Hill stroked at his chin for several moments while he thought it through. Then he looked at Jimmy and nodded. 'Well,' he said, 'for the plague to kill them where they were, on the beach, it must have been a particularly virulent, fast-acting strain. And from what you say, this Nick certainly contracted it. Yet he recovered. So either his immune system is particularly strong – or this old woman's medicine works. If it does it would certainly be unusual, but not unique. Hundreds of years before we had antibiotics old women just like her were curing people by mixing up herbal remedies. They were also killing a lot of people. It was a bit hit and miss. But she may well have stumbled on something . . .'

'So you think there's a chance . . .?'

'I just don't know, Jimmy – but I do know I've tried everything I can. I know that all the scientists in the world have tried their best to come up with a cure and that they're probably all dead now. So what have we got to lose trying this one out?'

'OK – then I'll get some, we'll try it on you, see if it works. If it doesn't we'll squeeze Barney until he pops, and we'll try whatever he has as well.'

The doctor shook his head. 'No, son, I've a couple of days in me yet.' He picked up his medical bag from the floor and opened it. 'I'm going to show you how to make an injection. Then I want you to fill half a dozen of these syringes with the medicine and somehow get them up to the hospital. Just inject everyone you can. They're in a much worse condition than I am. Find your girl. Inject her.'

He wanted to say, *She's not my girl.*

She's just 'a' girl.

But he couldn't.

The doctor quickly showed him what to do. He took the syringes and turned to hurry back across to where he'd hidden the pot. Then he stopped. 'Doctor?' he asked. 'What if it isn't the medicine? What if I inject them with soup?'

'They're dying, Jimmy. Just do it.'

Jimmy nodded once and dashed away.

A nurse sitting on the other side of the doctor, who'd been listening in, waited until Jimmy had gone before touching the doctor's arm. 'Doctor – what are the chances of it working?'

Dr Hill took a deep breath. 'About one in a million, I'd say.'

Her brow furrowed. 'But then why send him off with such . . . hope?'

'Because, Nurse Hathaway, hope is just about the only thing we have left.'

Jimmy knew the *Titanic* better than virtually anyone on board. Others might know their specific areas well

– Pedroza in his kitchens, or Jonas with his engines – but Jimmy now had an almost encyclopaedic knowledge of the entire ship and reckoned he could work out a way to get out of the theatre unnoticed by the guards Pedroza had posted. They had guns, certainly, but they also had beer and wine and spirits and several of them were openly smoking drugs. They were in charge, but not very alert.

He quickly discovered a ladder at the back of the stage which led up to a lighting gantry; he was able to cross this to a narrow walkway which in turn led to a small control room from which the entertainment director normally oversaw his productions. This led directly on to an unguarded corridor one level above the theatre. Jimmy nipped along this as fast as he could while still trying to protect the contents of the syringes. He had to stay hidden for a few minutes in order to get into an elevator undetected, but from there on he was fairly certain he'd be safe. Pedroza had abandoned the hospital patients to their fate. They didn't need guarding.

It was like a scene from hell.

The dead were left in their beds. The fevered cries of the dying went unheard. Jimmy pulled his T-shirt collar up over his face in a hopeless attempt to block out the smell as he tramped first through the hospital, then the adjoining cabins used for the overflow, looking for Claire.

When he eventually found her, he was shocked by her appearance. She must have lost half of her body weight. Her blonde hair lay dank on the pillow and her red eyes rolled back in her head. Her lips were dry and cracked and her face was covered in red blotches. She was breathing, but it was very shallow indeed. Her mother and father were in beds on either side of her. A family, dying together.

Jimmy took Claire's hand in his. He gave it a squeeze. 'Claire . . . can you hear me?' A foamy bubble issued from her mouth. Jimmy tutted. He set the syringes down on the bed and chose one. 'Claire . . . I'm going to inject you now . . . and if it kills you . . . I'm sorry.'

What else could he say?

Well, he could have said how much he'd hated her when they first met, but that now he really liked her and she was his best friend and they had great fun and incredible adventures. That he didn't want her to die because the *Times* needed her and *he* needed her to help him fight back against Pedroza. That he didn't really think her ponies had been eaten. Or perhaps only parts of them had been. A leg, maybe. Or he could have said, 'If you can hear me, Claire, I've just had a look, and your arse isn't so big any more.'

But he didn't. Instead he took a deep breath and plunged the syringe into her arm. He had no idea whether it was soup or medicine: or, if it really was medicine, what the correct dosage was.

He wasn't the type to say a prayer.

But he said one anyway.

He wanted it to be magical. Instantaneous. He wanted Claire to sit up and yawn and say something sarcastic. But there was no reaction at all. She just lay there.

Jimmy sighed. There was nothing else he could do for her now. Or for any of the others that he injected over the next thirty minutes. They would die, or they would get better.

'Shoot Someone'

Jimmy returned to the theatre in time to find Captain Smith and his officers being threatened with guns and knives. A ragged group of mutineers were demanding that he accompany them to the bridge for a meeting with Pedroza. Captain Smith's position was that he was still Captain of the ship, so Pedroza could 'damn well come to me'.

The leader of the group, a small man with a sunburned scalp and a tattoo of a dolphin on his arm, radioed this information to the bridge. Pedroza's response could be heard very clearly.

'If he doesn't come – shoot someone.'

The leader shrugged, raised his pistol and aimed it at old Miss Calhoon, who had chosen to sit close to the Captain in the mistaken belief that it might be safer. After an initial intake of breath, she stared defiantly back at the mutineer, but thoughtfully brought her hands down over Franklin's eyes so that her four-legged companion wouldn't be frightened.

As the mutineer's finger tightened on the trigger, Captain Smith suddenly snapped, 'Enough! Tell

Pedroza I'll meet him, but not because of his pathetic threats! Tell him I'll be bringing my best people with me. Running a ship is a team effort, as I'm sure he's discovering.'

Captain Smith picked three of his senior officers – although his *most* senior, Jeffers and Jones, were still stranded in Charlotte Amalie – then pointed at Jimmy. 'You too.'

'But . . .'

'I've told you, Jimmy, I want a record kept of everything.'

Jimmy swallowed nervously. It was fantastic that the Captain considered him important enough to include in his team – but also somewhat worrying, as he wasn't exactly friends with Pedroza.

Nevertheless, he checked his notebook and pen, then slung Claire's camera over his shoulder and joined the small group as it was escorted out of the theatre. Captain Smith and his officers marched along the corridors with their shoulders back and chins high, looking very impressive. Jimmy snuck along in their wake, trying to look small and insignificant.

The bridge was not as he remembered it. It had been pristine and quietly efficient, but now it was raucous and overcrowded. Beer bottles sat everywhere; slices of pizza were strewn across the floor. The mutineers had been partying, toasting their success at taking control of the ship, and only now were they realizing that they didn't have the first idea about how to sail her – that there was slightly more to it than switching the engine on and pointing her in the right direction.

Despite the state of his bridge, Captain Smith kept his eyes focussed on Pedroza, who was sitting in his chair facing a bank of computers and smoking a cigar.

'Ah, Captain,' he said. 'So good of you to come.' Captain Smith said nothing. Pedroza's eyes roved across their small party and came to rest on Jimmy. 'Why him?'

'I thought it only right and proper that your mutinous actions should be properly recorded, so that when it comes to your trial we have photographic evidence.' The Captain nodded at him. 'Jimmy – take a picture.'

Jimmy looked at Pedroza, and the gun he had resting on the desk before him. 'The light isn't quite . . .'

'Take it now, please.'

Jimmy somewhat reluctantly raised his camera. 'Ah . . . say cheese?'

'Cheese?' It was supposed to widen Pedroza's mouth into a smile, but it didn't work. He just looked even more menacing. Jimmy took the photo. The flash didn't go off, but it didn't matter, it wasn't really about the picture at all. It was about establishing who was in charge. Pedroza nodded at the man with the dolphin tattoo and he immediately grabbed the camera and hurled it against the wall behind them. It fell to the floor in several pieces. Jimmy looked up at the Captain. 'Do you want me to draw him?'

Captain Smith didn't respond. He kept his eyes fixed on Pedroza.

The chief mutineer clapped his hands, and this time he did smile. 'You see, Captain, everything has changed. We do not work for you. The ship is ours.'

'You, sir, are a mutineer. A pirate.'

Pedroza suddenly slammed his fist down on the table. Jimmy jumped. Captain Smith didn't even blink. 'And what are *you*? The world is dying and you cruise from island to island as if nothing is wrong! You make little newspapers! Food is running out and you bring *more* people on board! And this plague – you keep the sick *here*, so they can infect us all! What *we* are doing, this may be piracy, but it is not madness!'

Captain Smith was silent for several moments, then said quietly, 'What do you want of me, sir?'

'You will take us to Port Amalie. We will refuel and take on more supplies. We will unload the sick and any passengers who do not wish to serve under me. And then we will go exactly where we please and do exactly what we want with whatever time we have left!'

Captain Smith shook his head. 'I cannot agree to this. We must continue to care for the sick. We must look after our passengers until this crisis—'

'Crisis?' Pedroza exploded. 'The world is *over*, Captain, and this ship is ours! Now you will do as you are told.'

'And if I don't agree to this piracy?'

'Then we will *act* as pirates!'

Pedroza suddenly leaped out from behind his desk, grabbed Jimmy by the front of his shirt and began to drag him towards the door. One of the officers tried to block his way, but he was struck down hard from behind. Jimmy tried to resist – he sensed that whatever was coming wasn't going to be pleasant – but he was no match for Pedroza. The rest of the mutineers hurried out on to the deck after them. Pedroza snapped out a number of commands. A sunbed was quickly turned on its side and its wheels snapped off. The flat base was then pushed under the gap at the bottom of the security rail so that it jutted out over the water. Pedroza heaved Jimmy up and over the rail and on to the sunbed. Then he let go of him. Jimmy staggered and almost fell. As he regained his balance, he couldn't help but look down.

Fifteen levels above the sea!

Fear and shock and horror instantly turned his legs to jelly.

'I am a pirate!' Pedroza cried. 'So now he walks the plank!'

The mutineers clapped and roared. Captain Smith stood ramrod straight.

Jimmy had absolutely no qualms about begging for his life. He loved the *Titanic* and he loved the newspaper and Claire, but what was the point of loving anything or anyone if he was dead? He was quite willing to become a pirate if it meant extending his life, even a little. But as he turned to plead his case Pedroza slapped him hard across the face. The force of it almost knocked him over the side, but again he just managed to regain his balance. Blood dripped from his nose.

'If by any miracle you survive the fall,' laughed Pedroza, 'then the sharks will smell the blood and tear you to pieces.' He turned to Captain Smith. 'So Captain, do you follow my commands, or does the boy jump?'

Jimmy swallowed hard. 'Captain . . .'

'I do not negotiate with terrorists or pirates.'

'Captain Smith . . . *please* . . .'

Captain Smith shook his head. 'I'm sorry, Jimmy, but we can't give in to him. He may kill you, he may kill five, ten or a hundred more. But he can't kill us all.'

'I don't care about the others!' Jimmy wailed.

'Terrorism must not prevail!'

Pedroza nodded at his drunken comrades. 'Does he walk?'

'Walk!' yelled one.

'Walk!' yelled another.

'Walk! Walk! Walk!' they chanted.

'Captain, this is your last chance! Will you sail the *Titanic*?'

Jimmy Armstrong looked from the Captain to Pedroza to the sea below. In an attempt to look as pathetic as possible and thus possibly earn some very,

very late sympathy, he delved into his trouser pocket for a tissue in order to dab forlornly at his bleeding nose, but as he pulled it out something else came with it, falling down on to the sunbed and rolling across it before coming to rest precariously on its very edge. His lucky penny.

Jimmy let go of the tissue and it instantly vanished on the breeze. He crouched down and reached for the coin and was just able to claw it back into his grasp. He then held it tight in his fist as he straightened, and found himself wishing and praying that just this once it might bring him some luck.

'Walk! Walk! Walk! Walk!' the mutineers sang.

Jimmy gave Captain Smith one final look of profound desperation.

Please work!

But the Captain shook his head. 'I can't,' he said simply.

'Walk! Walk! Walk! Walk!'

Pedroza turned to Jimmy. 'I can push you, or you can jump.'

Jimmy could hardly breathe. He opened his fist and stared at the coin. 'You're bloody useless!' he hissed. He slipped it into his shirt pocket. It was finally going back where it belonged – the bottom of the ocean. 'You and me both,' Jimmy whispered. Then he turned and walked to the end of the sunbed.

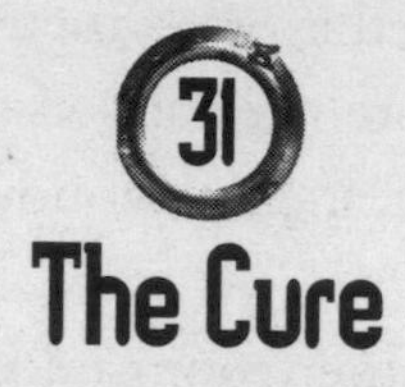

The Cure

Jimmy stared at the water far below. He closed his eyes. He thought of his mum and dad and granda, and his baldy headmaster and the bus driver falling off the dock and fighting with Claire and the thrill of producing his first newspaper. But after this he wanted to think some kind of big important thought before dying.

The meaning of life.

God.

But the best he could come up with was:

I wonder if there's a McDonald's in heaven?

Or hell?

He wasn't even that big a fan of McDonald's, but he couldn't seem to get the thought out of his head.

All he could hear was the wind and the steady hum of the *Titanic*'s engines. Even the chanting mutineers had fallen silent. They were, despite their drunkenness and their deadly weapons, just cleaners and cooks and tourists, and murder was new to them. Forcing a boy to walk the plank was a unique introduction to it. They had not really expected it to actually happen. They were certain the Captain would give in. Or that Pedroza would show mercy. But neither was prepared to give an inch. And it was just exactly an inch that now separated Jimmy from death.

He wasn't, however, going to give Pedroza the satisfaction of pushing him. If he was going to go, he was going to jump.

And now, he couldn't put it off any longer.

Jimmy took a deep breath, then stepped . . .

'*Stop!*'

Jimmy hovered on the very edge. Even the motion involved in looking round might have caused him to overbalance and fall.

All he knew was that it wasn't the Captain's voice – or Pedroza's.

'Step back, Jimmy!'

He recognized it now.

Jimmy turned very, very, very slowly, and saw that Dr Hill had pushed through the crowd of mutineers and had managed to get as far as the security rail. The mutineers would certainly have restrained him, if it hadn't been for the large red blotches that were clearly visible on his face and hands.

Pedroza scowled at him. 'Who do you think—?'

'Listen to me! Both of you!' Dr Hill pointed at Pedroza, then Captain Smith. 'You can't allow this to happen!'

'You, sir, are out of order!' Captain Smith growled back.

'He will jump or I will throw him!' Pedroza declared.

'No – wait. Please . . . you don't understand. Jimmy – he has a cure for the plague!'

This set the watching crowd to murmuring.

Pedroza's eyes narrowed. 'What are you talking about? What cure?'

'I swear! He brought it back from the island! We injected some of the infected with it . . . and I've just been up to see them and they're . . . damn it, man, they're starting to recover! There *is* a cure for this plague!'

But Pedroza wasn't easily swayed. 'You lie!' he cried. 'Nothing can—'

'Look!' shouted Dr Hill. He pointed through the crowd. They turned, and Jimmy saw what they saw, standing a little way across the deck.

'Claire,' Jimmy whispered.

She looked desperately thin and pale and unsteady, but she was standing unsupported, and the enflamed red blotches which had covered her were now grey and fading.

'She was dying half an hour ago, and now look at her! There's a dozen more like her! Don't you see what this means? We can all live through this!'

The mutineers began to jabber excitedly amongst themselves – only Captain Smith and Pedroza seemed untouched by this revelation.

Pedroza called for quiet, and his men immediately fell silent. 'This . . . this is good . . . *if* it's true. Maybe it's just an attempt to save this rat's life. Well, it won't work. Captain Smith still refuses to pilot the ship, so the boy must die.'

He turned back towards Jimmy, who had allowed himself a brief moment of hope. 'Now you must . . .' Pedroza indicated the end of the sunbed, and made a little fluttering sign with his hands.

'No!' cried Dr Hill. Pedroza turned impatiently. 'You don't understand! There isn't enough medicine for everyone! But if we return to the island we can make more, and only Jimmy knows where to find it!'

Pedroza shook his head. 'There was another sailor with him.'

'He collapsed soon after coming back on board – he has it as well. Only Jimmy knows.'

Pedroza stared at Dr Hill. Then he slowly pulled up his sleeve. 'It will cure this?' There was a small red blotch, halfway up his arm. Dr Hill nodded. 'Then whoever owns the cure, owns the world.'

Pedroza smiled. He turned to Captain Smith. 'Even you, Captain, cannot refuse to do this if it will save the lives of your precious passengers.'

But the Captain was stubborn. 'My orders are to continue the—'

'Your orders are changed!' It was a new voice. Mr Stanford had appeared beside his daughter. He looked even weaker than Claire, but his eyes blazed with determination. 'We must find the source of this medicine, Captain, and save ourselves. We can worry about the rest later!'

Captain Smith nodded slowly. 'If you're absolutely certain, sir.' He turned to Pedroza. 'Very well. I will take her to port, Mr Pedroza, in the interests of my passengers and crew. But be warned. This ship will be mine again.'

Their eyes locked for fully ten seconds before Captain Smith brushed past him and strode back towards the bridge.

Claire said, 'You saved my life.'

'Nah.'

'You did. You really did.'

'I just happened to be passing by.'

'It was weird, because I was unconscious, but I was dreaming all these crazy things. I dreamed you came in and started talking about my big bum.'

'I wouldn't do that,' said Jimmy.

'I know you wouldn't,' said Claire, and she kissed him.

It was quite unexpected. Right on the lips. Jimmy didn't know where to look or what to say. His face became very red indeed.

'D-d-don't. . . .' he stammered. 'You're probably still infected, it might wear off in a few minutes . . . just . . . don't . . .'

She bent in to kiss him again. He ducked away.

'What are you scared of, Jimmy?' Claire asked, laughing.

'*You*,' said Jimmy.

Defiant Times

While the ship refuelled at Charlotte Amalie, Jimmy led Dr Hill and a team of his nurses back to Mamma Joss's cottage, picking Nick up from his bar on the way. With his help, and after investigating a barely legible handwritten recipe and the various bits and pieces left over in Mamma Joss's kitchen, they were able to identify the ingredients that had gone into her marvellous medicine. Nick was then able to lead them to the different plants and bushes and trees from which these ingredients originated. The resulting concoction wasn't *exactly* the same as Mamma Joss's, but it was as close as they could get it. It was then administered to the passengers and crew of the *Titanic* as it sat in the deserted dock. After that there was nothing to do but wait.

And wait.

And wait.

But then, gradually, it began to do its work. Those who had been on the point of death began to pull back; those who had most recently become infected, including Dr Hill himself and Pedroza, saw their blotches fade.

This made Pedroza deliriously happy. Not only was he cured, but he could see great things ahead for himself. Controlling the medicine meant riches and power and respect. There would be a new world order, and he would be in charge. It was therefore important to build up a huge stockpile of medicine. Pedroza kept teams of passengers and crew working up and down the mountain, gathering fresh ingredients. Dr Hill then transformed these into medicine, which was then stored in huge plastic containers in the freezers, ready to be called on when required.

After three days in port the passengers and crew were almost completely well again and the ship was refuelled and resupplied (after ransacking a number of supermarkets on the island).

Nick was invited to join the ship's company, but again refused. However, realizing that he'd made yet another valuable contribution to the future health of mankind, he naturally demanded payment. He flashed the IOU for $14 million that Benson had given him. First Officer Jeffers studied it intently, then wrote him a new one, this time for $30 million. Nick was more than happy. He also had some new customers for his bar. Just over a hundred passengers and thirty crew chose to remain on the island, preferring to take their chances there than on a cruise ship under Pedroza's command.

Jimmy and Claire did not have that choice. They

were herded back on board and waved a sad farewell to Nick from Level Twelve. Pedroza and his fellow mutineers spent most of their time watching over Captain Smith and his officers on the bridge. Dissenting passengers and crew were no longer confined to the theatre, but were put to work performing the tasks that had previously been carried out by the mutineers. Jimmy and Claire, knowing better than to approach Pedroza directly, asked the mutineer they now knew as Dolphin Arm if they could restart production of the *Times*. He laughed at them, produced a pair of vacuum cleaners and told them to get busy.

In any country in the world where there is a despotic ruler, you can also find a group willing to work against him (or her). They are sometimes known as freedom fighters or 'the resistance', and the same was true on the *Titanic*. Jimmy and Claire, needless to say, were the instigators of the resistance. Their campaign consisted of many minor acts of sabotage – the fusing of lights, the snipping of telephone lines, the addition of vomit-inducing minor poisons to the food served to the mutineers – and one major act. This was the continued production and distribution of the *Titanic Times*.

It was difficult and dangerous but hugely exhilarating. The first thing that had to be done was to secretly remove the computers and printers from Scoop's office and to redistribute them to different cabins around the ship. Thus the typing up of a story criticizing Pedroza's latest set of commands could take place from behind the safety of a shower curtain on Level Six; the story was then transferred to a computer hidden inside a mini bar on Level Nine, where, after being slotted into the page design, it might then be sent to the printer, which was set up in a neglected alcove close to Jonas Jones' engines, where the noise of the printer wouldn't be so noticeable. Once printed, the *Times* was distributed by a hundred different methods, but they always made sure that a copy somehow arrived with Pedroza.

He knew they were responsible.

They knew he knew they were responsible.

But he could never quite catch them at it.

He could, quite easily, have just had Jimmy and Claire tossed over the side. But at least until they reached Miami he had to rely on Captain Smith's sailing abilities to get them there, and doing something horrible to the daughter of the ship's owner would hardly encourage him to continue, so it wasn't *yet* an option. Instead he gave Dolphin Arm strict instructions to halt production of the paper, a task he undertook with relish. The printer was discovered and smashed. The paper store was hurled overboard. Anyone caught handing out copies of the *Times* was confined to their cabin. But *still* the newspaper continued to appear. Jimmy, Claire and their team built another printer out of spare parts; they tracked down alternative supplies of paper; when one method of distribution failed, they thought up another one.

The *Times* appeared for four days in a row without fail.

The fifth day began dark and overcast with a strong swell on the sea. The *Titanic* was so huge, and its stabilizing system so unique, that most storms could hardly be detected by passengers, but today there was a definite rolling sensation on board. Nearly everyone was feeling a little queasy. Both Jimmy and Claire had been wondering why it was taking so long to get to Miami. As they were no longer following the cruise itinerary, it should have taken no longer than two days. Yet they still didn't seem any closer. Every time they saw Pedroza – albeit from a distance – he looked grimmer and grimmer, and there was a definite shift in mood amongst the mutineers. Neither Captain Smith nor Jeffers emerged from the bridge, and when Jimmy and Claire tried to question Jonas Jones he chased them out of the engine room with a flurry of curses. Claire tried asking her dad what was going on, but he was taking less and less interest in the affairs of the ship. He had been a very rich man before the plague, but now his money was worthless. His fleet was gone – even the *Titanic* was no longer his. He spent his time in his cabin, mostly sleeping. Her mother, on the other hand, who had married a happy, rich man, had found herself stuck with an unhappy, poor one. She was now almost permanently drunk.

'We're newsmen,' said Jimmy. 'We have to find out what's going on.'

'News*people*,' corrected Claire.

'Which means hearing it from the horse's mouth.'

'Captain Smith or Pedroza?'

'Pedroza is the horse's *arse*,' said Jimmy.

'You have a foul mouth, Jimmy Armstrong. But accurate in this case.'

'To the bridge then.'

They worked out a pretty lame story on the way there, but in the end didn't have to use it. Pedroza had retired seasick to his penthouse cabin and left a squad of grey-faced guards in charge of the bridge. Captain Smith and First Officer Jeffers were hunched over their computer screens, debating their course, when Jimmy and Claire hurried in, soaked by the torrential rain sweeping the decks.

Jeffers saw them approaching first and immediately snapped: 'Not now – we're busy! Out!'

Claire started to turn away, but Jimmy stood his ground. 'Captain – sir . . . you said it was important to record everything. We're still doing that.'

The Captain's eyes flitted up, and for a moment they twinkled happily. 'Yes – so I hear. Very well, my young friends – this is the situation.' He waved them forward, then glanced up at the guards and lowered his voice. 'For the past few days we've been driven west by a hurricane that's been developing off the coast of the

Dominican Republic. However, now there's a second one coming in from the Atlantic and we're caught right between them.'

'That, ahm, doesn't sound good,' said Jimmy.

'Can we outrun them?' Claire asked.

'That would be a distinct possibility,' said the Captain, 'if we weren't about to run out of fuel.'

'What?' said Claire. 'But we only just . . .'

'We're a big ship and we use a lot of fuel. That's why it was so important to stick to the itinerary – that way we could always rely on the supplies waiting for us on our islands. We had just enough fuel for a straight run to Miami, but any deviation was always going to cost us. I'm sorry to tell you that quite soon we'll be running pretty much on fumes alone.'

'But . . .' Jimmy began, 'if we've no . . . and we . . . and then the hurricanes . . .'

'We'll be smashed to pieces,' said Captain Smith.

The Olympic

Jimmy wrote another headline for the *Times*: WE'RE ALL GOING TO DIE – AGAIN.

'I don't think that's funny,' said Claire.

Jimmy shrugged. 'What do you think, Ty?'

'Uggggghhhhhhshhhhiiiiiittt,' said Ty, who was throwing up in the bathroom. He had recovered from the Red Death, but now claimed he was dying of seasickness.

'I think he likes it,' said Jimmy. 'And he'll *love* this one . . .'

Claire looked at the screen.

VOMITING PASSENGERS CREATE NEW WORLD RECORD.

'Jimmy – have you gone mental on me?'

'I thought it was kind of interesting. Jonas Jones tells me that this heap of junk was designed to be environmentally friendly, so no waste gets pumped into the ocean. It's all kept right here. So if this is the biggest cruise ship in the world, and virtually everyone on board has been throwing up nonstop for the past few hours, then I'm certain that we must have broken some kind of world record for the greatest amount of vomit to be found in any one location. Wouldn't you say?'

'You *are* mental.'

At that precise moment the lights went out. They were now in complete darkness but for the glow from the battery powered laptop they were using to write and design the *Times*.

'Have I died?' Ty called from the bathroom.

'Not yet,' said Jimmy. He looked at Claire's ghostly face in the light from the screen. 'They're trying to save power. They did warn us.'

Claire nodded grimly. 'The sea's getting rougher. You can feel it.'

They had moved back and forth between the bridge and this temporary newspaper office several times in the past few hours, gathering information as subtly as they could under the watching eyes of the guards. On their last visit Pedroza had recovered sufficiently from his seasickness to have a blazing row with Captain Smith, who wanted to have the passengers standing by to board the lifeboats. Pedroza maintained that no one was going to leave the *Titanic* until he said so. Captain Smith said they would have to use the lifeboats before all power was lost, because as soon as the engines failed the ship could easily overturn in the high seas. Pedroza finished the argument by holding a gun to the Captain's head and yelling, 'No lifeboats.'

* * *

The rain was still lashing the decks as they made their way back to the bridge. Much to their surprise they found it wasn't all doom and gloom, but the scene of sudden and intense activity. Half of Captain Smith's officers had their faces pressed to their computer screens, the others were standing at the front window with binoculars raised, scouring the waves. Pedroza stood with them, anxiously puffing on a cigar. Claire recognized the aroma. She was sure it was one of her dad's. She was just beginning to imagine that Pedroza must have done something awful to him, when she saw Mr Stanford standing just a few metres away, puffing his own cigar and scanning the waves. Last time she'd checked on him he'd been refusing to leave his bedroom, so this was a real surprise. She hurried up and tugged his arm.

'Daddy – what is it?'

'It's the *Olympic*, Claire!'

'Are you sure?'

'Radar confirms it! Just trying to raise her!' He lowered his glasses for the first time and looked along the line of officers and mutineers scanning the mountainous seas. 'A dozen cigars to the first man who spots her!'

Jimmy didn't know what they were talking about.

Claire turned suddenly and gave him a hug. 'It's *fantastic*!'

'*What* is?'

'It's the *Olympic*! Our sister ship!'

'Our what?'

'*Jimmy!* Our *sister*. She was built in Belfast last year! She's slightly smaller – but who cares? Daddy thought the whole fleet was lost – but she's out there . . . and if she has enough fuel we can transfer some and get out of the way of the hurricanes!'

'There she is!' First Officer Jeffers yelled suddenly. 'All lit up like a Christmas tree!' He pointed, and half a dozen sets of binoculars shifted.

'It's her, by God!' cried Mr Stanford. 'We're not finished yet! Look at her, Claire, isn't she beautiful!' He handed Claire his glasses.

It took her just a moment to focus in, and then she let out a little yelp of excitement. 'Look, Jimmy, look!' She passed them on.

Jimmy had to admit the *Olympic* was a fantastic sight to behold, storming through the waves like . . . he was already thinking of how to write the story . . . like *an avenging angel*.

'Any contact, Mr Benson?' Captain Smith asked.

'No, sir, not yet, sir!' shouted the young radio operator.

'What course is she making, Mr Jeffers?'

Jeffers quickly returned to his computer screen and studied it intently. 'She's . . . erratic, Captain.'

'She must see us by now! Try raising her again!'

But there was still no response from the *Olympic*. They tried several different methods of contacting her, but without success. As the two ships drew closer Captain Smith and his crew grew more and more anxious.

'What's wrong?' Pedroza demanded. 'Why are they not responding?'

'Maybe they're sick,' said Jeffers.

Captain Smith nodded grimly.

Pedroza looked from one to the other. 'You are planning something. You've sent secret messages.'

'No,' the Captain responded simply.

Pedroza jabbed the gun at him. 'Then we board her, take her fuel.'

'Impossible,' said Jeffers. 'Not in these conditions.'

Pedroza exploded: 'We have no fuel! We will die here! We *must*!'

Jeffers shook his head. 'If the *Olympic* is drifting out of control and we try and get any closer she could smash into us and then we'll both go down. We must keep trying to contact her, and keep our distance for now. That way we have a slim chance of pulling through. Captain?'

Captain Smith continued to examine the brightly-lit ship through his binoculars. Then he slowly lowered them. 'We need the fuel. We'll have to rig up a bosun's chair—'

'Sir, with all due respect – that's madness! Whoever you send, in these conditions, across that distance, it's a death sentence.'

'Mr Jeffers, I understand your concern. But we're

already facing a death sentence. Better to go down fighting, don't you think?'

Jeffers glared at him. Yet within a few moments his anger had faded. 'In that case, sir, I'd like to volunteer to go across.'

'I was counting on it,' said Captain Smith.

Jimmy gripped the guard rail outside. The rain pounded, the wind howled and the waves, as high as apartment blocks, threatened at any moment to throw the *Olympic* against the *Titanic*. Claire, beside him, had to yell to be heard. 'They shoot a rope from . . . here . . . to *there* and try to make it secure on the other side, then there's like a swing chair he sits in and a pulley system and he slides across . . .'

Jimmy stared at the waves. His hands were numb from just a few moments' exposure to the wind and rain. He yelled back: 'You would have to be . . . really . . . really . . . *really* mental to try that!'

It is a sad fact that once you say something out loud, it has a habit of coming back and biting you.

Claire and Jimmy were still debating the foolishness of any sane being attempting to take a bosun's chair ride between two giant ships in a hurricane, when First Officer Jeffers somewhat sheepishly called them back to the bridge. He handed them each a cup of coffee and a towel to dry their hair. Then he led them across to Captain Smith, who was back behind his desk. Pedroza, his pistol jammed into his trouser belt, sat on the edge of it, grinning as they approached.

'Claire . . .' Captain Smith began gravely, clasping his hands and leaning forward, 'sometimes compromise is the—'

'Enough!' Pedroza exploded suddenly. He jabbed an angry finger at Jimmy, then moved it to Claire. 'I know you two are responsible for that little rag of a newspaper. You think you're very smart, don't you?'

Jimmy shrugged. Claire looked at the floor.

'When you strike me, little children, I always strike back, and twice as hard. It's just a question of waiting for the right opportunity. And now here it is.' He smiled at them, because he knew what was coming. 'You see, Captain Smith and I do not trust each other. He wants to send this man – Jeffers – and this man – Jones? – to the *Olympic* to get fuel. But how do I know what they will do when they're over there? Perhaps they will sail away and save themselves. Or find weapons and try to lead a mutiny against me. So I have decided to go with them. I am curious about this *Olympic* – I might just make it part of *my* fleet. However, if I do go, what's to stop them cutting the rope when I'm halfway across? Captain Smith promises that his men wouldn't do something as *uncivil* as that, but I'm not so sure. So we've reached a compromise. I will go to the *Olympic* on the chair, and *you*,' he pointed at Claire, 'will go across on my lap. No one is going to cut *that* rope. And *you* . . .' he nodded at Jimmy, 'will go across with my second in command.'

Claire wasn't having any of it. 'My daddy—'

'Claire,' Captain Smith said bluntly, 'your father agrees.'

She stared at him in disbelief. 'My daddy would *never* . . .!' She turned to confront him, but Mr Stanford had conveniently left the bridge.

'He has, Claire. If you don't go, we may lose both ships.'

'But what if he loses *me*?' Claire wailed.

'It would be unfortunate,' said the Captain, 'but we have no choice. Jimmy, what do you say?'

'Does it matter what I say?'

The Captain smiled ruefully. 'Regrettably, no. But I want you both to know that this is the bravest thing you could possibly do. Ordinarily I would never, ever consider putting the lives of children at risk, but this . . . this *pirate* . . . has given us no alternative. All of our lives depend on it. If you were in the Royal Navy, you would most certainly receive a medal for even attempting this.'

'Gee, thanks,' said Jimmy.

The Ghost Ship

Fear.

Fear and horror.

Fear and horror and sheer *terror*.

Jimmy stepped up to the bosun's chair. The wind was howling, the seas raging and the *Olympic* was drifting dangerously close, threatening at any moment to crash into the *Titanic* and sink both ships.

And yet – he also felt curiously exhilarated. Hundreds of passengers and crew were crowded along the deck to watch the spectacle. Captain Smith and his senior officers stood outside the bridge. The mutineers jabbered excitedly. Because he was going first, Jimmy was pretty much the star of the show. It felt quite good, and would probably continue to feel quite good right up to the point where he died.

After a dozen failed attempts, a line had finally been secured between the two ships: but there was no real way of telling just how safe it was except by sending the first two passengers across.

'Let me just get this straight,' said Jimmy. 'If we

get across alive, then we'll know it's safe, but if we fall into the water and drown, then we'll know that it's too dangerous.' Jeffers nodded. 'That's not very reassuring.'

'It's safe, trust me.'

'Why should I trust you? What do you base that opinion on?'

'Instinct,' said Jeffers. 'And experience.'

'Do you have experience of sending a helpless child between huge ships in the middle of a hurricane?'

'*Two* hurricanes,' said Jeffers. 'And no. So it's just you and *him*.' Jeffers nodded at Dolphin Arm, who was already sitting in the bosun's chair. Dolphin Arm patted his lap and waved Jimmy over.

'Oh God,' said Jimmy. 'It's bad enough as it is, without having to sit on someone's *knee*.'

With the change in weather Jimmy had gone back to wearing his overalls over his stolen T-shirt and shorts, and these were now further augmented by an inflatable survival suit. Benson, who had helped him into it, had assured him that if he fell into the sea the suit would keep him afloat and alive for at least an hour.

'And how long will it take to rescue me?'

'In these seas? We won't be able to get near you.'

'This isn't funny.'

Benson had looked at him gravely. 'I know,' he said. But then he added, 'Look on the bright side, Jimmy. It's not me out there.'

'Thanks. I'll try and remember that.'

If Dolphin Arm and Jimmy were successful Jeffers would follow. Then Pedroza with Claire. And finally Jonas Jones.

As Jimmy prepared to step forward, Claire came up and hugged him. 'Good luck,' she said. She was wearing her own inflatable suit.

'Claire – there's something I should tell you.'

'I know. I love you too.'

'No. I can't swim.'

Claire laughed. 'It won't make any difference, Jimmy. Just concentrate on getting to the other side. I'll see you there. And I don't really love you, it's just the sort of thing you say when someone's about to die.'

Jimmy swallowed.

Jimmy could hardly take his eyes off the swirling waters far below. He was sitting awkwardly in Dolphin Arm's lap with only a very thin leather strap keeping him in place. The spectators, whom he had expected to cheer him off, had fallen ominously silent.

Pedroza came up to Dolphin Arm and patted him on the shoulder. 'Good luck,' he said. 'If he starts to squirm, throw him off.'

'OK,' said Jimmy.

Pedroza scowled at him for a moment, then stepped back and shouted: 'Go!'

They were suddenly at the very edge; it was the very

last moment when they could step back; Jimmy closed his eyes; Dolphin Arm whispered a prayer; then their feet lifted off the deck and they were pulled up and away from the ship. The wind caught them immediately and hurled them to one side. Jimmy could hear screaming and he knew it was him doing it. He was sure they were falling, yet he couldn't open his eyes.

Jimmy was sitting on a pirate's lap on a flimsy chair, strung on a rope between two ships which could at any moment clash together and squash them to a pulp, and yet . . . and yet . . . he was experiencing a huge rush of adrenaline. They had made slow, gut-wrenching progress at first, but now they were speeding up. Jimmy had never been to one of the big theme parks, but this had to be what it was like on one of those mad rides. The difference was that whereas they made you feel like you *might* die but were actually perfectly safe, you really *could* die on this one, and that multiplied both the terror and the excitement of it a thousand times.

As they raced towards the *Olympic* Jimmy screamed again, but this time with a mad kind of joy. Even Dolphin Arm joined in.

They were three-quarters of the way across, with their speed still increasing and the huge bulk of the *Olympic* looming before them, when the thought suddenly struck Jimmy that the emphasis had been put on getting them across quickly and safely, with no thought actually given to braking and landing. In fact, they both seemed to come to this conclusion at the same time. They were *hurtling* towards a crash landing.

'Ohhhhhhhh . . . shiiiiiiiiiiiiit . . .!' Jimmy yelled. They cracked into the guard rail with considerable force, the security strap across the chair snapped and they were both hurled into the air before landing hard on the deck and tumbling head over heels several times before coming to rest flat on their backs. They lay there for half a minute, hardly sure if they were alive or dead.

Then Dolphin Arm said, 'You OK?'

'OK,' said Jimmy.

They sat up – aches and pains, but nothing broken. They almost gave each other high fives, but then remembered that they were enemies.

They had made it, and the line was still secure!

It took forty minutes to get everyone across. Dolphin Arm kept his gun trained on Jeffers, even though the First Officer managed to half concuss himself on landing. Pedroza fell heavily on top of Claire when they were thrown out of the chair on landing, then rolled off and stood without even looking at her. When Jimmy asked her if she was all right she just stared at the deck. She seemed to be trying to stop herself from crying. Jonas Jones was the only one to make a perfect landing. He stepped out of the chair, smiling broadly, as if he was just stepping out of an elevator.

'Fantastic!' he cried.

But his good mood soon faded.

The *Olympic* was so like their own ship and yet at the same time utterly different, and for just one reason: it was completely empty. There were no survivors, no putrid corpses. The corridors were clean, the kitchens freshly scrubbed. Even the hospital wing had neatly folded beds and cupboards full of untouched medicines. Eerily, muzak continued to play on an endless loop over the public address system as the little party moved along the corridors.

The *Olympic* was a ghost ship.

It was vital to get the transfer of fuel underway as quickly as possible. The hurricanes were getting stronger, buffeting the ships hard and making it increasingly difficult to keep them apart. But this wasn't like filling your car at a petrol station on a windy day. Hundreds of thousands of litres of fuel had to be moved from one ship to the other. It would, Jonas Jones confidently predicted, be 'an absolute nightmare'.

Pedroza stood guard over Jonas and Jeffers while they worked on the fuel problem. He ordered Dolphin Arm to lock Jimmy and Claire in a cabin, and to then search the rest of the ship for weapons.

Dolphin Arm warned them against causing trouble

on the way up and gave them a filthy look as he thrust them into a cabin and locked the door from the outside. As soon as it closed, Claire whispered urgently: 'Pedroza tried to kill me again. On the bosun's chair the seat belt was broken so I had to hang on to him, but halfway across he started bending my fingers back – he was trying to make me fall . . .'

'God! But you didn't . . .'

'No – I hit him right in the . . .'

Jimmy winced. 'And he . . .'

'. . . he was in too much pain to throw me off, but he swore and swore, he said he was going to do all sorts of terrible things to me . . .'

'Claire – why didn't you tell Jeffers or—'

'I couldn't – don't you see? What could they do? Pedroza and Dolphin have the guns – what if there's a fight and Jonas and Jeffers get shot? There'll be no one else to get the fuel across, everyone will die.' Claire shook her head. 'Jimmy, I don't think we're going back. He's going to kill us.'

'Claire – you don't know that.'

'Yes I do! Why do you think he made such a big deal about bringing us across? Why us?'

'So Jeffers wouldn't try anything, because you're the owner's daughter . . .'

'Then why *you*?'

'Because . . .' Jimmy suddenly wasn't sure. Pedroza could have used any one of the many passengers or crew who didn't support his mutiny, but it was

Jimmy and Claire he'd insisted on.

'See? He said he wanted revenge – and we thought he meant just making us take the chair, but then he tried to kill me, and now he's going to try again, I'm certain . . . That's why he locked us in here, so he knows exactly where to find us. He'll leave Dolphin in charge of the others and come up here and . . .'

Jimmy was suddenly convinced. 'He'll say we fell overboard by ourselves or we had an accident and got chewed up by the elevators or . . .'

'Then we don't give him that chance. Come on, Jimmy – we have to get out of here!'

Claire tried picking the lock with a straightened-out paperclip they found in a folder advertising future cruises, but failed. They tried kicking it, but it held firm. Jimmy opened the balcony doors and hurried across to the guard rail. He had to take a firm grip because of the howling wind and then he hung himself out just enough to be able to see around the dividing wall on to the balcony next door.

'What are you doing?' Claire shouted as she struggled out to join him.

'If we can get over here, their balcony doors mightn't be locked. Maybe we can get out that way.'

'You mean climb over the rail, without even the tiny amount of safety the bosun's chair gave us?'

'Exactly.'

'OK – but this time, let me go first.'

'OK.'

'Aren't you going to ask why?'

'No.'

'Because you took the risk last time with the chair. Now it's my turn.'

'OK. Whatever you say. Personally I just think you're trying to prove you're braver than me.'

'I don't have to prove that. I *know* I'm braver than you.'

In ordinary circumstances it would not have been *that* difficult a manoeuvre. It was, essentially, nipping over a neighbour's fence. But if you fell from a neighbour's fence you might graze your knee. If you fell from this one, you would lose your life. Jimmy took a firm hold of Claire, supporting her as she forced herself up the rail in the face of hundred mile an hour winds. She gripped the rail on her side and then felt around the corner for something to hold on to.

'All right – I'm just . . .'

Her foot slipped suddenly on the damp rail and she screamed. The wind seemed to grab at her and pull her out, but Jimmy held tight. Slowly, slowly, he pulled her back down over the rail and they both collapsed, defeated.

Two minutes later she said: 'I'm trying again.'

'It's my turn,' said Jimmy.

'No – it's *still* my turn. It was the shoes – no grip.'

She showed him the sole of her shoe. Then she took them both off and stuck them inside her jacket. 'C'mon!'

Jimmy helped her back up on to the rail, and this time held her even tighter. She felt for her grip on the other side, made sure it was secure, then nodded at Jimmy to let her go.

He held on.

'Jimmy – now! I'm fine!'

Jimmy took a deep breath and released his grip. Claire pulled herself around the fence and dropped down on to the balcony next door.

'OK,' Jimmy shouted, 'here I come.'

He just about made it round – the force of the wind was *incredible*. But when he landed, Claire was already looking grim.

'The doors are locked!' she shouted. 'What do we do now?'

'We keep going until we find one that *is* open!'

'But what if they're *all* closed? The wind is going to rip one of us off eventually!'

'It's the wind or Pedroza – up to you!'

Four times they climbed from balcony to balcony, growing colder and weaker with each attempt, but finally they found an unlocked door and collapsed into the cabin. They lay on the big double bed and laughed and laughed and laughed.

It wasn't funny, but they couldn't help themselves. It

was a heady mix of adrenaline and relief. When they could manage it they rolled over to the mini bar and feasted on Toblerone and Diet Coke. Claire opened a bottle of champagne and drank. Jimmy refused. 'I drink it all the time with Mummy,' she said. 'She buys a new bottle every time one of my ponies wins a . . .' Then she stopped. 'My poor ponies. Do you really think they're dead?'

Jimmy thought about it. He liked Claire, and knew the right thing was probably to spare her feelings. On the other hand, he was who he was. He said, 'Of course they are. Their flesh has been consumed by wild dogs and their bones boiled for soup by starving plague victims.'

'Sometimes you're very cruel, Jimmy Armstrong.'

'Sometimes you have to be cruel to be kind.'

Claire's eyes blazed. 'No! You should *never* be cruel to be kind. It's horrible. The truth is horrible.' She wiped at her tears. 'Everyone is dead, Jimmy. The world is dead. I have to believe my lovely ponies are still alive. I *have* to.'

'All right,' said Jimmy. 'I'm sorry. If it makes you feel any better, then they are still alive. Albeit in soup form.'

Claire hurled a Toblerone at him.

Pedroza

From the fourth deck, Jimmy and Claire could see that a second line now connected the *Titanic* to the *Olympic*, a flexible pipe used for ship-to-ship refuelling. It was being blown violently from side to side and looked as if it might be swept away at any moment. The wind seemed to be getting even stronger.

They ducked back inside and took seats opposite each other in the *Olympic*'s library. They had to decide what to do next.

'If we go down and stand with Jonas,' Jimmy suggested, 'then maybe Pedroza won't try anything.'

Claire shook her head. 'No, Jimmy. Jonas said it could take four or five hours to refuel. Pedroza could just take us away again and they wouldn't be able to do anything about it.'

'Well what then?'

'What if we wait until the last possible minute to go down? Once we see the pipe being retracted, we'll know it's safe. Or safer.'

'But it'll just be the same when we get back, won't

it? We know he wants to kill us. We have to do something to stop him, right here, right now.'

'Like what? If Captain Smith and the whole crew haven't been able to get rid of him – how can we?'

'I *know*. But over *there* he's got his whole band of mutineers; over *here* there's just him and Dolphin Arm. And if he has to leave Dolphin Arm to guard Jeffers and Jonas, then there's just him . . .'

'And a gun. And several knives.'

'But he hasn't got what we have.'

'What's that?'

'Your big arse and my lucky penny.' Claire gave him a look, and he quickly apologized. 'Look, all we need is a plan. Something not too complicated. Something that doesn't depend on him doing this, and this and this, before we can do this, and that.'

'We need to lure him somewhere, trap him and . . .'

'Kill him.'

They stared at each other.

'We can't kill him,' said Claire.

'Why not?'

'Because that makes us as bad as he is. And I couldn't do it. I couldn't . . . stick a knife in him. Or shoot him.'

'What then? Tell him he's been a very, very naughty boy and give him detention?'

'I don't know! Could *you* kill him? Stick a knife right into him and watch the blood burble out of him?'

'Burble?'

'*Jimmy* – could you?'

Jimmy was from a rough, tough part of Belfast, but he'd never stabbed anyone. 'I killed a gerbil once,' he said.

'That's hardly the— Did you kill him with a knife?'

'I knelt on him. It was an accident.'

'Oh. Well you may not have the opportunity to kneel on Pedroza.'

'So we still need a plan.'

'Yes we do.'

Jonas Jones was the first to see Jimmy as he came running into the fuel depot ninety minutes later, his face flushed, barely able to grab his breath.

'Jimmy, lad, where did you spring from?'

Jeffers was overseeing the pumping, while Dolphin Arm and Pedroza kept guard. Before Jimmy could respond Pedroza strode angrily across, grabbed him and threw him to the ground.

'How'd you get out of that cabin, you little rat?'

He took his gun out and pointed it down at him.

'Easy now!' said Jeffers.

Pedroza immediately swung his gun around to point at the First Officer. 'Get on with your work!'

'Just . . . just . . . take it easy, then . . .'

Jeffers turned reluctantly back to his labour. Pedroza snarled down at Jimmy.

'Where's the girl?' he snapped.

'She stayed with it . . .'

'With what?'

'The gold!'

Pedroza's eyes narrowed. 'Gold? What gold?'

'Please,' said Jimmy. 'I'm sorry . . . we were bored. It was easy to get out of our cabin . . . But listen, please, we came to tell you what we found! You won't believe it . . . incredible – an entire room, just full of it . . . gold bars . . . thousands of them!'

They had guessed, correctly, that Pedroza's face would light up at the thought of a room full of gold. He already had one potential fortune on his hands with Mamma Joss's medicine, but gold was something else entirely – paper money might now be worthless, but gold never loses its value. He had seized power on the *Titanic* and had grand plans to take the *Olympic* back to port. But it still meant that he would have two ships guzzling enormous amounts of fuel. In a broken world, where oil would be jealously guarded by the few survivors, gold would become the means by which such commodities could be bought. Civilizations come and go. But gold remains constant. Through all of history it has been prized above all other metals. It is, was and always will be completely irresistible.

All of these thoughts were whirring through Pedroza's brain as he marched Jimmy towards the eleventh floor. The chef's eyes were wide with excitement, the pulse in the side of his forehead was visibly thumping away and his breaths were coming fast and furious.

Jimmy egged him on the whole way.

'I've never seen anything like it! Bricks made from gold! From floor to ceiling! Claire thinks her dad put all his money in gold and hid it on the *Olympic* when he realized how bad the plague was! That's why he was so miserable when he lost contact with his fleet! But now it's all ours! We'll be the richest pirates on the high seas!'

Pedroza thumped him hard in the back with the butt of his gun. 'I'm not a pirate! And shut up!'

'Sorry! Sorry! But you should see it! It's incredible! It's . . .'

Completely made up.

Their plan was based on their assumption that:

(a) Pedroza would completely fall for their story, and rush up to see the gold for himself.

(b) Claire had the ability to jump out from behind the door and stab him with a syringe.

They had both seen Dr Hill administer a certain drug to plague sufferers in the *Titanic*'s hospital. They'd been thrashing about in agony one minute, and fast asleep the next. It was a simple matter of breaking into the *Olympic*'s medical supplies room and identifying the correct drug. Jimmy, being a good reporter, had previously noted its name.

They thought it was better that Jimmy, rather than Claire, lure Pedroza into the trap. Or, to put it another way, Claire refused to go, on the grounds that Pedroza might elect to hurl her overboard on the way up. The fact that he might do the same to Jimmy did not seem to unduly worry her.

Jimmy, having had experience with Mamma Joss's medicine, filled up a test syringe then showed Claire how to inject it, using an over-ripe orange they found in the doctor's office. Claire was a little bit hesitant at first, barely pricking the skin and looking away squeamishly. Jimmy showed her again. Her next effort was little better.

'Claire,' Jimmy said finally, 'it's an orange. You can't hurt it.'

'I know that. It's just . . .' She made a face.

'Forget it's an orange. It's Pedroza. If you don't get this into him, he will kill you, and, more importantly – me. Now do it again. Stab him. Stab Pedroza.'

Claire held the syringe tightly, with her thumb over the plunger, raised it, then brought it back down with such force that the orange collapsed flat down on the desk, spraying juice across the room.

'I think you've killed it,' said Jimmy. 'You're officially lethal against fruits. Now let's try the real thing.'

They chose a windowless store room on the fourth level. Jimmy removed three light bulbs so that Pedroza would not immediately realize that the shelves were filled with bed linen as opposed to gold. Claire, meanwhile, had tracked down the *Olympic*'s own newspaper office and found a camera.

Their plan was this:

1. Jimmy warns Claire that he's about to arrive with Pedroza by talking loudly and generally making a racket.
2. Jimmy opens door, pretends to feel for light switch.
3. Pedroza enters darkened room.
4. Claire sets off camera flash, temporarily blinding Pedroza.
5. Jimmy trips him up.
6. Claire plunges syringe into Pedroza.
7. They flee room, lock door, allow 30 seconds for drug to work.
8. Re-enter room, find Pedroza asleep, remove his gun, lock room.
9. Return to fuel depot, hold gun on Dolphin Arm, disarm.
10. Return to *Titanic*, disarm mutineers.
11. Live happily ever after.

It was a good plan. All good plans remain good plans up until the point where they don't work, and then they suddenly look like bad plans. All good plans usually work up until the point where you add humans, at which point the difference between complete success and utter catastrophe is a very small one.

You cannot blame what happened on the plan, or on Jimmy's or Claire's or even Pedroza's part in it.

If any plan went like clockwork, it was this one.

Jimmy hurried along the corridor in front of Pedroza. As he approached the door he clapped his hands happily together and waved the mutineer forward. 'In here! In here! You should see it! It's fantastic! Gold! Gold! Gold!'

Jimmy pulled the door open and stepped inside. 'I'll get the lights . . .'

Pedroza stepped into the room.

Claire set off the flash.

Pedroza automatically closed his eyes . . . but too late! He was blinded!

Jimmy kicked at the back of his legs, causing him to fall forward.

They jumped on him as he tried to get up, forcing him down again.

Claire rammed the syringe into his leg and pressed the plunger down flat, forcing its entire contents into his body.

They leaped off him, charged out of the door, slammed it shut behind them and locked it before collapsing down.

'We did it,' said Jimmy, breathing hard.

'We did it!'

They were just in the act of giving each other high fives when the door was suddenly thumped, causing them both to jump. The handle was rattled. Then again – but with slightly less power. Then for a third time, weaker still.

They held their breath.

Finally . . . complete . . . silence.

'We *have* done it . . .' Jimmy whispered.

'We *really* have . . .'

'How long should we give it?'

'It took half a minute in the hospital – and we probably gave him three times the dose.'

'But still . . .'

'I know . . .'

'Three minutes then . . .'

'Five . . .'

'To be safe.'

It was probably the longest five minutes of their lives. The *Olympic* was rolling beneath them, making them feel queasy, but they were determined to let nothing spoil their moment of triumph. They had outwitted and overthrown Pedroza, and they were going to enjoy every moment of it. No throwing up over the side of the ship for them. They were conquering heroes. They would fling open the door of the storage room and sweep in to retrieve Pedroza's gun. They would shake their heads over the fallen pirate and say, 'Let that be a lesson to you, evildoer.'

When the five minutes were up, Claire said, 'You first.'

'*Ladies* first,' said Jimmy.

'Age before beauty,' said Claire.

They smiled at each other.

'Together,' they said together.

Jimmy turned the lock. They both gripped the door handle. They silently counted off one-two-three and pulled open the door.

Pedroza stood in front of them, his gun raised and pointing, the syringe still sticking out of his leg. 'Get in here *now*!' he growled.

'Oh *crap*,' murmured Jimmy.

Death

Pedroza made them stand against the back wall of the storage room.

'No gold,' he said.

'No gold,' agreed Jimmy.

Claire just looked at him. Her bottom lip quivered.

'Plenty of bedding,' said Pedroza, nodding at the shelves. 'Useful for muffling the sound of a gun.' Jimmy swallowed. 'You think you're very clever, don't you? Your great plan! Jab me with a needle, kill me, eh?'

'No,' said Jimmy, 'just put you to sleep.'

'So you say. Yet for some reason, the drugs don't work. Why do you think?'

'I don't know,' said Jimmy.

Pedroza reached down and plucked the syringe out of his left leg, then hurled it suddenly towards them. Claire let out a scream as it embedded itself in the wall just by her left ear.

Pedroza laughed. 'I'll show you.' He closed his free hand into a fist and punched himself in the leg. It sounded – hard, yet hollow. 'This leg is wooden. Lost it when I was a boy.' He moved to the other leg and knocked it as well. He pulled his trousers up a fraction to show a couple of centimetres of swarthy skin. 'This leg is flesh and bone. You picked the wrong leg, little children. So now I must kill you.'

'Why?' Jimmy asked weakly.

'Because you are my enemy. And because of you I killed fifteen people.'

'Me?'

'Both of you.'

'I don't under—' Jimmy began, but Claire cut him off sharply.

'The people in the freezer.'

Pedroza nodded. 'I was smuggling them to a new life in America. Their relatives were to pay me once I delivered them safely, but then you two stuck your noses in. If the Captain found them then I'd lose my job and go to prison – but they'd still get to America. That wasn't fair, was it?'

'What did you do to them?' Claire asked.

'I told them I'd managed to get them cabins, but that I had to take them one by one to avoid being discovered. So I threw them overboard, one at a time. Not pleasant, but essential.'

'You are . . . *evil* . . .' Claire whispered.

'All your fault.'

'No,' said Claire, '*no* . . .'

'And now that I've told you, it is time for you to die as well.'

Pedroza raised his gun.

'Would it help if we said sorry?' Jimmy asked.

'No!'

'Is there *anything* we can do?'

'No!'

Jimmy had a sudden, desperate, last thought. 'Please – just wait a minute . . . It's important . . . listen to me . . . My granda used to tell me this story . . .'

Pedroza's brow furrowed. 'I do not wish to—'

But Jimmy continued right on, '. . . about this gang leader who caught two of his enemies. He was going to shoot them both, but then he realized that if he did that, there'd be no one to spread the word about what he'd done. So he just killed one of them . . . and let the other one go, and he told everyone he knew about how tough and ruthless this gang leader was, and nobody ever dared tell on him or challenge him again.'

Claire was staring at him, wide-eyed and incredulous. 'Is that supposed to help?'

'Well, I just thought, if one of us survives it's better than neither of us sur—'

'Quiet!' They both looked back to Pedroza. 'It's a good story. And wise. Fortunately I am already feared by everyone on the *Titanic*, and once we have refuelled I will kill everyone who does not support me. You two have been particularly troublesome, so I'm giving you the privilege of being killed first. So . . . which of you would like to die first?'

Claire glared at him. 'You are a cruel and horrible man. I hope you burn in hell.'

Jimmy knew what she was doing – she wanted to be killed first, as if it might somehow give him a better chance.

He wasn't having that. He nodded at Pedroza. 'You're not only cruel and horrible, you've got one leg missing, and the other one looks pretty crap.'

Claire wasn't going to be beaten. 'You're a violent, vicious, ugly little man and your children will be vicious and ugly . . .'

Jimmy cut in with: 'Your scrambled eggs taste like shit and everyone laughs at your cooking behind your—'

'ENOUGH!'

They fell silent.

'*You* die!' He pointed the gun at Claire and squeezed the trigger.

Without really knowing why, Jimmy hurled himself at Claire, shoving her out of the way just as the gun exploded. The bullet thumped into his chest. There wasn't time to register pain, hear Claire scream or even to have a final thought about McDonald's. Everything just went black.

The Afterlife

Darkness.

Complete and absolute.

Jimmy couldn't tell if his eyes were open or not, or even if he had any eyes. He might just be a formless shape, floating in the universe. But no . . . he had hands – he felt his left with his right, and vice versa. He had legs.

Or maybe I just think I have them.

He had read about people who lost their legs in road accidents, but could still feel them. Something to do with nerve endings.

I'm in a bed. I can feel the pillow, sheets.

Or I'm imagining them.

I am dead.

I know I am dead.

I have to be dead.

He remembered very clearly: pushing Claire out of the way of Pedroza's shot, feeling a dreadful pain in his chest and then . . . nothing.

OK – I was shot in the chest. If by some miracle I'm alive, there'll be bandages, tubes . . .

Jimmy moved his hand up his chest and felt – skin. No wound, no bandages, just his normal self.

That's it. I'm dead. I'm not in a bed. I'm not anywhere. I'm just . . . a thought. Or a soul on my way to heaven or hell. Or maybe there's nothing, and I'll just exist in this darkness for ever.

He didn't like that thought *at all.*

He squeezed his imaginary eyes shut.

'Jimmy.'

Claire's voice.

No, she was dead.

'Jimmy.'

How mad would I have to be to start talking to a ghost?

'Jimmy – for goodness' sake, I can see you moving. Will you come out from under your blankets and talk to me?'

No. Once I start talking to imaginary creatures then I'll be lost for ever.

'Can you not give him some sort of an injection?' Claire said.

Then another familiar voice – Dr Hill's. 'No, Claire. He's still in shock, he'll come out of it in his own time.'

Jimmy felt for the corner of the blanket, then cautiously raised his eyes above it. The light was so harsh that he was half blinded and could only see two vague, shimmering outlines.

Lost souls like his own, or real live human beings?

'Ah, the sleeper awakes,' said Dr Hill.

'Only because you mentioned injections,' said Claire. 'He's a scaredy cat.'

Slowly, slowly, they came into focus.

It *was* them. It was Claire. She was alive! Which meant . . . *he* was alive!

He was in the hospital wing. The *Titanic*'s hospital wing.

When he tried to speak his voice was ragged. 'I . . . don't . . . I was . . . Pedroza . . . what the . . . hell . . . is going on?'

Claire beamed down at him. Dr Hill took hold of his wrist and checked his pulse. Satisfied, he smiled at Claire and said, 'I'll leave you to fill in the details.'

As he left the wing, Claire sat on the edge of Jimmy's bed. 'What do you remember?' she asked.

'I . . . don't really . . . I . . . was . . . shot . . .'

'You don't remember the aliens coming down and encasing you in a bubble of ectoplasm?'

Jimmy stared at her. '*What?*'

Claire cackled. 'Only joking. Jimmy, you saved my life. You threw me out of the way. You took the bullet that was meant for me.'

'I must have tripped.' He wasn't sure he liked the way she was beaming down at him. 'But . . . if I was shot I . . .' His hand felt about his chest, but it was still as wound-free as before. 'I don't understand.'

'Well, perhaps this will help.'

Claire delved into her trouser pocket and produced a small piece of twisted metal.

'Is that . . . the bullet?'

'No, Jimmy, it's the coin.'

'Coin?'

'Your lucky penny, Jimmy! Don't you see? Pedroza shot you in the chest, but the bullet struck the lucky penny in your pocket. The force of it knocked you out – but the bullet ricocheted right back at Pedroza and went straight through his forehead and killed him stone dead.'

'It *what*?'

'He's dead, we're alive, we beat the hurricanes, the ship's back in the Captain's hands, the—'

'Hold on! Too much information! Just . . . slow . . . down . . .' Jimmy took a deep breath. He put his hand out and Claire dropped the battered coin into his palm. 'So it *was* lucky, after all . . .'

'Or *you* were. Or Pedroza was *un*lucky. Anyway, something worked. It knocked you out, and it killed Pedroza. It was horrible . . . but kind of fantastic at the same time. I got his gun and took it downstairs and slipped it to Jeffers when Dolphin wasn't looking, and then he put it against Dolphin's head and advised him to give up. And he did.'

'But . . . but . . . there were still all the other mutineers?'

'Yeah, but there was only about half a dozen of them who really, really wanted to follow Pedroza: most of them just wanted to get back to Miami as quickly as possible. They all have families, relatives, you know? So they didn't put up much of a fight, and now everything's back to normal. We've outrun the hurricanes, and we'll be back in Miami this afternoon.'

'That's . . . incredible . . . it's *fantastic*! Isn't it?'

'Yes it is. You saved my life.'

'Pedroza dead like that . . .'

'You saved my life.'

'And overpowering the mutineers . . .'

'You saved my life.'

'And even beating the hurricanes . . .'

'You saved my life.'

'Yes,' said Jimmy, 'I realize that.'

'I'll never forget it,' said Claire.

'All right.'

'Why did you do it?'

'Like I said, I tripped. Or fainted.'

'You jumped. You were going to sacrifice yourself for me.'

'I had every confidence in the lucky penny.'

'Jimmy Armstrong – you love me, don't you?'

Jimmy blinked at her. 'Are you sure *you* didn't get shot in the head?'

'You love me.'

'Claire – I don't even like you.'

That was harsher than he intended, but sometimes when you're cornered you say things you don't especially mean.

It had taken a lot for Claire to say what she said, and his instant rejection hurt. She flared up immediately.

'Why don't you get out of bed anyway? There's nothing wrong with you! For all I know you probably did trip! And I'm glad you don't even like me, because I'm getting off the ship this afternoon, and you'll probably never see me again. Do you hear me? You'll never see me again!'

She stormed out.

Farewell

'Well, Jimmy, what's it to be? Are you staying with us?'

Captain Smith stood beside him at the rail outside the bridge, looking down at the dock and the steady stream of people disembarking. They had been leaving like this for the past hour. Without even admitting it to himself, Jimmy was waiting to see if Claire really was leaving the ship. They hadn't spoken since their bust-up.

'I suppose I am,' said Jimmy.

'That's good. We've missed the newspaper these past couple of days, would be good to get it started again. I think it helps the passengers a lot. And the crew. At least those who are left.'

He had gathered everyone in the theatre shortly before the ship docked and told them that he intended to remain in Miami only as long as it took to refuel and forage for food supplies. He didn't believe the city to be safe, but he understood that many people wished to leave and they were free to do so.

'I didn't think so many would get off,' said Jimmy. 'It's safe here. Even after everything that's happened. Out there . . . isn't everyone dead?'

'We just don't know. Some places the plague hits, like St Thomas, it kills everyone, others – remember San Juan? – there are really quite a lot of survivors. Here, millions are dead for sure, but there will be survivors, there has to be, and if one of them is your son or daughter or dad, wouldn't you want to find them? Or just make sure they get a decent burial? I expect most will take a look around when they get ashore, realize just how bad it is, then get back here quick as they can. Others will try and make it home – might be twenty miles, might be two thousand. But they'll try.' They watched the line of disembarking passengers for several more minutes. 'Mr Stanford wants us to sail up the coast towards Texas; he's pretty certain we'll be able to refuel there. Then we'll just keep going from fuel depot to fuel depot, long as we can.'

'Does that mean the Stanfords are staying on board?'

'No, son. He hasn't the patience. He's going to try and get to the airport. He keeps a private jet there and he's hoping to fly his family out to the Midwest. They own a big farm – ranch, whatever you call it. Not too many people live out there anyway, so he reckons it will be safer than sticking it out on the *Titanic* or trying to make it in one of the cities.'

'But it's *his* ship. Doesn't he cares what happens to it, or to the people on it?'

'Of course he does, Jimmy. But he's done all he can do. He's letting us take the ship, he's brought as many passengers as he possibly could right back to port, and now he has to think of his family. I think that's only right.'

Jimmy understood. 'Do you have a family, Captain?'

Captain Smith took a deep breath. 'It sounds very corny, Jimmy . . .' he waved a hand across the prow of the ship, 'but this pretty much is my family.'

'No wife,' said Jimmy.

'Oh yes,' said the Captain, 'but she's an absolute cow. Don't tell anyone, but this plague is the best thing that ever happened to me. Now I've got an excuse not to go home to her.'

He winked at Jimmy, then turned and re-entered the bridge.

Jimmy knew he was only joking.

At least, he *thought* he knew he was only joking.

Twenty minutes later Jimmy spotted Claire as she left the ship with her parents. She had a pink bag slung over one shoulder.

'Claire!'

She didn't look up. He shouted again, but got no response. She was already too far away.

Well.

That was it.

She was gone.

Jimmy sighed.

Good. She was no friend at all. He'd be fine by himself.

He kicked at the guard rail.

And then he started running. He took the stairs six at a time. He moved faster than any elevator. By the time he reached the gangplank he could hardly breathe for the effort of it. First Officer Jeffers was on duty there, with a gun at his side, reminding everyone to check their watches.

'We sail at six, if you're coming back make sure . . .'

'Don't you worry, young man,' the elderly Miss Calhoon was saying, 'my watch has perfect time, and if by any chance I forget to check it, why Franklin will remind me.' Franklin was nestled in her arms. She raised one of his little paws and waved it. 'Won't you, darling? Franklin always— oh!' Miss Calhoon was spun around as Jimmy flew past. Franklin yelped and hid his little head, frightened.

'Jimmy, are you leaving us?' Jeffers shouted after him.

'No!'

Claire was now several hundred metres away along the dock, standing close to the main entrance to the passenger terminal, where, ordinarily, returning travellers would have had to pass through passport control then wait to retrieve their suitcases. But not today. The arriving passengers were hauling their own luggage, and there was nobody there to check their documents. They were back on dry land, but it wasn't the land they'd left. Doors blew back and forth in the stiff breeze, luggage carts lay upturned, cars abandoned.

Several bodies lay around the door itself. They were not only rotting, but they appeared to have had most of their flesh torn away from them. Claire stood clutching her father's arm as they looked down at them.

Mrs Stanford said, 'Dreadful . . . dreadful . . .'

'Claire.'

She turned. She tried extremely hard not to smile when she saw Jimmy. Her eyes were red-rimmed from crying.

'I'm sorry,' said Jimmy.

Claire shrugged. She looked at the ground.

'I wish you weren't going,' he said.

'*I* wish I wasn't going.'

'It's those ponies, isn't it?'

'No . . . Jimmy, why don't you come with us?'

'What? Where to?'

'Our farm. Daddy's going to fly us there.'

He looked at the ground. 'I can't.'

'But why not? We'll be safe there, I'm sure of it.'

'I can't, Claire. I need to stay on the ship. Captain Smith thinks one day he'll take her back to Ireland. It's the only way I'll get to see my family again.'

'But they're probably . . .' She stopped herself. 'I'm sorry.'

'I know they probably are. But still.'

'*Claire*. Will you hurry up?'

It was her mother, standing in the doorway.

'Mum, it's not like we're going to be late for anything!'

'Don't be cheeky! Now hurry up!'

Claire looked at Jimmy.

Jimmy looked at Claire.

'So,' said Jimmy.

'So,' said Claire.

'I'm going to keep doing the paper.'

'That's good. No – that's great. I wish . . .' She sighed.

'Well. See you around.'

'Suppose.'

Jimmy nodded, then began to turn away.

'Jimmy?'

As he turned, she just jumped on him. She wrapped her arms around him and planted a kiss on his lips.

He didn't quite know what to do. So he kissed her back.

The Flesh Dogs

Jimmy was miserable. He went to the *Times* office and tried to start work on the next edition of the newspaper. All of the equipment had now been retrieved from the various hiding places they had used during Pedroza's brief reign, and Claire had even persuaded her dad to order that some extra equipment be sent across from the *Olympic* before the ropes were cut and it floated off to its doom.

But he couldn't concentrate.

Ty, who had also chosen to remain on board, told Jimmy to relax, that Claire could easily be replaced. 'There are plenty more fish in the sea,' he said.

Jimmy threw a printer at him.

He imagined Claire at that very moment, flying through the air, on the way to a new life on her farm.

He could not have been further from the truth.

Mr Stanford had commandeered a Miami Port Authority transit bus. He had also, somewhat reluctantly, agreed to drop Miss Calhoon, Franklin and half a dozen other passengers in downtown Miami.

They had been driving for over an hour, but had

only managed to travel about a mile from the port because the roads were almost impassable. Wrecked and abandoned cars, bodies, burned out and collapsed buildings – everything combined to make their progress agonizingly slow.

Claire stood behind her dad. 'This is impossible,' she said. 'It will take for ever.'

'Nothing's impossible,' her dad snapped.

From behind her her mother said: 'Your father didn't become a billionaire by saying things were impossible. He went out and did them.'

'Isn't that nice,' said Miss Calhoon. Franklin barked.

The closer they got to the city centre, the worse it got. There was nothing but devastation and destruction. Fires had burned out of control, laying waste to entire blocks. There did not appear to be any survivors.

'Oh *damn* it!'

Smoke began to pour from under the hood. A few metres further on the bus shuddered, then ground to a halt. Mr Stanford quickly ushered them all off. Just as he prepared to take a closer look at the engine, it burst into flames.

'*Great*,' said Claire.

They began to hunt for an alternative means of transport capable of carrying them all. Mr Stanford himself was desperately keen to go directly to the airport, but he had accepted the responsibility of giving the other passengers a ride into the city and didn't feel that he could abandon them – especially with a dog like *that* eyeing them up.

It was a huge beast, like a cross between a German shepherd and a Rottweiler, standing less than a dozen metres away, its teeth bared and dripping.

'Easy, boy,' said Mr Stanford.

At about the same time, another passenger, a Mr Greening – an elderly man with a hearing aid and walking stick – stumbled across what he thought was a survivor. A man was lying face down on the sidewalk – but still appeared to be moving.

Mr Greening struck the ground with his stick to attract the others' attention. 'There appears to be someone . . .' But then he stopped. A small dog had wriggled out from beneath the body, and was now snarling at him. Its teeth were bright red. Strips of rotting flesh hung from them. The old man began to back away.

Mr Stanford, sensing danger, was just beginning to usher them all back towards the safety of the bus – even though it was still smoking – when two more snarling, snapping animals wriggled out from beneath it, cutting off their approach to the open doors.

Then there was another dog, and another, and soon they were surrounding the little group, pressing them closer and closer together.

'My God!' Mr Greening cried. 'They've been eating the dead! They have a taste for human flesh!'

The dogs were now a mass of spitting, snapping beasts, intent only on tearing them apart and devouring them.

They drew closer and closer.

Claire clung to her father. He tried to kick at one, but instead of ducking away it lunged at him and sank its bloody teeth into his shoe. Mrs Stanford screamed. The dog was now attempting to drag her husband away. Claire kicked at it. Momentarily surprised, it lessened its grip for just a fraction of a second – enough to allow him to twist his foot out of his shoe and scramble backwards.

The dogs moved closer again.

'Oh, they just need to know who's in charge!' It was Miss Calhoon. She patted Franklin's fluffy head and stepped forward.

'No!' Claire shouted.

But the old lady wasn't frightened at all. Miss Calhoon raised a warning finger to the flesh dogs and shouted, 'Sit!'

The flesh dogs growled and roared.

'SIT!'

One dog actually did.

'*SIT!*'

Then another sat, and another, until one by one all of the dogs surrounding them were sitting obediently.

'Now,' said Miss Calhoon, turning and beaming triumphantly at her companions, 'why don't we all get back on the bus. I'm sure it will be perfectly safe.'

They hesitated. It was Claire who made the first move. 'Come on, Mum, let's go.'

She took her hand and moved towards the encircling dogs. Mr Stanford ushered the others forward. One by one, and hardly daring to breathe, they passed through them and began to climb back on to the bus. Only Miss Calhoon stayed where she was, her finger raised and repeating over and over: 'Stay . . . stay . . . good boys . . . *stay* . . .' until they were all on board.

'You see?' said the old woman, 'they're all just scared and hungry, aren't they, Franklin?' She raised the little poodle up to kiss the top of his head, but as she did Franklin suddenly snapped at her. He was a spoiled little creature, and had snapped a thousand times, but this was the first time in his entire life that he had actually bitten her. Probably, he didn't mean to. Possibly he was just nervous, with all those other dogs there. But his little sharp teeth jagged into her nose, drawing blood, and causing a shocked Miss Calhoon to drop him.

The watching dogs, smelling fresh blood, immediately stood and began to snarl.

Miss Calhoon only had eyes for Franklin, who was scampering away. 'Franklin!' she cried, and began to shuffle after him. 'Franklin!'

The dogs growled and edged closer.

'Miss Calhoon!' Claire shouted from the bus doorway. 'Don't . . .!'

The Rottweiler snapped at her. Miss Calhoon immediately ordered it to sit again – but her moment was gone.

The flesh dogs attacked.

The New Voyage

Chief Engineer Jonas Jones reported that refuelling was completed. First Officer Jeffers presented the figures for the returnees – of the two hundred passengers who'd gone ashore, eighty-five had returned. Out of fifty crew who'd left, twenty-six were back on board. The cruise line's dockside food storage facility was found to be intact and an emergency generator used to keep it frozen had apparently only failed within the past few days, leaving nearly all of it in edible condition. This had been brought on board, together with several tonnes of tinned foods which Jeffers had 'liberated' from various supermarkets.

'Very well, gentlemen,' said Captain Smith, 'let's get her underway.'

Jimmy was back in the *Times* office, typing up a story. He'd interviewed a number of the returning passengers about their experiences in Miami, and he was depressed even writing about it. The city was a mess.

He had paused as the engines started up, then forced

himself to continue writing. They were off now, on the next voyage of the *Titanic*. There were new adventures to come, he was sure of it. Yet he felt empty.

Alone.

He *was* alone, as Ty Warner was too frightened of being attacked again to return yet. But – *alone* alone.

Jimmy typed for another five minutes. He reread what he'd written.

It was rubbish.

He deleted it and started again.

There was a knock on the door.

'Get lost, Ty, I'm busy.'

It was knocked again.

'I'm serious. Just leave me alone.'

When it was knocked for a third time, Jimmy leaped from his chair and yanked it open. 'Will you just . . .!'

He stopped.

'Hello,' said Claire.

'Oh.'

'What's got you all fired up?'

'Uhm. Nothing. What are you doing here? I thought . . .'

'Job to do, haven't I?' She slipped past him into the office and crossed to her desk. She pulled out her chair and sat down.

Jimmy remained in the doorway. '*Claire?*'

'It's no big deal. We couldn't get anywhere near the airport – every road is blocked. Miss Calhoon got eaten by wild dogs. We decided to come back to the ship.'

'Miss Calhoon . . .?'

'Torn to pieces, actually.'

Jimmy cleared his throat. 'I don't suppose you . . .'

Claire gave him a look. '*No*, I didn't get any photos of it. And you are one sick individual.'

Jimmy closed the door. He returned to his own desk. He typed something. Without looking up he said: 'I passed by the gangplank two or three times, you know, interviewing people. I didn't see you come back.'

'No, we were late. Daddy borrowed a little speedboat and we caught you up.'

'Ah. Right.'

Claire studied her own computer. Without looking up she said: 'All that stuff, you know when you woke up, and then on the dock, when we said goodbye . . . I was just upset about Pedroza getting shot dead like that, and then me having to leave the ship. I didn't really mean any of it.'

'I know that.'

'I just want to do the paper.'

'That's OK. Me too.'

'It's important, and it's fun, and there's no point in spoiling that.'

'Absolutely not.'

They both nodded.

'Ladies and gentlemen, this is the Captain speaking.'

Captain Smith's voice crackled out of the public address system. Jimmy and Claire looked up at the speaker on the wall. All over the ship, people stopped what they were doing. In the engine room the engineers paused; in the kitchens the catering staff wiped their hands and stood listening; by the swimming pool mothers stopped applying sun cream and children quietly trod water.

'We are now setting sail on the second voyage of the *Titanic*. Our journey will take us along the east coast of the United States of America. We at White Star Line and the *Titanic* take very seriously our responsibility to our passengers and crew. We have already been through difficult times, and you may be sure there will be many more ahead, but it remains our primary duty to ensure your safety. Only the good Lord above knows how long our journey will be, but it's important that we all work together to ensure our continued survival. If you're a doctor at home, volunteer here. If you're a carpenter or an electrician, a baker or an accountant, we need your help. Even if you have no profession, you can be trained. The *Titanic* is the greatest ship ever built, but it needs your support. Thank you for your cooperation, and enjoy the trip.' There was a short pause. 'And now for an important message from First Officer Jeffers.'

'Thank you, Captain.' Jeffers cleared his throat, then gravely announced: 'The public toilets on Level Four are blocked, please avoid using them until further notice. And Dr Hill has reported an infestation of fleas which is believed to be due to a small dog that boarded at St Thomas. If you spot this dog, please notify a member of the crew immediately. Approach it with extreme caution. Thank you.'

THE END

ANOTHER BOOK BY COLIN BATEMAN:

Eddie's new in town, hanging out on his own while he waits for school to begin. Drawn in by a gang of boys infamous for their elaborate scams around town – the Reservoir Pups – Eddie finds his initiation involves breaking into the very hospital his mother works at. That's bad enough, but then he overhears a plan to kidnap babies from one of the wards. Soon Eddie and the Pups are on the trail of a gang of baby-snatchers...

ANOTHER BOOK BY COLIN BATEMAN:

Eddie's got great plans for world domination. The trouble is that none of them look likely to come off. How is his gang of One ever going to rival the Reservoir Pups?

Then a dark, wizened, shrunken object in a glass case is stolen. The thief sparks a chase and the chase sparks a battle for what is right. Eddie Malone and his cronies are back in business – so Captain Black, watch out!

HODDER